The Western Writers series is edited
by Bill Pronzini and Martin H. Greenberg.

Also in the series

The Best Western Stories of Steve Frazee
Edited by Bill Pronzini and Martin H. Greenberg

THE

Best Western
Stories

OF

Wayne D. Overholser

Edited by BILL PRONZINI
and MARTIN H. GREENBERG

Introduction by Stephen Overholser

SOUTHERN ILLINOIS UNIVERSITY PRESS
Carbondale and Edwardsville

Copyright © 1984 by the Board of Trustees,
Southern Illinois University

Introduction copyright © 1984 by Stephen Overholser

All rights reserved

Printed in the United States of America

Edited by *Dan Seiters*

Designed by *Design for Publishing, Bob Nance*

Production supervised by *Kathleen Giencke*

Library of Congress Cataloging in Publication Data

Overholser, Wayne D., 1906–
 The best western stories by Wayne D. Overholser.

 1. Western stories.   I. Pronzini, Bill   II. Greenberg,
Martin Harry.   III. Title.
PS3529.V33A6   1984   813′.54   83–20111
ISBN 0–8093–1145–3

87 86 85 84   4 3 2 1

Contents

Acknowledgments

"They Hanged Wild Bill Murphy." Copyright © 1947 by Fictioneers, Inc. First Published in *15 Western Tales*.

"Book-L'arnin' and the Equalizer." Copyright © 1947 by McCall Corporation. First published in *Blue Book*.

"The Petticoat Brigade." Copyright © 1948 by The Hawley Publications, Inc. First published in *Zane Grey's Western Magazine*.

"Debt Canceled." Copyright © 1948 by The Hawley Publications, Inc. First published in *Zane Grey's Western Magazine*.

"The Hero." Copyright © 1949 by Street & Smith Publications, Inc. First published in *Western Story Magazine*.

"The Steadfast." Copyright © 1950 by The Hawley Publications, Inc. First published in *Zane Grey's Western Magazine*.

"The Patriarch of Gunsight Flat." Copyright © 1950 by McCall Corporation. First published in *Blue Book*.

"High-Grade." Copyright © 1952 by The Hawley Publications, Inc. First published in *Zane Grey's Western Magazine*.

"Winchester Wedding." Copyright © 1953 by Best Books, Inc. First published in *Ranch Romances*.

"Outlaw's Wife." Copyright © 1953 by The Hawley Publications, Inc. First published in *Zane Grey's Western Magazine*.

"Smart." Copyright © 1959 by Popular Publications, Inc. First published in *Argosy* as "The Law-Abiding Outlaw."

"Mean Men Are Big." Copyright © 1959 by Western Writers of America, Inc. First published in *Frontiers West*.

"The O'Keefe Luck." Copyright © 1967 by Fawcett Publications, Inc. First published in *Iron Men and Silver Stars*.

"Beecher Island." Copyright © 1970 by Western Writers of America, Inc. First published in *With Guidons Flying*.

Acknowledgments

Introduction:
A Critical Memoir
By Stephen Overholser

Writing short stories for a large commercial market is all but lost to today's authors. But half a century ago magazines of all descriptions and shapes and sizes formed an important part of American culture, and the fiction pieces in them provided entertainment much as televised dramas do today. This marketplace in the 1930s provided an opportunity for a budding author like Wayne D. Overholser to try out and perfect his skills as a writer, a place to make a private dream come true.

The youngest of four children, Wayne was born on September 4, 1906, in Pomeroy, Washington, of pioneer parents. He was raised on two different farms in the Willamette Valley of western Oregon, and most of his early schooling occurred in a one-room schoolhouse called Scrabblehill. The teacher boarded on the Overholser farm, and Wayne often walked the mile and a half distance at her side. In the evenings by the light of a kerosene lamp he read his school assignments, practiced penmanship, and drew pictures with colored pencils.

Although Wayne performed all the chores expected of a farm boy of that day, raising crops and tending animals for a livelihood was not for him. Born left-handed and nearsighted, he was not in the least mechanically inclined, a source of consternation to his father who could not understand why everything from harness buckles to threaded nuts and bolts looked backwards to the boy.

Wayne's interests were more creative and adventuresome, at least in a vicarious way. As a youngster he gave serious consideration to becoming a clown in the traveling circus. He read a great deal, devouring such books as *Scottish Chiefs, Ivanhoe, Lamb's Shakespeare Tales,* and the King Arthur tales and many of the Greek myths. He also read the thick, leatherbound *Ridpath History of the World* volumes that his parents had purchased by subscription.

As Wayne grew older he drew cartoons and began writing poems and adventure stories. He liked stories of the West and read serials in copies of *Country Gentleman* that he borrowed from a neighbor. He also read the novels of Zane Grey; for him the high point of a Saturday shopping trip to the town of Eugene was the movie matinee where he watched silent films such as Grey's *Man of the Forest.*

In high school Wayne was keenly interested in politics and social issues and enjoyed debate. At home he found himself disagreeing on the issues of the day with his father, a staunch, unquestioning Republican. Wayne was breaking away from the stern views of his parents, fundamentalist Christians who believed that the infidels who drank, swore, danced, played cards, or practiced other faiths were bound for the fires of hell.

The move to the second farm had proved to be ill-advised, and the Overholser family was experiencing hard times when Wayne graduated from Pleasant Hill High School. Years earlier they had paid for his brother Roy's college education, but in 1924 the family was in no position to make a similar offer to Wayne.

Wayne's grades had been excellent, almost straight A, and he was valedictorian in a graduating class of four students. Fortunately he was awarded a one-year scholarship to Albany College. The next year he attended Oregon Normal School, financed through part-time jobs and money borrowed from the school. He graduated with a certificate to teach. During his schooling he never considered a profession other than teaching. For one thing he could not afford more education; for another, he simply knew of no other line of work that he could do.

No job offers came his way that summer of 1926. He tried selling books door to door for a time, but did not do well at it. He traveled out to Garibaldi where he worked in a sawmill for a few weeks. Then he went to Portland in search of any kind of employment he could find. While walking the streets he went on impulse to a fortune teller who read his palm and solemnly advised him that if he went home a job would come to him.

In truth Wayne had no other choice. He did return to the farm, hoping one of his resumés had brought a favorable reply. None had, but he had been home only a short time when a call came offering him a job teaching a seventh-grade class in Tillamook. He eagerly accepted, and in the fall traveled out to the fishing and sawmill town on the coast, where he began a teaching career that was to last nineteen years.

As a teacher, Wayne attended summer school six out of seven years from 1927 to 1934, when he received a Bachelor of Science degree from the University of Oregon. So much schooling, along with his philosophical turn of mind, earned him the nickname of "Prof" from his students.

At a botany class during one of those summers he met a pretty student named Evaleth Miller, daughter of a registered nurse in Portland. They dated, and after Wayne returned to Tillamook they corresponded. In November of 1934 Wayne asked for her hand in marriage. Evaleth accepted, but her mother vigorously objected. Divorced, she wanted her eldest daughter to stay home so they could make a life together. Instead the couple eloped to Yakima, Washington.

Wayne spent much of his spare time writing poems and stories, having a vague idea that someday he might sell one to a magazine. He wrote mysteries, fantasy and love stories, and westerns, and he attended monthly meetings of a local creative-writing group where would-be writers shared readings and criticisms. He also subscribed to *Writers Digest* and every month he read how-to articles and pored over the market guide in each issue. And while in pursuit of his degree he'd signed up for as many creative writing classes as his schedule permitted.

By the time of his marriage, Wayne was writing regularly and had sent out a few of his stories to magazines, receiving printed rejections for his trouble. He did not entertain serious thoughts of a writing career, but he sensed that if he kept working at it he would sell a story someday.

In the summer of 1935 Wayne and Evaleth drove to Missoula, Montana, where writing courses were being taught by E. Douglas Branch and Robert Penn Warren. In the classroom Wayne felt the most rapport with Branch, who unlike Warren encouraged his students to write for the current markets.

The trip to Montana strained the young couple's finances, and often they ate meals of sandwiches and soup heated on a hot plate. But Wayne was much encouraged and returned to Tillamook more determined than ever to continue writing fiction. Through the school year he spent many evenings in an unheated upstairs room working at his typewriter, but his sole reward was a growing stack of unsold short stories—and a lonely wife.

But Evaleth was a woman of great patience. Then, as throughout their marriage, whenever Wayne's determination faltered Evaleth urged him to continue. He did continue, but not until the fall of the next year did the moment arrive that is most memorable in the career of a writer. Instead of the usual returned manuscript Wayne found a business envelope in his mailbox containing a check for fifteen dollars. One of his stories had sold to *Popular Western*, a pulp magazine edited by Leo Margulies in New York. The story was to be published in the December, 1936 issue.

Wayne sold a second story that year, and then in 1937 he sold four more. His total income from writing in those two years was $127.57. These sales came slowly, and while the money supplemented a teaching income of less than $1600 a year, Wayne still had no more than a vague dream of earning a living by writing stories for the magazines.

In the Tillamook group of amateur writers Wayne became acquainted with a woman named Lily Kerr who had sold a number of love stories through the Lenniger Literary Agency in New York. She suggested he inquire to find out if the agency would represent him. After sending a letter detailing his sales to date, Wayne received a reply by return mail from August Lenniger: "You sound like the kind of writer I can go to town with. Send me a story."

With those words began the professional relationship between Wayne and the literary agent he came to know as "Gus." This association lasted more than four decades and saw the sale of over 400 short stories and novelettes in pulp magazines and 100 full-length novels published in hardcover and paperback editions.

Results of Lenniger's work in the marketplace were soon apparent. In 1938 Wayne's writing income shot up to $344.00. In the summer of 1939 he and Evaleth drove to Los Angeles where "Prof" had signed up for six weeks of graduate work at the University of Southern California. Now they traveled with a two-year-old son, and expenses for the three of them were much higher than anticipated. After three weeks their money was almost gone and they were faced with the prospect of having to pack up and go home. But then in mail forwarded from Tillamook came two checks from Gus, enough money to allow Wayne to finish the term. His earnings that year totaled $472.65. And in 1940 the dream seemed even larger when he cleared $614.20.

As his confidence grew, Wayne's literary output increased, too. So did his sales. A memorable year for him was 1942 when his earnings from writing totaled $1704.62, a sum that exceeded his annual salary as a teacher. He began to think more seriously of a career change. Having taught in Tillamook for sixteen years, he began to feel that he had gone stale. In addition to teaching social studies, he had coached basketball and had sponsored a chess club. He was ready for new challenges, but not quite ready to give up a regular paycheck and support his family solely by writing stories.

In the spring of 1942 Wayne applied for a teaching position at the high school in Bend, a small, picturesque town in the middle of Oregon where the Cascade Mountains face out toward a great stretch of high plains known locally as the Oregon Desert. He got the job and moved to Bend the following summer.

In many ways living in Bend gave Wayne a new outlook on life. He wrote more stories than ever, and he began work on a western novel. In 1943 and 1944 his earnings from writing totaled over $3,000. And in 1945 alone he made $3,162.82, and his first novel was published by Macmillan under the title, *Buckaroo's Code*.

The decision that proved a major turning point in Wayne's life came in the spring of 1945. Now father of two sons, he decided not to return to his teaching position in the fall. He wanted to write full-time and believed he could substantially increase his income if he devoted all of his energies to the typewriter.

While the decision did not come easily and involved a great deal of discussion and soul-searching with Evaleth, it was one that neither ever regretted. Wayne's earnings soon reflected the change. In his first year away from the classroom, he sold forty stories and made $4,383.72. His salary during his last year of teaching in Bend was $2,300. The writing career of Wayne D. Overholser was established.

Through the next several years he wrote more than half a million words per year, paid at a rate from half a cent to a cent and a half per word. During that time he moved to Colorado where his third son was born, and he shifted his literary production away from the magazines to books. He accurately foresaw the demise of the pulp magazines and by 1950 knew that if he was to sustain a writing career he would have to create 60,000 word novels.

This was a transition he made successfully while other authors who had been well known in the pulps fell by the wayside. These writers were either unable to create full-length novels, or had become so mired in the clichés of dialect and plot situations common to the pulps that they were unable to make the change. In addition, some of these authors were growing old and found it difficult to adapt their skills to new markets.

A partial explanation for Wayne's later success in the writing business is that he conducted a great deal of research into the history of the West, and as much as possible—given the speed with which he turned out short stories, sometimes as often as one finished story every two days—he gave his stories historical backgrounds or at least imbued them with historical realities. This approach would serve him well in later years.

But perhaps more important to his success in the highly competitive book market was the fact that he envisioned his stories through the eyes and through the emotions of the characters he created. This reversed the method of many other prominent pulp magazine authors, who imposed a few plot situations on all of their stories. While this technique may have made for consistent action-story formulas that guaranteed sales, it also led to shallow characterizations that could not carry a story for 60,000 words.

While Wayne wrote stories in other genres early in his career, he naturally gravitated to westerns. This was partly due to the encouragement of August Lenniger, but to a larger degree it was a reflection of his background and interests. His boyhood reading had steeped him in classic adventure stories. Elements of the King Arthur tales can be found in westerns, and certainly the traditional elements of all adventure literature are present in this uniquely American genre of fiction.

Also, in his boyhood, Wayne witnessed firsthand a life very similar to that depicted in fictional accounts of the West—a life based on the seasons, a life dependent on animals for transportation and power, a life without electricity or running water. He remembered hearing his maternal grandfather tell of crossing the Great Plains to western Oregon in a covered wagon. He saw uniformed Civil War veterans in Fourth of July parades. These boyhood memories made pioneer times quite real to him. And in later years Wayne interviewed men and women who had lived through that period of American history made so famous in literature.

Wayne greatly admired the work of Ernest Haycox, and believed that his short stories constituted some of the best fiction ever written about the West, better even than Haycox's more famous novels. The writing of Ernest Haycox always had power, and he had the rare ability to portray the more subtle emotions of his characters, giving them a greater sense of reality. Wayne studied Haycox's stories carefully and while he never consciously imitated that unique style, he was unquestionably influenced by this master and was inspired to develop his own sense of characterization.

Perhaps the background influences on Wayne's work are best demonstrated by passages in the short story, "Book L'arnin' and the Equalizer," published in the October, 1947 issue of *Blue Book*. (This story was later produced for television under the title "Schoolmarm," with Will Rogers, Jr., playing the lead role.)

In the opening paragraph Wayne brings an historical perspective to the story: "Grass had grown again to cover the scars of battle at Shiloh and Gettysburg and Five Forks, but there was nothing that could hide the scars in the hearts of men that strife had made. Even in Oregon where no battle had been fought, bitterness still lay like a motionless, evil-smelling pool."

The story's protagonist is a teacher in a country schoolhouse, a man of ideas who is forced by circumstances to face the reality of physical violence: "Except for the war years, Neil Hartley had taught school since he was sixteen. Tall and ungainly and awkward, he was far from a handsome man, but had a rare understanding of people, both young and old, and for that reason he was a successful teacher. . . .

"In Missouri old hatreds were still festering sores, but Hartley had not expected to find the same thing true here. He rose now, and putting his hands palms down on the scarred desktop, leaned across it, his mouth drawn tight across his bony face."

Clearly, in the lines quoted above, Wayne has projected his own experiences into the character of Neil Hartley, drawing both on his background as a teacher and on his memories of attending a one-room school in rural Oregon.

On another level of experience, Wayne as a storyteller is drawn to two sources of conflict. One is simply between opposing forces, Unionists and Secessionists, with the protagonist caught in the middle. The second concerns a deeper problem: applied book l'arnin'. One day the man who teaches lessons embodying concepts of honesty and integrity will have to take a stand and back up his moral values. That this teacher is not physically equipped to take such a stand adds to the drama and mounting suspense of the story.

A gangling school teacher with flawed vision but a sure grasp of the fundamental issue at stake is a character drawn from Wayne's own background, and while this story is representative of pulp fiction published in the United States during the post-war years, it is at once vastly superior to most "Westerns." This one rises above cliché, both in language and in plot situation, offering insights into the characters' motivations while giving the reader an accurate historical background for the fictional events depicted in the narrative.

In another short story, "The Steadfast," first published in a 1950 issue of *Zane Grey's Western Magazine,* pioneer hardships and suffering are vividly portrayed: "When disguised by the darkness of a prairie night, Gunlock seemed like a pleasant place with its one wide street and the pools of yellow light spilling out across the dust from Clem York's hotel and saloon. But the sunrise drew away the disguise. Then Gunlock could be seen for what it was, a huddle of buildings dropped here among the empty miles, an evil, almost deserted town with broken hitch rails and walks that had more splintered boards than sound ones, with cobwebbed windows and doors that hung askew from bent hinges."

In the second paragraph the protagonist is introduced and the theme in the opening paragraph is enlarged: "Each morning Dave Lowrie viewed Gunlock with distaste as he walked from his house at the east end of town to his livery stable. He always had the weird feeling he was looking at something that should have been a corpse but stubbornly refused to become one."

And in the third paragraph the dramatic theme of the story is indicated: "There was something painful about seeing Gunlock this way; he had seen the settlers come filled with hope and leave with no hope at all, humbled by drought and hard times. He had seen his father die here in front of Clem York's hotel, shot in the back by parties unknown, or so the coroner's jury had said."

Like other short stories in the western genre, "The Steadfast" is constructed round a male who is young and unmarried, faced with a seemingly impossible conflict. Through the course of the story he conquers evil and wins the girl. While this story is typical of other westerns, it, too is superior to the cliché because of the believeable characterizations that give the story a certain complexity and depth that are found in the best of Wayne's stories.

In the beginning of his career in the 1930s Wayne's goal was simply to sell the stories he wrote. He studied magazines that were potential markets for his work. Then he wrote stories that he hoped would appeal to the editors in New York. He was, in effect, honing his skills to fit the demands of the existing marketplace.

In those days the best pulp magazines were helmed by strong-minded editors who had specific concepts of the types of stories that would compel readers across the country to buy their publications. These editors stamped their imprints into the content of their magazines, requiring within a genre fast-paced action stories, or violent stories, or suspenseful stories, or stories with a strong romantic angle. The result was that the most successful authors of the day slanted their material toward the known requirements of a particular market.

As a maturing writer in his forties, Wayne had learned to write for the western magazines, but over the years he had gradually developed his own voice and his own techniques in the craft of storytelling. While his goal was still the same as it had been in the beginning, his talents emerged and he put more of himself into his stories.

This fact is clearly demonstrated in "The Patriarch of Gunsight Flat," first published in a 1950 issue of *Blue Book*. The narrative begins not with an action scene or with violence designed to capture the reader's interest, but with a philosophical statement, one that is even more direct than the opening cited in "Book L'arnin' and the Equalizer" published three years earlier:

"The sins of man are many. He will kill. He will take that which belongs to others—money and cattle and all that can be turned into money. Aye, and other things: a good name—a woman's virtue—a man's home—a friend. And who can say with certainty that murder is a greater crime than thievery?"

This strongly moral tone appears again near the denouement of the story:

"Aye, the sins of man are many, and there must be compensation for them. There must be life, as there is death; there must be love as there is hate. . . .

"There would come a day when the empty miles would not be empty, when train whistles and the shrill scream of whirring saws slicing pine into lumber would cut the high thin air. There would be people and cities; there would be the echo of children's laughter. There must be compensation, the companionship of tomorrow to replace the loneliness of yesterday, the goodness of the Gramps to balance the sins of the Jim Sollys. It takes time to understand these things: time and human dignity and a willingness to understand."

The growth and maturing of Wayne's literary talents made it possible for him to move on to a long and successful career as a novelist. (More than one hundred of his Western novels have been published; many of these have been made into feature-length films, and two— *The Lawman*, under the name of Lee Leighton, and *The Violent Land*—received Spur Awards from the Western Writers of America as the best novels of 1953 and 1954, respectively.) Rather than being trapped—or worse, outmoded—by his background in the pulp magazines as so many writers of that day were, he was able to use the experience to develop his own skills. The magazines served as a rigorous apprenticeship for a young writer who learned much about the art of storytelling and about the discipline required to sit down at the typewriter every day, day after day, and write fiction.

Money earned by his written word was always of great importance to Wayne. In the beginning nearly half a century ago the earnings from his typewriter supplemented a meager income from teaching. Later the extra money helped support a young family. Wayne always haunted the mailbox when a check was due. After he became a full-time writer he experienced great anguish if an expected check from the sale of a story was overdue. The pressure on him to produce was relentless, yet there was no other career that he wanted more in his life. And somehow the money always arrived in time to avert disaster.

But even though money loomed so large in his thoughts and was such a frequent topic of discussion among his fellow writers, Wayne was philosophical by nature and a historian by training. He always believed that his work had a purpose beyond the obvious one of entertaining readers. His stories are distinguished from the run-of-the-mill pulp action yarns with wooden characters marching through familiar plots. He wrote for money, but in a greater, more profound sense, he wrote to explore hidden aspects of human nature and he attempted to cast a beam of light, no matter how small, into the past.

Throughout his career he believed that his ultimate success as a writer would not be measured by his earnings or his awards or his recognition among critics, but by his readers. A deep, private communion exists between writer and reader, and to Wayne D. Overholser that knowledge was always at the heart of his work.

The following is a complete list of magazines that published stories by Wayne D. Overholser. With the exception of *Argosy,* all are pulps. Some were well-known publications with long traditions in the first half of this century; others were short-lived, some lasting only an issue or two. *Blue Book* was the best of these pulp magazines, and paid the best, too, at three cents a word. Typically, the pulps paid from one-half cents to one and one-half cents a word.

Popular Western
Clues Detective
Lone Ranger
Red Seal Western
Thrilling Western
Romance Roundup
Western Trails
Western Story
Western Aces
Detective and Murder Mysteries
Two-Gun Western
Masked Rider Western
Western Romances
Blue Ribbon Western
Romantic Range
Stirring Detective and Western
.44 Western

Uncanny Stories
Wild West Weekly
Ranch Romances
Western Novel and Short Stories
Two-Gun Western Novels
Complete Western Book
Rio Kid Western
Complete Cowboy
Western Yarns
Fifteen Western Tales
Big-Book Western
Ace-High Western Stories
New Western
All Western
Complete Western
10 Story Western
West

Western Adventures
Big Book Western
Thrilling Love
Lariat
Mammoth Western
Western Action
Leading Western
Star Western
Six-Gun Western
Famous Western
Exciting Western
Complete Western Book
Action Stories
Giant Western
Frontier Stories
5 Western Novels
Triple Western
Three Western Novels

Rodeo Romances
Western Short Stories
All Story Western
Zane Grey's Western Magazine
Western Novels and Short Stories
Western Short Stories
Dime Western
Two Western Romances
Complete Western Book Magazine
Golden West Romances
Texas Rangers
Best Western
Thrilling Ranch Stories
Two Western Book
Two Western Action Books
Top Western Fiction Annual
Blue Book
Argosy

In addition King Features Syndicate, Toronto *Star,* and *Grit* published stories written by Wayne D. Overholser

THE
Best Western
Stories
OF
Wayne D. Overholser

They Hanged Wild Bill Murphy

Sheriff Cole Drager had never known how true the old saying was that a man's eyes are the windows of his soul until Wild Bill Murphy came to Custer County. They were mad eyes, and Murphy was a wild madman who loved his horse and his wife and hated everything else. He killed with provocation or without, and there was nobody in Custer County, including Cole Drager, who could stand before his guns.

But it was not Wild Bill Murphy who had brought the trouble. That went back through the years to an old festering sore, and Murphy had been attracted by the smell of it, the same as a coyote would be attracted by the stench of a long dead steer. On this spring day, with lush green staining the valley and a life-giving sun sweeping upward from the Needles into a cerulean sky, trouble was ready to explode into death. Cole, who had seen it build through the years, knew that neither he nor any man was big enough to stop it.

It was Silver Wade and his Rocking H boys from the other side of the Needles who rode into town first, as salty a crew as you'd find west of the Rockies. Wade rode in front, straight-backed and arrogant, confident of what the day would bring, a dozen buckaroos strung out behind him, each sitting his saddle with the same insolent grace that characterized his boss.

Racking their mounts, the Rocking H hands swaggered into the Fashion saloon. There was an hour of drinking time before the hearing, and Cole, thinking of what whiskey would do to them, felt his nerves tighten until they were ready to twang like an overwound fiddle string.

3

Then the nesters. Wild Bill Murphy led them, riding with as much arrogance as Silver Wade himself, two black-butted .45s tied low on his long-boned thighs. But the men behind him were something else. Murphy was like a tall wind-resisting pine in a juniper forest. The others came in buggies and buckboards, rifles in callused hands, mud caked on their shoes, farmers who knew the art of tilling the soil but not that of gunfighting. That was the reason they looked to Murphy for leadership, the reason he was able to levy his high tribute upon them.

Cole, standing in his office doorway, raised a hand in greeting. Ash Barto, who drove the buggy directly behind Murphy, nodded, but the rest looked straight ahead, faces as grim as the badlands that were the Needles. Cole Drager was the law, and the events of this day might well pit them against him.

For one short moment Murphy's mad eyes swept Cole's face. They were black, as black and shiny as chipped obsidian, and the look was a direct challenge. Then the cavalcade moved past the jail, dust hanging motionless in the still air. Hopelessness deepened in Cole Drager as he watched them hitch their rigs before the Gold Moon, and go in.

Then another buggy wheeled into Main Street to complete the parade, Ruth Barto driving, Delight Murphy beside her. According to Wild Bill, his wife was the prettiest woman in Custer County, and nobody disputed the point with him. She was pretty all right, Cole thought, as pretty as a sleek rattlesnake sunning herself on a rock. For his money, Ruth was Custer County's beauty. She was everything that was fine and decent, the same as Delight Murphy was everything else.

Cole raised his hat to them. Delight smiled and waved, but Ruth's nod was barren, her lips stiff and frigid. The same thought was in her mind that was in the minds of the nesters. Now, reading that thought, Cole felt a tightening of his insides. He had loved Ruth Barto since they had been in school together, but her answer had always been no. She'd said a dozen times that they'd have to wait until this trouble was settled.

Stepping back into his office, Cole built a smoke, but he found the taste bitter against his tongue, and threw the cigarette into the street. He took out his gun, checked the loads and fell to pacing the floor.

Whiskey would hone tempers already sharp, tempers that would not take defeat. Then it would come, the moment he had long known was inevitable. Guns would snarl their lethal message, and blood

would stain the boardwalks and streets, and death would be there in
all its ugliness. And every fiber of Wild Bill Murphy's mind would
thrill to the echoes of those shots.

There had been suits and court battles, letters shuttling back and
forth between Custer County and the national capital, special agents
galore, and some dead homesteaders who had been pulled out of the
tules around Coffin Lake. Now, after a decade spent fighting over
what was home to the nesters and fertile hay land for Rocking H, the
decision was to be made.

The general land office should have sent an army instead of another
special agent. Lacking the army, it was Cole's job to keep the peace
with a single deputy—or maybe two of them! He laughed. A dozen
gunslingers on the side of the Rocking H, and twenty on the other, led
by a man who would rather kill another human than eat turkey on
Christmas day. Might as well try to stop a tornado by waving his
bandanna.

Glancing at his watch, Cole saw that there were still forty minutes.
He slanted across the dust strip, Stetson brim tilted against the sun.
The batwings gave to his shoulders, and with the first whisper of their
movement, Wild Bill Murphy wheeled, long fingers splayed over gun
butt.

"What's biting you?" Murphy demanded in his shrill voice.

Murphy was a trigger trap needing only the touch of a hair to set
him off. With Cole Drager dead, except for little Bunk Eddes, the
deputy, there would be no law in Custer County.

Cole looked past Murphy to Ash Barto, who stood with his back to
the bar. Barto was one of the first settlers on Coffin Lake, defying the
early survey that called the old lake bottom swamp land, and until the
coming of Murphy, had been regarded as the nesters' leader. He could
be blamed, if anybody could, for accepting Murphy, but Cole knew
how it was. Barto was like a man riding a grizzly. It was tough to stay
on, but hell to get off.

"You boys are a mite early," Cole said mildly.

"No polecats are gonna put anything over on us." Murphy snarled.

"I dropped in, Ash," Cole said, ignoring Murphy, "to ask for your
help in keeping the peace. Wade's bunch won't start anything if you
boys ain't armed, so maybe you'd better leave your irons here in the
Gold Moon."

Murphy took two quick steps toward Cole, eyes wide and glittering. "We ain't leaving our guns here, Drager. The decision is going our way. Savvy?"

"You'll accept the decision, or you'll be outside the law, and I'll treat you accordingly," Cole said curtly.

"You treat me like that," Murphy taunted, "an' I won't waste powder shooting you. I'll just spit in your eyes."

"It takes more'n your mouth to make me pull my gun," Cole said, his voice still mild, and wheeled out of the saloon.

Murphy fired a stream of curses at his back, but the sheriff kept on across the street to the Fashion. He'd cut one bridge behind him, he thought grimly. From now on, Murphy would dog him until he forced a fight, and there was only so much any man, sheriff or not, could take from another.

Cole pushed through the Fashion's batwings, and grinned when Wade called, "Howdy, Sheriff. Drink up, boy. This is our day to howl."

It was false friendliness, bait to relax Cole's vigilance. Silver Wade was backing more than Wild Bill Murphy was. He'd spent a fortune fighting a legal battle, another in gunslicks' wages. If he lost in the court, there was always the last appeal to gunsmoke.

"No thanks, Silver. I'm not drinking today."

Cole's eyes raked the men at the bar. A dozen of them—tough, hard-drinking and hard-riding. Fast with their guns. Good with their fists. Wade had tested all of them except possibly young Tommy Cotter, who had been on the Rocking H less than a month, and found that they filled the bill. Pres Phelan, the red-headed ramrod, held his job because he could lick any man in the outfit with either a six or his fist.

"Not drinking?" Wade asked as if affronted. "Why, this is the day you lose 90 percent of your trouble. Soon as we get the formality of this hearing over with the nesters will pack up and roll out."

"I don't think so," Cole said quietly.

Wade lifted black brows. He was in his early forties, but his hair was completely white and had been as long as Cole had known him. He was not a killer like Murphy or Phelan, but he was cool-thinking and cunning, and without a conscience that would stop at bloodshed. Now, the forefinger of his right hand twisting his watch chain, his mouth holding a small smile, he was to Cole Drager a merciless and formidable man.

"What makes you think they won't pull out?"

"You know Murphy."

"Sure. He can stop a slug the same as any man."

"While he's doing it, there'll be hell to pay. Silver, I'm asking you and your men to leave your guns here in the Fashion."

"Is that an order?"

Cole shook his head. "I'm just asking for cooperation in keeping the peace."

Pres Phelan laughed, a booming laugh that was echoed all along the line, even by young Tommy Cotter.

But Silver Wade barely smiled. His expression was almost contemptuous. "Rocking H isn't cooperating, Drager."

"I'm warning you not to make trouble if the decision goes against you. If you do, you're outside the law."

Wade's grin was definitely contemptuous now. "We'll get back in."

Cole strode out, Rocking H laughter beating against his ears. He heard Phelan say, "Tough, ain't it, Silver, to have some of your tax money go to pay that star-toter's wages."

"It sure is, Pres, when a man expects something for his money."

Cole fought down his impulse to go back and beat Pres Phelan to his knees. To knock Silver Wade's teeth down his throat. But this wasn't the day to lose his temper. He glanced at his watch. There was one more thing he could do.

Ruth Barto was the only woman among the nesters who was close to Delight Murphy's age. That, Cole thought, was the reason Delight and Ruth were together a great deal. It couldn't be a matter of mutual interests, for they were as unlike as two women could be. But today there was one thing they had in common, and Cole nursed a small hope that he could make them see it.

He passed through the hotel lobby and climbed the stairs. Murphy kept the best room in the hotel rented for Delight because she hated the cabin on the Barto place, and spent most of her time in town.

"Why, Ruth, it's Cole!" Delight cried when she opened the door to his knock. She drew him into the room. "Imagine Cole coming to see us." She stood so close to him that the fragrance of her gold-tinted hair reached him. Her wide mouth was smiling; her eyes were warm-tinted emeralds.

"I came to see you two about your menfolks," Cole said evenly. "To see if you could do anything about them. Bill Murphy's set to blow the roof off—an' nobody wins a row like that. It means defying the law in the end, if the loser won't accept the decision."

Delight breathed, "We can watch the fight from here—if there is one!"

Cole looked past her to Ruth, who was standing by the window, a tall black-haired girl who had the power to quicken Cole's pulse with her presence. Usually her mouth held a sweet shape, and her blue eyes hinted at her feeling for him, but he saw neither today. There was only a bleak soberness on her face.

"Can't you do anything, Ruth?" he asked.

"Nothing, Cole."

He turned from them, ignoring Delight's half mocking, half mischievous, "Don't go, Cole." He closed the door, and heard Delight's soft laughter. "The man isn't human. . . . He thinks. . . . Ruth. . . ."

He stopped at a door down the hall and knocked. "Time to go, Dan."

"All ready, Cole." The door swung open, and Dan York, special agent from the land office, stepped into the hall, a satchel in his hand.

York was an old hand at sifting evidence and settling disputes like this one, and he understood the danger that lay barely beneath the surface. He was a heavy-set man, a few years older than Cole, with a shock of iron-gray hair that stubbornly pointed skyward, regardless of how many times a day he applied comb and brush to it. His hair, Cole thought, was symbolic of his character.

"I've seen 'em all," Cole said tonelessly. "No use. Everybody's set to shoot hell out of each other."

"It's understandable." York locked the door and walked down the stairs with Cole. "How much does Murphy charge the settlers?"

"I could never get anybody to say, but it's plenty. He gives Delight everything she wants."

"And she wants it all," York said with unexpected bitterness. He shrugged his meaty shoulders. "You've got to educate people to obey the law, and it's tough to do that when they're in the habit of buying everything they get." He tapped his satchel. "I've got evidence that could send half a dozen local officers and special agents to the pen, but it would do no good now."

Leaving the hotel, they strode along the boardwalk to the courthouse, an unpainted frame building that stood beyond the county jail, without care and without dignity, a fair index of what Custer County

people thought of that intangible known as law. The courtroom was
deserted. York took his place at a front table, laying the satchel and a
.45 in front of him.

Cole glanced at his watch. "Five minutes."

"They'll be here," York said grimly. "Stand at the back door, Cole.
Plug the first man who shows fight."

They were there before the five minutes were over, the nesters
filing in behind Murphy and Ash Barto and taking seats on the east
side of the room, Rocking H following Wade and ranging across the
aisle from the nesters.

It would take no more than a loud creak of one of the seats to set it
off. Cole, staring at the backs of the nesters, felt a pity for them. They
bristled with the most nondescript collection of weapons he had ever
seen: Kentucky rifles, Civil War muskets, needle guns, shotguns, a
Sharps .45–90, dragoon pistols. Only Murphy with the .45's thonged
low on his thighs could compete with the gunslicks who drew Rocking H wages, and Murphy was mad enough to believe he was equal to
the dozen of them.

Strangely enough, the settlers had that same blind faith in Murphy's gun wizardry, arising, Cole thought, from a fear of Wade that
went back over a decade. Now, like drowning men, they clutched at
this flimsy straw, hoping that by some miracle Murphy could save
their lives and homes from Wade or the law if it decided against them.

"I'm proud of the fact," York began, "that I have never had any
kick about my work. My honesty has never been questioned. I won't
stand for its being questioned now. I hope that both sides will accept
my decision without making trouble."

York paused to let this soak in. There was no sound in the room but
asthmatic breathing of one of the nesters. York, Cole thought, would
do well to save his breath when it came to warnings.

"I've spent months going over the previous testimony." York patted the satchel. "I have proved to my satisfaction that evidence which
was given in hearing after hearing adds up to the biggest collection of
lies I ever ran into. This case should have been settled years ago. You'd
have saved money, Wade. Maybe some lives."

"You can—" Wade began.

"Shut up, Wade," York said sharply, bending his gaze on the Rocking H owner. "When I'm ready to listen to you, I'll say so."

Dan York was tough, made tough by his profession. The fingers of his right hand were never far from his gun butt, and it was a question in Cole's mind as to whether either Pres Phelan or Wild Bill Murphy would be on his feet after a smokeout with York.

"I've boiled this down to a few words." York removed a sheet of paper from his satchel. "It's not new to either side, but it bears repeating."

Picking up the paper, York read, "The settlers have consistently denied that the lands in dispute around Coffin Lake were swamp and overflowed in eighteen-sixty. Therefore they claim that these lands were subject to selection under the general land laws of the United States. However, surveys of Alex Jones and Henry Simmons returned these lands as the bed of Coffin Lake. Thereby the state received them as swamp lands, subject to sale as such.

"After the survey was made, the general land office received many complaints from settlers who argued that there were thousands of acres of dry land within the boundaries of the meandered lake, and they maintain that they have made *bona fide* settlements upon such land. These settlers"—York motioned to Barto and his friends— "claim that fraudulent returns have been made by various officials so that land actually desert was described as swamp and overflowed in order that it could be certified under the Act of March, eighteen-sixty."

York rose and leaned on the table. "I have studied the evidence, I've ridden around the lake and looked at the disputed land, and I've talked to every man whose testimony was accepted at previous hearings. I was given this case to examine the claims of fraud which have been made. Now, before I give my decision, Wade, do you want to say anything?"

"You're damned right." Wade came to his feet, thin-lipped mouth pulled against white teeth. "I saw this disputed land in eighteen-sixty-eight. Reckon I was about the first one who did see it. I climbed one of the Needles, and had a hell of a good look. It was tule marsh. Cane and swamp grass all over it. Water in the tules."

Wade shook a fist at York. "I'm saying this, and I'll keep saying it till I get justice and the damned trespassing clodbusters off my land. The state got it from the government as swamp land. I bought it for swamp land, and by hell, it was swamp land. Now you'd better see I get it."

The expression on Dan York's square face did not change. "You didn't say anything new, Wade." He patted his satchel. "I have plenty of such testimony, but saying doesn't make it true. Barto, you got anything to say?"

Barto rose, the corners of his mouth twitching under the stress of deep emotion. "Nothing new, I reckon. I saw the land a year or so after Wade made his deal with the state. It was desert with sagebrush on it. We put water on the land so now we can raise hay. Still we can't get a clear title. We've had court fights and everything else trying to get us kicked off our land. Even had murder—"

"You don't need to listen to that," Wade bellowed. "When he talks—"

"Sit down, Wade, before I have you thrown into jail for contempt."

"Contempt, hell. I've got plenty of it."

"So have I," York snapped. "Always did have it for liars. Sit down."

Wade kept his feet for a moment, eyes locking with York's, and Cole, still standing in the back of the room, gripped his gun.

He thought this was the moment. Then he saw it wasn't. Wade dropped into his seat and grinned at Pres Phelan. Cole wouldn't have been more surprised if Wild Bill Murphy had stepped across the aisle to kiss the Rocking H owner.

"Go on, Barto," York said imperturbably.

"That's all," Barto said, "except that we think the law oughta be big enough to protect us little fry from range hogs who can buy lying surveys. If it ain't, we aim to fight."

"All right." York nodded for Barto to sit down. "I won't take time to read the complete report I'm sending to the land office, but I promise it'll curl a few hairs.

"In eighteen-seventy the state passed a law allowing its citizens to buy the acreage they wanted. 'Swamp angels' bought huge empires for paltry sums. My report names deputy surveyors and local officers who, with agents of the state, made fraudulent returns regarding swamp land surveys, selection, and inspection in the field."

York laid his gaze squarely on Wade's face. "When I gained a full knowledge of the fraud which was back of these reports, I found no question in my mind concerning my decision. These lands were never swamp or overflowed. No one but Wade or men in his employ have

sworn that they were. Therefore the state has no title or interest in
them and could not have sold them. Without reservation, the settlers'
claims are upheld."

York paused, fingers touching his gun. "You can keep on fighting,
Wade, but I think you will not find the land office of a mind to listen.
If you have any idea of violence, you'd better forget it. The report is in
the mail and on its way to Washington."

"You sound a mite worried, York," Wade said contemptuously.
"You don't need to stay awake nights waiting for me or my boys to
plug you."

Wade tramped down the aisle and out of the building, completely
ignoring Cole. Phelan and the others followed, young Tommy Cotter
bringing up the rear, his bright-cheeked face showing his astonish-
ment. He'd been primed for a fight and for some mysterious reason, it
had failed to come off.

Not until the door was closed behind Tommy Cotter did Cole turn
his eyes to Dan York, and he saw that the special agent was as puzzled
as he was. He gave the agent a tight-lipped grin, and swung his gaze to
the nesters. They sat as if stupefied—all but Murphy, whose long-
jawed face showed his disappointment.

Ash Barto wiped his face with his bandanna and, coming to his feet,
crossed to York and shook his hand. "I take back those things I said
about the law. You're the first honest man the government's sent us."

"There are plenty of honest government men, Barto. You just got a
bad deal on the ones they sent here."

"He ain't got no thanks coming, Ash." Wild Bill Murphy was in the
aisle and moving to the door. "York was too smart to decide it any
other way. Come on. Long as Wade's around, we've got trouble."

York's face flamed. He started to say something, but closed his
mouth when Cole shook his head at him.

Murphy paused when he came opposite Cole, mad black eyes raking the lawman. "I never did like a star-toter, Drager. One of these
days you and me are gonna smoke it out."

"Mebbe."

"Today's as good a day as any."

He was a gaunt, ugly man, this Wild Bill Murphy, with a wolf's taste
for blood. Cole wondered why a woman like Delight had married him,
but there was no judging him by normal standards. With an inordi-
nate pride in his gun speed, and an insatiable desire to take human

life, Murphy would not rest until Cole Drager had gone down before his gun.

"I guess not," Cole said.

"I said today was a good day. Make your play, tinstar."

"If either one of you go for your gun," York bellowed, "I'll plug you."

Slowly Murphy's long-jawed face came around. He stood motionless, staring at York. Cole, who could see only the left side of his face and that one eye, thought again of chipped obsidian, bright and wicked.

"You honing for trouble?" Murphy asked.

"Not me," York snapped, "but you'll get some if you aren't careful."

The black eyes narrowed. "I guess you and me—"

"Barto, why in hell did you hire a killer like that?" York demanded.

"We need him," Barto said slowly. "Come on, Bill. We've got no fight with either Cole or York."

Barto jerked his head at the nesters, and they filed out. Murphy held his place at the door, bleak face mirroring his inward struggle. He yielded only when Barto was within a pace of him and, wheeling, stalked out ahead of the settlers.

The door remained open, and Cole heard Delight ask, "How did it go, darling?"

"Just like you knew it would, honey," Murphy answered in the soft tone he used only on his wife. "York was so damned scared he couldn't do nothing but give it to us."

"Then we're done here?"

"Not till Wade and Phelan are in hell," Murphy said darkly.

They moved out of earshot then. It was a reprieve. Nothing more. The fuse was longer than Cole had guessed, but it was still sparking and still connected with a powder keg. Turning, Cole said, "I ain't hungry, Dan, but let's put the feed bag on."

It wasn't until they'd finished their pie and the second cup of coffee in the hotel dining room that Cole put the question which had been bothering him from the moment Silver Wade had walked out of the courtroom.

"Why didn't it bust, Dan?"

Scowling, York spooned sugar into his coffee. "Damned if I know.

I figured Wade and Phelan would start smoking their irons the minute I got done."

"Wade's got something cute cooked up or he would have."

York stirred his coffee, biting the corner of his lip thoughtfully. "He isn't done. That's the only thing I'm sure about."

"When are you pulling out, Dan?"

"Not till I see how the wind blows," York said with affected carelessness.

"I can get along."

"Sure, Cole. I'm just curious to see how it's going to turn out."

They left the dining room, Cole knowing that the aftermath of this decision would be more than any sheriff and one deputy could handle. It was dynamite that no official in a plush-bottom chair in Washington could understand. York understood it, but Cole, watching him as they moved across the hotel lobby, had a feeling that the special agent had a private ax he hadn't finished grinding.

Ruth Barto was waiting for them near the door. She held out her hand to Dan York as she said, "I want to apologize for what I've been thinking."

York's craggy face was softened by a quick smile. "We always accept apologies from pretty women."

But Cole said a little angrily, "If your dad doesn't boot Murphy out of the country, this'll still blow up in our faces."

"That's right," York agreed gravely. "He's as dangerous as a hydrophobia skunk. And as crazy."

Ruth drew back, eyes searching one and then the other. "You don't understand," she said finally. "We've got to keep Bill as long as Wade hires gunslingers."

"Murphy lives on trouble, Ruth. As long as he's in the valley, there'll never be peace."

A gunshot broke into Cole's words. It came from the Gold Moon. For a moment his eyes locked with York's, and he knew the same unspoken fear was in the agent's mind that was in his own.

"Come on, Dan." Cole stepped around Ruth and left the lobby on the run.

Townsmen raced out of stores and offices and crowded into the Gold Moon behind Cole and Dan York. The medico was there ahead of them, bending over a still form on the floor. Seeing Cole, he rose. "Dead. Shot an inch above the left eye."

It was then that Cole saw that the dead man was young Tommy Cotter. His gaze swept the motionless nesters to Ash Barto, ignoring Wild Bill Murphy. "Who did it, Ash?"

"I did," Murphy said. "He came in gunning for me."

"That right, Ash?"

Barto nodded glumly. "I hate this like hell, Cole. He was just a kid. Came in like he was drunk. Started cussing Bill and went for his gun."

Still ignoring the killer, Cole nodded at the barman. "Get that shutter you've got in the back room. We'll take him over to Doc's place."

Murphy swaggered away from the bar. "Calling me a liar, Drager?"

Cole met the man's black eager eyes. "Routine questioning, Bill, but you got out of line on this one. You don't always have to kill a man."

"When a man kicks up a gunfight, I kill him." Murphy's lean jaw jutted forward. "Savvy?"

"I savvy, all right."

The eagerness in Murphy's mad eyes deepened. "Drager, you arresting me?"

"No. You won't run away. Give me a hand here, Dan."

They lifted the body to the shutter, Cole acting as if he didn't hear Murphy's jeering laugh. When Cole and York reached the door, they found Silver Wade and Pres Phelan waiting.

"Tommy?" Wade asked unnecessarily.

"You've got eyes," Cole said. "I want to ask you some questions."

"Sure." Wade shook his head sadly. "Hell of a thing. He was just a kid."

It wasn't right, Cole was thinking as they carried the body through the medico's office to his back room. With a dozen gunslingers on his payroll who might have stood a chance with Murphy, it made no sense at all for Wade to send a boy like Tommy Cotter to do a man's chore.

Wade and Phelan were in the doctor's office when Cole and York came out of the back room. "What are you going to do about Murphy?" Wade asked with more courtesy than was his habit.

"You've got some questions to answer before I do anything," Cole said grimly. "Why did you send Tommy after Murphy?"

"I didn't," Wade squalled. "I wouldn't do a thing like that. Damn—"

"All right," Cole said testily. "What did happen?"

"I don't rightly know," Wade admitted. "We were standing around talking, giving Murphy a hell of a cussing. All of a sudden Tommy was gone. Next thing, we heard the shooting. He did whatever he did on his own."

"The kid never could do anything right," Phelan added. "Came from the other side of the mountains where they didn't know nothing about buckarooing. He was getting laughed at all the time for messing things up. Reckon he figgered plugging Murphy would be a good way to play big."

"I should have left him at home," Wade said with exaggerated regret, "but he could shoot pretty good. I thought we'd need every gun we had."

They were lying. Cole Drager was sure of it, but he knew he couldn't break their story down, and they had committed no crime he could hold against them even if he could get the truth.

"Get your boys out of town before anything happens," Cole said.

"Not just yet." Wade's black brows lowered over shrewd hazel eyes. "Shooting Tommy's different than plugging Pres, here, for instance. Murphy can't claim it was a fair fight. I've seen Tommy draw. Slow ain't the word. I make murder out of it, Drager."

"We're staying here till you get Murphy," Phelan said truculently. "If you don't, we'll smoke him out ourselves."

Cole saw it then. Somehow Wade had worked Tommy Cotter into making his suicide play, and that made Wade as guilty of murder as Murphy. But there was no court of law that would call Wade's action murder, nor was he sure that even Murphy could be convicted.

"If I arrest Murphy, you'll take your boys out of town?"

"You've got my word," Wade promised.

"All right. Get back over to the Fashion and stay there."

"We'll give you a hand."

"We don't need any help."

"You ain't enough to take Murphy."

"I'm not Tommy Cotter," Cole said sharply. "I expect you to stay in the Fashion and keep your boys inside."

"All right," Wade snapped. "Go ahead and get yourself a slug. After you're dead, we'll show the nesters how to handle a coyote."

York waited until Wade and Phelan had gone. Then he asked, "What have you got in mind, Cole?"

"I'm going to arrest Murphy. It won't stick, but it'll get Rocking H out of town till things cool off."

"Where's your deputy?"

"Bunk's asleep. Been down in the south end of the county, and didn't get back till sunup."

"Get him. It'll take three to do this job."

"You've done your chore, Dan."

"I just started it," the stocky man said grimly.

Bunk Eddes was asleep in a little room off the sheriff's office. Knuckling his eyes when Cole shook him, he muttered, "Why in hell do you have to get me up the minute I go to sleep?"

"This is the day you get out of bed. We've got trouble."

Eddes swung his feet to the floor and shook the cobwebs out of his head. "We ain't had nothing but trouble since you got this office."

Eddes dressed while Cole told him what had happened. He was a little man with a bristling moustache that gave him a ferocious appearance that was deceiving, for actually he was a softhearted, easygoing man. But when the chips were down, he was, as Cole expressed it, "all guts and vinegar," and he looked up to Cole.

"Let's go get him," Eddes said confidently as he buckled on his gunbelt.

"There's a back door to the Moon, isn't there?" York asked, and when Cole nodded, the special agent went on, "Only one way to handle Murphy. Give the same chance you would any sidewinder. If you're easy with him, he'll get all three of us, and then Wade would hold the high cards."

"That's what Wade's working for," Cole grunted.

"We'll fool him. You boys make the arrest. Give me a shotgun, Cole. Won't hurt my conscience to let Murphy have it in the back."

Cole took a shotgun down from the rack above his desk and handed it to York. "We'll take it easy so you'll get to the back door by the time we hit the front." He checked his gun. "Let's get at it."

Cole and Bunk Eddes moved slowly along the walk, giving York the time he'd need. When they reached the Gold Moon, Cole said, "Move away from me, Bunk, when I jump him."

They pushed through the batwings, the deputy instantly angling into the middle of the room so that he stood facing the bar while Cole strode along it toward Murphy. The nesters spun away, even Ash Barto, so that nobody stood within twenty feet of the gunman.

"I'm arresting you for the killing of Tommy Cotter," Cole said evenly. "You'll have a fair trial, Bill. If you make a move for your gun, you're a dead man."

Pleasure washed across Wild Bill Murphy's face. He licked thin lips that held a small smile as if wishing to make this moment last a little longer. "I didn't think you was man enough to try it, Drager. I'll get both of you. You know that, don't you?"

"The first move you make for your irons will get you a dose of buckshot."

The smile widened on Murphy's long-jawed face. "That's so old it stinks, Drager."

Ash Barto yelled, "York's got a shotgun."

There was silence then, doubt narrowing Murphy's eyes. Both hands were splayed over gun butts as he slowly made the turn. Then he saw York, and anger lashed him into a fury.

"You damned yellow rabbits," Murphy shouted, "Wouldn't be a man among you if you was all boiled into one."

"Take his guns, Ash," Cole said quietly. "Hook the moon, Bill."

"I never give my guns to nobody," Murphy snarled.

"Cole's square, Bill." Barto pulled Murphy's guns.

"You get me out, Barto. You hear? Get me out soon as it's dark. Then I'm gonna hunt these coyotes down and plug 'em in the guts."

"You'll stand trial," Barto said, stepping back. "If the law's gonna mean anything, we've got to back it. Your pay'll go on."

"You get me out tonight. You hear?"

"Get moving." Cole jerked his head at the batwings.

They went out of the saloon and down the walk, Murphy with his hands high, mouthing a steady flow of curses. When they reached the jail, Cole searched him and removed a derringer and a thin-bladed knife. He locked the gunman in a cell and, returning to his office, stood in the doorway while Rocking H rode out of town, Silver Wade in front, as straight-backed and arrogant as when he'd come in that morning.

"What's he up to, Dan?" Cole asked.

"Just him and the devil know," York growled.

Cole built a smoke, thinking about Silver Wade and how his scheme had failed. He'd sacrificed Tommy Cotter's life in order to force Cole's hand, thinking that Cole would ask for Rocking H help in making the arrest. Then, operating on the side of the law, Wade and his men could wipe the nesters out. Or, if Cole had been killed in making the arrest, they could piously claim they stood for the law in going after the killer.

"Like sitting in front of a tornado," Cole said sourly. "You never know what it'll do or how it'll do it, but you sure as hell know it's gonna tear the guts out of something."

Eddes had stepped to the door. Now he called, "There's a feller coming into town from the west. Looks like that Laredo hombre."

"Riding like the devil was on his tail," Cole said, coming to stand behind his deputy.

They waited until the rider pulled up in front, dust whipping around him. "Get out to Wildcat Creek," Laredo bawled, "as fast as your bronc can bust the breeze getting there. Orrie Morgan killed Jim Fergus and he's forted up in his cabin now. The boys were closing in when I left."

Cole swore. Another ruckus that he'd momentarily forgotten under the pressure of the trouble between Rocking H and the nesters. "All right," he growled. "Thanks for riding in."

"I'll tell 'em you're coming." Laredo pulled his lathered animal around, and left town in the same killing pace he'd used coming in.

"He's murdering that animal," Eddes raged.

As Cole turned into his office to get his Winchester, York asked, "Does that sound on the level?"

"Afraid it does." Dan loaded his rifle and slid a box of shells into his pocket. "Fergus and Morgan have been jawing about a fence."

"Don't look good, coming just now," York said. "With Murphy in the jug, Wade and his bunch could come back and wipe the nesters out."

"Tell 'em to light out for home, Bunk. And keep a watch tonight. They might make a try at getting Murphy out."

Cole left his office, and taking his sorrel from the public stable, rode westward toward Wildcat Creek.

Despite the note of urgency in Laredo's message and the certainty that Silver Wade would make trouble, there was an undercurrent of optimism in Cole's thoughts that had not been there for months. He had been sure, until he'd been elected sheriff, that Ruth would accept his ring when she was old enough to know her own mind.

But the instant he'd pinned on his star she had become suddenly aloof. Today was the first time she had softened toward him since he had been elected sheriff, and the memory of their meeting in the hotel lobby filled him with a warm pleasure that lingered in his thoughts.

It was dusk when Cole topped the Wildhorse hills that lay between Bucktail Valley and the steep-walled canyon of Wildcat Creek. He listened for gunfire as he came down the twisting trail, but he heard no sound that would mark a battle.

It took him two hours to reach the bottom; another two hours before he came to Jim Fergus' cabin. Orrie Morgan's shack was another half mile downstream, and he would be hearing gunfire now if there was any. Either Laredo had brought him on a wild-goose chase, or the fight was finished.

Coming opposite Fergus' cabin, Cole saw there was a light in the front window, and belief grew in him that he had been tricked. Turning his horse across the creek, he called, "Jim."

The door swung open, and Jim Fergus' gaunt figure stood silhouetted in the yellow rectangle. "Who is it?" Fergus shouted.

Cole rode into the finger of light falling through the doorway. "Laredo brought word that Orrie Morgan had killed you. Looks like he exaggerated."

A laugh boomed out of Fergus. "He must have wanted to see you ride, Cole. Orrie and me buried the hatchet. He bought me out, and I'm fixing to leave the country."

"Sorry to see you go, but glad you're alive." Cole wheeled his sorrel and put him back across the creek, anger a white heat in him.

He'd break Laredo's neck the first time he caught up with the homesteader. Riding all night. . . . Suddenly he remembered York's suspicions and his own certainty that Silver Wade would pull a trick out of his hat. Laredo could have been waiting west of town with orders to ride in when he saw Rocking H leave. Or it might have been a nester trick. A sick emptiness came into Cole Drager's stomach as the certainty of disaster washed through him.

Cole kept his gelding at as fast a pace as the trail allowed, but the night was black with no moon and the stars were hidden by thick clouds that had scudded in from the west, and the trail was steep and crooked. It was well after midnight before he reached the sagebrush flat of Bucktail Valley, and dawn when the dark blot that was the town appeared before him.

Riding the length of the street, Cole was obsessed by the feeling that something was wrong. He put his sorrel away in the stable, still seeing nothing that was wrong. Pulling his Winchester from the boot, he swung back to his office. Then he stopped in the doorway, pinned there by horror. Little Bunk Eddes lay twisted on the floor, his head bent at a grotesque angle.

Cole knelt beside him, knowing he was dead before he tried to find a pulse. He came to his feet, still dazed by what he saw. Eddes had been slugged to death by blows on his head, probably from a gun barrel. Cole thought of Murphy, and ran back to the cells. The gunman was gone, and his cell door open.

The nesters had ridden back to free Murphy; Eddes had tried to stop them and they'd killed him. That was Cole's first thought, but in a moment it didn't add up. Ash Barto and his neighbors weren't that kind of men. It was the sort of thing Pres Phelan would do, but it was crazy to think that Rocking H would break Wild Bill Murphy out of jail.

"Hell, ain't it, Cole?"

Cole wheeled, hand instinctively dropping to gun butt, and fell away when he saw it was Dan York. "I'm a mite jumpy," he muttered. "Didn't hear you."

"I should have sung out." York ran a hand over his face. "I'm not thinking straight. Just saw something that made me air my paunch."

Cole followed York into the gray light that was filtering across the valley from a reluctant sky. Turning the corner at the courthouse, they followed the path to the back. York pointed upward. There, below a thick cottonwood limb, Wild Bill Murphy dangled from a rope, his body swaying in the slight breeze, his weight bringing an eerie creak from the tree.

"Dead," York croaked. "I didn't want to cut him down before you saw him. They must have got him and your deputy an hour ago. Maybe two."

Cole turned away, nausea sweeping over him. The spasms convulsed him and passed. He stood motionless, listening. There was no sound in the town. Only the stillness of a sleeping world at dawn.

"I told Eddes I'd spell him off, seeing as he'd been up all of last night. I dressed and came down and found him. Then I started looking around. Beefing Eddes didn't make much sense. Not till I found Murphy."

Cole started back to his office, York falling into step with him. He had never before seen a man who had been lynched, and the picture would be in his mind for years. "I ain't gonna overlook this, Dan," he said darkly.

"We'll get Doc up and cut the body down."

"I ain't gonna overlook it," Cole repeated.

"Who are you going to start on?"

"I dunno, but Bunk was my friend."

"Bunk being your friend don't make any difference," York said bluntly. "Looking at it from the side of the nesters, it was just as great a crime to hang Murphy as it was to beef Eddes. You think it was some of the Rocking H outfit, but you don't know. They were mighty quiet about it. Don't reckon anybody was up to see what went on."

"When I get done with Wade, he'll talk."

"You're gabbing like a fool," York snapped. "There's one thing that may help. I set my alarm for four, and when I was dressing, I heard somebody come up the stairs. I looked out. It was Wade, and he went into Delight Murphy's room. He stayed two, three minutes, and came out."

"Now you're talking like a fool. They'd have been done with the hanging by then."

"I'm thinking Wade told Delight what they'd done," York murmured.

"Delight would have killed him."

"Maybe not. If one of us is a fool, it's you when it comes to women. You'd better have a talk with Delight."

Silver Wade was the only Rocking H man who had the temerity to attend Murphy's funeral. Tommy Cotter had been buried the day before, Bunk Eddes that morning. The townsmen and a handful of ranchers from the west end of the county were there for Eddes' funeral, along with Cole and Dan York. That was all, but it was an even smaller crowd that stood through the short ceremony at Murphy's grave. There were the nesters, Ruth Barto with her arm around Delight, and Wade, York, and Cole standing away from the others.

Cole kept his eyes on Delight, remembering what York had said about Wade visiting her, but he could tell nothing from her expression. Her eyes gave no indication that she had been crying.

When the last prayer was finished, York muttered, "I never thought I'd grace Murphy's funeral with my presence. Let's drift."

They turned down the path toward the street. Cole didn't look at the fresh mound of earth marking Bunk Eddes' grave. He thought now, with grim detachment, that the little deputy had taken with him the deep respect and affection of everyone who had known him. Then he wondered if anyone, even Delight, had felt the keen edge of sorrow because of Murphy's death.

Looking back when they were a block from the cemetery, Cole saw Ash Barto and Ruth lead Delight away from the grave. They stepped into a buggy and wheeled by before the three men reached the hotel.

"It strikes me," Wade said soberly, "that the nesters were relieved by Murphy's passing. He was like a load chained to their backs. They don't need him any more, but they'd have had a hell of a time getting rid of him."

Cole held his silence, knowing Wade's words had been carefully chosen to mislead him. The nesters might need Murphy as much as they ever had.

When they reached the hotel, Wade said, "Tell Barto I want to see him."

It was a blunt order given as if Wade had not considered the possibility of Cole's refusing to carry his message.

"I'll tell him," Cole said curtly.

Nodding in the manner of one expecting immediate obedience, Wade turned into the hotel.

"Why didn't you jump him?" York demanded.

"The sign ain't right," Cole murmured. "When I get the proof I want, I'll have a talk with him. I figger to let him play his string out."

"I suppose you figure on letting Delight play her string out," York said with unnecessary heat.

"That's right."

"Only she'll leave the country, and where'll you be? I tell you she and Wade are in this up to their necks. The sooner you bust down on her, the sooner you'll get somewhere."

Cole had instinctively liked Dan York from the moment the special agent had ridden into town and showed his credentials. Now he realized that he didn't understand the man, and distrust began to gnaw at him.

"I don't reckon Delight has got anywhere to go."

"She won't stay here," York snapped. "I know her, Cole, and know how she'll act. She's got the devil's own soul. The only thing she gives a damn about is how much she can gouge out of a man."

"You said you know her?"

"I know her kind," York said quickly as if trying to erase a mistake. "I've got a hundred dollars that says she'll be on the stage in the morning if you don't hold her." York glared for a moment, as if angered by the sheriff's stubbornness. "Oh, hell, it's your business." Wheeling, he stamped into the lobby and up the stairs.

Cole kept his place in front of the hotel, shoulders against a post, hoping he would see Ruth and afraid that he would. The nesters drifted back from the cemetery, the women going into the stores, the men heading for the Gold Moon. Cole was still there when Ruth and her father came out. Cole said, "Wade wants to see you, Ash."

"I don't want to see him," Barto said uneasily.

"Mebbe you'd better."

Ruth had gone on to the steps, entirely ignoring Cole, her presence a chill pool touching him. Turning now, she pinned her gaze squarely on him. There was no softness about her, no hint that she had ever loved him.

"You took the one man who could have protected us," she said coldly. "You locked him up in jail, and sent York to tell us to go back home so there would be nobody to protect him. You even rode out of town so you'd be out of the way. Then Wade murdered him. Haven't you done enough damage?"

He stared at her, shoulders suddenly slack. It wasn't possible that she could believe all that. Yet he saw that she hated him with a deep and cutting bitterness.

He turned his eyes to Barto, masking the hurt that was in him, and said evenly, "Better go up and see Wade, Ash."

"Let's go home, Dad." Ruth stepped down from the porch.

"Reckon I will, Cole," Barto said, and moved beside his daughter to his buggy.

Cole waited until they had left town. Swinging into the lobby, he asked at the desk for the number of Wade's room, found it and knocked. When Wade opened the door, he said, "I told Barto, but he didn't want to see you."

Wade ran a hand through his white hair, anger staining his cheeks a dull red. "I'll stop there on my way home."

"Where were you the night Bunk was murdered and Murphy hanged?" Cole asked bluntly.

"Home." There was no break in the composure on his face, no sudden stirring of emotion. "You think I had something to do with it?"

"Who else would want Murphy dead but you?"

"The nesters. Like I said coming back from the funeral. They don't need him now, and they didn't know how to get rid of him. This way they made it look like my boys did it."

It was bold and shrewd, exactly the sort of play Cole could expect from Wade, and if it hadn't been for Bunk Eddes' death, he might have believed it. He nodded, thinking it was better for the moment to let Wade believe he had accepted the rancher's explanation, at least tentatively.

"I'll find out," Cole said. "When I do, I'll bring the men in. Make no mistake about that."

"Might be a foolish try."

Cole swung away and, leaving the hotel, moved down the street to his office. The nesters were leaving now, the wheels of their rigs stirring the dust of the street and the road that lay eastward across the sage flat and ran a twisting course through the Needles to Coffin Lake.

Presently Wade left the hotel, mounted, and took the same road the nesters had followed. Cole, watching the Rocking H owner until he was a black dot in the sage, felt a grudging admiration for the man. It had taken a cold, calculating courage to come to town alone on this day, when the nesters buried Wild Bill Murphy.

For a time he moved aimlessly around his office. Everything reminded him of Bunk Eddes: his gun, his pipe and tobacco, the joke book he'd read a dozen times, the cot in the side room. Too, there was that intangible thing which is beyond all human measure—the place he had made for himself in the hearts of those who lived.

Cole sat down at his desk, emotion tugging at him and turning his mind into a wheeling whirlpool. He thought of Ruth, and tried to forget her, then of Dan York, and finally of Delight Murphy. He pondered York's interest in this business, and knew he was right and York was wrong. There was no use for him to talk to Delight yet. She could deny Wade had been to her room the night Murphy was hanged. Or, admitting it, she could contend it was none of the sheriff's business.

But York was right in one thing. Delight Murphy's actions were not those of a woman who had lost a beloved husband. Then he remembered he had neglected to question the medico.

The doctor put down the book he was reading when Cole stepped into his office, and said wryly, "Had more business with the dead than the live lately. How long's this going to last?"

"A while." Cole cuffed back his hat. "Doc, how did Delight Murphy act before the funeral? Or did you see her?"

The doctor had started to reach for the pipe on the desk. Now his hand dropped, and swiveling his chair, he gave Cole a straight look. "Why?"

"Most women bawl their heads off when their husbands are buried. She didn't. Struck me as kind of queer."

"She's a funny woman, Cole." The medico picked up his pipe and began filling it. "I've been thinking about her ever since she came in two, three hours after we cut the body down. I thought of telling you, but I ain't one to go around gabbing."

"It's murder, Doc."

"Like I said, she came in a little while after we put Murphy in the back room." He flamed a match, and sucked it into his pipe bowl, keen eyes fixed on Cole. "I was going after Bud to come over and shave Murphy when I saw her leave the hotel with a suitcase. I figured she wanted to see him, so I waited. She didn't though." He took a puff. "She'd brought his grave clothes. Now make what you want to out of that."

"Hell, it was natural enough to bring his grave clothes."

"Yeah, but she didn't have time to leave town and go to the cabin where they'd been living on the Barto place, and fetch them."

"Bill kept that hotel room rented all the time. Mebbe she had 'em there."

The doctor shook his head. "Delight's been sick several times since they came here. I've been in the hotel room and I've been in their cabin. Bill kept all of his clothes in the cabin because he stayed out there, figuring that was where they'd have their trouble."

Cole saw, then, what the medico was thinking. Delight Murphy had brought her husband's grave clothes to town hours before he had been lynched.

He said, "Thanks," and wheeling, left the office. He had enough now to talk to Delight Murphy.

Cole hurried along the boardwalk to the hotel, feeling some direction to the sense of urgency that had been in him since he had found Bunk Eddes' body. Before Cole had gone a dozen paces past the batwings of the Fashion, Dan York stepped out and caught up with him.

"You're moving like you were headed someplace," York said.

Irritation prodded Cole. The special agent acted as if he were afraid Cole knew something he didn't. Then, remembering it was York who had started him thinking about Delight, he said, "I'm gonna have that talk with Delight."

"It's about time. Wade had another visit with her before he left."

They swung into the lobby and climbed the stairs, a vague sense of uneasiness gnawing at Cole. Dan York was a human bulldog with a mind that had room for only one compelling idea at a time. Now that the hearing was over, he was pursuing another objective, and Cole had a feeling that it was entirely personal.

Glancing sideways at York's granite block of a face as they strode along the hall, the thought came to Cole that they might be enemies within the next few minutes. There was, to Cole Drager, such a thing as human mercy that was to be weighed in the balances with justice, a consideration that had probably never entered Dan York's stubborn mind.

Cole knocked on Delight's door. He had heard a movement inside the room; now there was only silence. He knocked again, and when there was no answer, York said impatiently, "Bust it in. She's here all right."

"It's Cole Drager. I want to talk to you, Delight."

"I'm dressing, Cole. You can't come in now."

"Hell, she lies faster'n a horse trots." York tried the knob, but the door was locked.

"No hurry, Dan," Cole said.

"Plenty of hurry," the special agent snapped.

York backed away and plunged at the door in a bull-like rush, the point of a beefy shoulder hitting it and smashing it open so that it slammed against the inside wall.

Clad in a flimsy negligee, Delight was backed against the window, a small gun in her hand. She said sharply, "What do you want, Drager?"

This was a new Delight Murphy, without the veneer of sweetness which she had always worn when Cole had been around her. Wildness made a bright shine in her emerald eyes. She was suddenly and violently afraid, Cole thought, and he probed for the reason of her fear with, "It's the guilty people who don't like to answer lawmen's questions."

"Am I guilty?"

"When you answer a couple of questions, I think I'll know. Want me to stand out here so everybody who goes by can hear?"

"All right," she said reluctantly. "Come in."

Cole and York stepped into the room, Cole heeling the door shut and standing against it, York moving to the bureau and stopping only when Delight turned her gun on him. Cole moved forward until she covered him, and then York came around the bureau and stopped within ten feet of her.

"That's enough," she said angrily. "I'll kill you first, Drager, if you keep sneaking up."

"I don't talk good with a gun in my face," Cole said. "Put it down."

"No." Her lips were a scarlet line curved by fury. "Ask what you want and get out."

"We think Wade and some of his men killed Bunk Eddes and hanged your husband. We know that Wade came to see you after the murders. Why?"

The wildness in her eyes became a green flame. She pulled back the hammer of her gun. "Both of you, get out."

"Why did Wade see you today before he left town?" York demanded harshly.

She whirled on York, finger tightening on the trigger.

Cole had eased up another step. Now he lunged forward, bending low, the sound of her bullet slapping at his ears. He had her then, one arm around her, right hand gripping her wrist. She began to curse and kick. She bit his hand before he could jerk away. Then the gun clattered to the floor and Cole, swinging her in a wild skirt-ballooning arc, dumped her violently on the bed.

"You called her right, Dan," Cole said, wiping blood from his hand.

York smiled a tight smile. "I told you I knew her. How do you figure on making the lady talk?"

"Jail her."

"Won't do. Wade will bust her out. Or even if he lets her stand trial, you'd never convict a woman with her face."

"I didn't have anything to do with it," Delight shrilled.

The desk clerk and half a dozen people had gathered outside, attracted by the shot. Moving to the door, Cole said, "It's all right, folks. Nobody hurt." Turning back, he said, "A prison term plays hell with a woman's looks, Delight."

She made a wild lunge toward the door. Cole caught her and threw her back. "Why did you bring Bill's grave clothes to town before he was lynched?"

"I'll be damned," York breathed. "How'd you find that out, Cole?"

"Doc told me."

"I'll be damned," the special agent repeated as if he was certain now of what he had suspected.

"What are you going to do?" Delight whispered, eyes shining emerald orbs.

"Let you rot in jail till you're ready to talk," Cole snapped.

"I reckon you might convict her," York said thoughtfully, "when the jury hears about Bill's grave clothes."

"Who are you?" Delight demanded. Her eyes were suddenly shrewd. "I mean, besides being what you pretend."

"Shawn Bellamy's brother. He had some trouble in Texas that made him change his name when he got into Colorado, but the trouble he'd got into wasn't anything to what he had after he met you."

She sat on the edge of the bed, staring at York, trying to hold to what was left of her courage. Then her shoulders went slack. "All right," she breathed. "I'll talk if you'll let me go."

"I'll make no promise," Cole said sharply, "but I'll do the best I can for you." He took pencil and paper from his pocket. "We'll take this down and you'll sign it?"

"I'll sign it," she said tonelessly, as if numbed by the pressure of her fear. "Three of Wade's men killed Eddes and hanged Bill. Wade was sure he'd lose the decision and he was done fooling. With Bill out of the way, the nesters would scare if he got tough, so he decided to go whole hog. His men were afraid to tackle Bill. That's why Wade schemed this up. He wanted you to ask him to help arrest Bill. Then there'd be a fight. Bill and most of the nesters would get killed. Wade would be on the side of the law. When it didn't work, they took this other way of getting Bill when he couldn't defend himself."

"Wade had Laredo suck me out of town?" Cole asked.

"He fixed that up in case things didn't work out. Laredo was to ride in when he saw them leave. They didn't figure on killing Eddes, but Phelan lost his head."

"How did they get Tommy Cotter to tackle Bill?"

"Got him drunk. Wade told him he would be a hero if he killed Bill."

"What about you and Wade?"

"I was going to San Francisco and he was coming there when he got this fixed. We were going to be married." She glared at Cole. "If you'd been married to a kill-crazy fool like Bill, you'd want him out of the way, too. I knew they were going to get him some way, but I didn't know about the hanging. Wade came up to tell me."

"Who killed Bunk?"

"Phelan. Jeb Lowell and Ras Olney were with him."

Cole scribbled for a moment and handed the sheet to Delight. She read it and signed her name without argument. "Now get out and leave me alone."

"I've got a job to do first," York said darkly. "She married my brother, Cole. He was the only living relative I had. I was in Colorado working on a Mexican land grant case, and Shawn and this devil were in a mining camp in the San Juan. Before I got up to see them, I had word he'd killed himself. When I got there, I found out she'd run away with Murphy. That was two years ago. I heard through an agent who'd been working on this case that they were here. That's why I pulled some wires and landed this job."

Cole folded the paper and stowed it in his pocket. Looking at York now, he felt again the bulldog qualities of the man. There was only one motive in him that was more powerful than his urge for personal vengeance—his sense of duty.

"You're lawman enough to know that I can't let you hand out personal punishment, Dan," Cole said.

"You can't stop me," the special agent said somberly. "Go after Phelan and let me do what I've got to do."

"I'll need Delight's testimony when these men come up for trial."

"You've got her signed statement."

"What's more," Cole went on as if he hadn't heard, "I'll need help bringing Phelan and the other two in. With Bunk gone, you're the only man in the county who can give me the help I need."

For a moment York's eyes locked with Cole's, and Cole sensed the battle that was going on behind those eyes. Then York nodded as if he saw the logic in what Cole had said.

"What's your plan?"

"We'll take Delight to Barto's. Then we'll go after Wade's men."

There was no humour in the grin York gave Cole. "I guess what I've got to do can wait."

The sun had dropped behind the Wildhorse hills before they were through the Needles, Delight Murphy riding between Cole and Dan York. They held a somber silence, Cole knowing that the moment for the final settlement of Delight's future had only been postponed.

It was a wasteland, this range of cliffs and spires and hideous monsters carved by a bitter cutting wind that was constantly at work. Shadows lay dark in the bottom of the canyon, and Cole, never liking this eerie region nor the high scream of the wind above them, felt relief when they came down into the grasslands that lay north and west of Coffin Lake.

The last glint of the dying sun was caught in the lake. It was a bright diamond framed on two sides by rocks and sagebrush, and a fringe of tules and hay lands on the others. Then the color faded, and it was nothing more than a pool of murky water, its momentary glory gone, as somber as the run of Cole's thoughts.

They turned north along the road that hugged the rimrock, and dusk became night, and the windows in homesteader cabins were yellow pinpoints. Then, swinging from the main road that ran on to Rocking H they made the turn to Barto's cabin.

"Ash," Cole called.

The door was flung open, and Barto stood there, the lamp behind him throwing his long shadow into the dusty yard. Cole helped Delight down, and gripped her by the arm, propelled her into the cabin. Ruth stood by the table, lips tightly pressed as she waited for an explanation.

"I'm going after the men who killed Bunk and hanged Murphy," Cole said. "Delight is my witness. No matter what you and Ruth think, or what this woman tells you, keep her here."

"We won't have any part of this," Ruth flung at him.

"Who runs this place, Ash?" Cole asked, pinning his eyes on the homesteader.

"We'll keep her," Barto snapped.

"I'll want three horses."

Barto nodded, "They ain't what you'd call saddlers, but they'll get your men to town."

Cole told Barto about Delight's confession as they threw gear on the horses. He added, "It ain't for me to judge the right and wrong of this, Ash. Being in love with Ruth put me on your side as far as my feelings go, but sheriffing is more important than favoring one side or the other."

Barto came directly under the lantern, the cone of light throwing an orange mask on his seamy face. "A man can stand so much, Cole. We've got to that place. Wade stopped here tonight, said he'd give a fair price for our places, and that if we didn't sell, he'd make it tough, starting before the week was out. We can't go on living this way." He turned away, blinking a little. "We can't forget it was you who locked Murphy up, so they could hang him."

"You ain't going on living this way," Cole said angrily. "Send Ruth to round up the settlers. Have 'em here when I get back."

"What good will the settlers do?" Barto demanded. "Murphy's dead."

"It's a good thing for you he is. Sooner or later he'd have made outlaws out of all of you. Now it'll be Wade who's outside the law. If I've got Wade figgered right, he'll be here after Delight."

Barto stood there until the sound of the horses died. Then, turning to saddle Ruth's mare, he muttered, "Two of 'em against Rocking H. They'll never come back."

Angling across the sageflat, Cole and York came to the Rocking H road. Less than an hour later they topped the ridge that looked down upon the ranch buildings. Cole noted the light in the big house. He was picturing the layout and planning his moves when York said, "If you don't have a brother, you won't know how I feel."

"I have two," Cole said quietly. "I know how you feel and I know what you're thinking. I won't let you."

A gusty sigh broke out of York's great chest. "I like you, Cole, but I'll kill you if you try to stop me. When I get done with that she-devil, she'll never do to another man what she did to Shawn."

"Right now we've got another job. We'll tie the horses a piece on this side of the house. You turn their horses out and shoot a few times. I'll get into the house while the fracas is going on."

"Your men won't be in the house."

"I'll get 'em," Cole said grimly. "Don't start fighting the bunch. Come back and wait for me where we leave the horses."

They split fifty yards from the house, York circling toward the corrals, Cole tying the horses and going the rest of the way on foot, gun palmed. The rear of the house was entirely black. Cole, moving swiftly, reached it and rounded the north side. Coming to the long porch, he waited at the edge of the pool of light cascading from the first window.

Cole heard the talk, Wade's soft tone and Pres Phelan's loud one. Phelan raised his voice to bellow, "Damn it, Silver, you've schemed up one trick after another. All the time I could have done the job for you in one night."

Wade flung back, "Cole Drager is a hell of a lot tougher than I figured. We've got to hide our tracks, or we'll wind up in the calaboose."

"The hell we will. If you want Drager out of the way—"

The racket broke out then: York's high yell, his shots piercing the night silence, jagged tongues of flame lashing into darkness, the thunder of hooves. Men boiled out of the bunkhouse, their minds sleep-fogged. There was a moment of chaos, and Cole profited by it. He raced across the porch, reaching the door just as Phelan bolted through. Cole tripped him, sending him into a jarring fall, and slid into the house.

"Hold it," he called to Wade, and turned to Phelan in time to see the ramrod pull gun. He fired, his bullet angling through Phelan's chest, and sending the redhead off the porch in a loose-jointed roll.

Cole wheeled again to Wade. There had been that moment when the other could have pulled gun, one precious second when Cole's back was to him. But he hadn't moved. He'd kept his position at the fireplace, black brows hooding his eyes. Whether it was shock or fear that had held him rigid Cole didn't know, but the moment was gone.

"Get out where the boys can see you," Cole ordered, his gun on Wade. "Holler for Lowell and Olney. Send the rest after the horses. Don't say anything about Phelan."

Wade obeyed, walking stiffly across the room, as if his legs were stilts. Standing in the doorway, he shouted, "Ras—Jeb! Come here. Rest of you boys get those horses back into the corrals."

Some of the hands had started toward the house to investigate the shooting. They stopped now, uncertainty gripping them.

"Get 'em moving, Wade," Cole prodded.

"Get in here, Ras. You, too, Jeb," Wade called, panic honing an edge to his voice.

Lowell and Olney came on to the house. The rest faded into the darkness.

"Step inside," Cole ordered. "Get back over by the fireplace."

Again the Rocking H owner obeyed. Olney and Lowell came in, and stopped abruptly when Cole said, "You're under arrest for the murder of Bunk Eddes and Bill Murphy. Unbuckle your gunbelts."

They faced him, Olney cursing as they unlatched their belts and let them drop.

"What'd you call us in here for, Silver?" Lowell demanded. "You want us to hang?"

"You won't hang," Wade said darkly. "He won't get you to Bucktail."

"We'll sure as hell start," Cole returned. "I have a signed statement from Delight Murphy saying these men and Phelan killed Bunk and Murphy. Delight's at the Barto place, and she'll stay there till the trial."

"Delight wouldn't—" Wade began. "Hell, Drager, you're bluffing."

"You'll see. All right. Let's mosey. Don't start throwing lead, Wade, if you want these boys to stay alive."

They crossed the porch and faded into the darkness, Cole following closely, gun cocked. Presently York called, "Who is it?"

"A couple of men on their way to a hanging." Cole answered. "Phelan didn't live long enough to taste the rope, but these boys did."

"Let's drift," York said. "They'll be after us like hornets on the prod soon as they get their horses."

Olney laughed, "You won't get far."

Cole and York tied the prisoners into saddles and lashed their hands behind their backs. Mounting, they took the road up the ridge, and had barely gained the top when they heard the thunder of hooves behind them.

Olney's laugh was more confident this time. "You didn't get all the horses, York. You won't even get to the Needles."

"Pull off the road and let 'em pass, Dan," Cole said. "I'll go on to the Barto place. You take these hombres to town."

"I'll jail 'em for you and then I've got another chore to do," York said.

Cole didn't wait to argue. Feeding his sorrel steel, he thundered through the sage, taking a straight course to the Barto cabin. Junipers fled by in a black blur. Then the cabin loomed before him, and he was pulling up, dust whipping into a suffocating cloud around him.

"The whole outfit's coming, Ash," Cole called.

Barto came out, a Sharps .45–90 in his hands. "Ruth ain't back," he said worriedly.

Cole stripped gear from his horse and slapped him on the rump. The weary animal disappeared into the darkness. Cole stood listening to the rolling thunder of hooves. "Looks like you and me, Ash."

They went inside, the settler barring the door and covering the windows with heavy shutters. "I built this solid, thinking of the Piutes."

Delight Murphy was sitting on the bed, the lamplight painting color on her cheeks.

"Get down on the floor," Cole ordered. "Less chance of getting hit."

Slowly she obeyed, emerald eyes bright.

"Plumb crazy," Ash Barto muttered. "Cussed me and Ruth good for not letting her go."

They came out of the darkness, blurred, swift-moving shapes that circled the cabin, guns roaring Rocking H's final challenge to the settlers who had clung so tenaciously to this disputed land, bullets slapping ominously into the logs. This was death drawing close, death in the flame-stabbed darkness, and only a miracle of luck and straight shooting and cold courage could save the lives of Cole Drager and Ash Barto.

"Hold your fire," Cole cautioned. "They'll get closer."

The shooting stopped; hard on the dying echoes came Silver Wade's voice: "We want Mrs. Murphy."

"Go to hell," Barto bellowed.

"We'll burn you out," Wade threatened.

"Burn and be damned," Barto raged.

There was sillence then. Cole, standing at one of the loopholes Barto had drilled long ago between the logs, could see nothing, but his thoughts were racing as a man's do when he stands at the threshold of eternity, seeking a way of escape, and failing.

Tonight would bring the flash. Ash Barto was showing a solid core of courage, but what about the others, the ones Ruth had gone to fetch—who should have been here before now? Without Wild Bill Murphy to lead them, they probably would not come at all.

Suddenly the firing began again north of the barn. Wade and his men had forted up in the corrals or were lying flat in the fields between the cabin and the haystack.

Cole began shooting, targeting the spots where he saw the gun flashes. Barto cut loose with his Sharps, the boom of it momentarily drowning out the sound of lesser guns. There was the nostril-sting of powdersmoke, the whisper of bullets across the cabin when they found a loophole or an entrance between the logs.

"They can't hurt us," Barto shouted jubilantly. "Ruth'll get here with the boys, and we'll have then varmints between two fires."

But Cole Drager did not share the homesteader's optimism. It would take just two of those stray bullets to finish the fight. Then, with opposition ended in the cabin, Silver Wade's hardcase crew would sweep the valley with lead and fire. And somewhere, out there in the darkness, Ruth Barto rode for help that might not come.

"What's that?" Barto cried in terror.

It was the unmistakable crackle of fire above them. "They've lit the roof!" Cole shouted, and wheeled to the opposite side of the cabin. Peering through a loophole, he saw a bright flame leave the earth and soar skyward, falling short of the cabin by a few feet. "They're shooting fire arrows, Ash. The damned coyotes were ready for this."

"I figgered they was from the way Wade talked today," Barto said harshly. "We're licked, Cole. The minute we go through that door, they'll drill us, and we'll roast if we stay here."

"Any way to get on the roof?"

"No."

"From the way that roof sounds, they don't need to waste any more arrows." Cole crossed to the other side of the cabin. "They've fired the stack, Ash."

"No sense in that. Now we can see 'em."

Barto shot again, the cabin trembling with the blast of the great gun. Cole emptied his .45, saw that another gun was in action on the other side of the burning stack and wondered who was firing.

The burning cabin on one side and the stack on the other threw a murky leaping light across the yard. Within a matter of minutes the Rocking H position was untenable. They broke, Wade and his men, and raced for new cover. One of them threw a shot as he ran, the slug ripping between two logs and raking the side of Cole's head. He cursed and, squeezing trigger, brought a man down before he swiped at the blood.

Neither Cole nor Barto, busy for the moment at the loopholes, had a thought for Delight Murphy. Crazed by terror, she slipped across the room, lifted the bar and jerked the door open. It was only when firelight danced across the floor that Cole saw what she had done. He leaped toward the door, but he was too late.

"I'm coming, Silver," the woman screamed, and ran into the yard.

Cole never knew who fired the bullet. It might have been another chance shot from Wade's men. Or from the man in the hayfield whose gun had kept up a steady fire. Slugs had been snapping across the yard in insensate fury. One of them caught her, bringing her to an abrupt stop as if she'd hit an invisible wall. Then she crumpled into the trodden dust.

A cry rose from Silver Wade, high and wild with fury. He lunged from his position at the edge of the light and bolted toward the cabin.

"I'm coming after you, Drager!"

As if by order the firing stopped when Cole stepped out of the burning cabin into the lurid light. Smoke billowed between them and was gone. They faced each other, then, across Delight Murphy's still form.

The guns thundered together, their echoes rolling out across the earth. Wade began to wilt, white head dropping forward. He spilled to his knees, and held himself there a moment, fighting against the payment of man's eternal debt while he struggled to bring his gun up for one final try at the lawman who stood before him. Then the last spark of life was gone and he fell.

Cole paced forward, gun held at his hip, knowing that he made a high target. Now that Wade was down, he'd be on the receiving end of Rocking H lead. It came, snarling at him, knocking him off his feet as Ash Barto was driven from the cabin by the heat and raced a dozen steps before he fell.

The man in the field was shooting again. Lead screamed over Cole or tugged at him or geysered into the dirt. He was vaguely aware of the cabin roof's falling, of the upsweep of sparks. He felt no pain, only a numbness in his chest.

This was the end of the trail, he thought. It had to be, for he heard the drumming of hooves and then Ruth was cradling his head in her lap. The shooting had stopped. Then he slipped off into a pool that was wide and black and without bottom. . . .

It was daylight when he came to, daylight that filtered through cracks in the roof and through cobwebby windows. He saw that he was in Barto's barn, that others were lying near him, and the medico was fussing over one and then another.

Dan York saw that Cole was conscious and came to hunker beside him.

"Hell of a fight, wasn't it?" the government man said. "When I get back to Washington I'm going to tell them that if a special agent stays on the job till it's finished, there's less ruckusing about it afterward."

"Were you the one who fired the stack?"

"That I did, and put a few notches on my gun to boot."

"Barto?"

"Got a shoulder wound. Your prisoners are locked up. I took 'em in as soon as I got done here." He grinned. "Never could stay out of a good fight."

Cole looked squarely at him then. "What about Delight?"

It was York who broke gaze. "Maybe the Almighty don't use me to hand out punishment like I figgered He did. She's alive, but her face is going to be scarred. She'll never turn another man's heart, but I'm damned glad I didn't do it." He held out his hand. "Got to be on the move. Just came back with Doc to see how you were."

He was gone then, and Ruth was there, a cool hand on Cole's forehead. Even now, bullet-shattered as he was, she still had the power to stir him in a way no other person could.

"There were so many things I didn't understand," she murmured. "Cole, I know now what it takes to be a sheriff. I'm sorry. . . ."

"I just want to know one thing, honey. Will you marry me?"

She brought her lips down to his, and he found the answer to his question. He had all this woman could give to a man. It was enough. He looked back along the trail, and found that he had no regrets. Ahead was the sun, a bright sun shining on the two of them, and he knew her presence would always stir him as it did this moment.

Book-L'arnin' and the Equalizer

Grass had grown again to cover the scars of battle at Shiloh and Gettysburg and Five Forks, but there was nothing that could hide the scars in the hearts of men that strife had made. Even in Oregon where no battle had been fought, bitterness still lay like a motionless evil-smelling pool.

Many who had been admitted Copperheads during the war had moved to other localities and started again among new neighbors; but the Vannings clung sullenly to old Enoch's donation land-claim in the foothills east of Oregon City, brooding and muttering defiance to those who kept alive the memory of their Civil War record.

Although the schoolmaster, Neil Hartley, was new to the Corners, he soon understood the situation. Hank Bonner, the postmaster and storekeeper who had been a Union Leaguer during the war, and a loud-mouthed one at that, stopped at the schoolhouse the first evening after the pupils had gone.

"Everybody in this community but the Vannings was for Lincoln and the Union, Hartley," Bonner said arrogantly. "I understand you came from Missouri. What are your politics, sir?"

Except for the war years, Neil Hartley had taught school since he was sixteen. Tall and ungainly and awkward, he was far from a handsome man, but he had a rare understanding of people, both young and old, and for that reason he was a successful teacher. His eyes, red-rimmed from much reading, fixed on Bonner and mirrored his instinctive dislike for the man. Bonner, small and over-proud and fuzzy-whiskered, was a trouble stirrer bent on keeping the Civil War alive years after Lee's surrender.

"My politics are my business," Hartley said shortly.

Bonner bristled. "You won't get along if you take that attitude. The Vannings will run you out in a month if you don't have the Unionists' help."

"I didn't have any Vannings in school today."

"It ain't that. They're Rebels. Allus was 'n' allus will be. Old Enoch Vanning was the Copperhead kingpin around here. Three of his boys fit with the Rebels. One of 'em died at Cold Harbor."

"I respect any man who fights for his belief," Hartley said gravely.

Bonner's little eyes narrowed. "All right, Hartley. You're a gone pigeon, and talking tough won't help you."

In Missouri old hatreds were still festering sores, but Hartley had not expected to find the same thing true here. He rose now, and putting his hands palms down on the scarred desktop, leaned across it, his mouth drawn tight across his bony face.

"There has been unnecessary suffering in the South because men like you keep the old fires alive. Every human being, whether his name is Vanning or something else, has a God-given dignity and an intrinsic worth because he is a human being. Good day, sir."

"The Vannings will make you trouble," Bonner cried. "I only wanted—"

"If you think you can embroil me in your neighborhood feuds, you're wrong. Good day, sir."

Bonner left, muttering about Rebel Missourians teaching loyal Oregon children. A sickness crawling through him, Hartley watched Bonner until he had crossed the schoolyard and disappeared into the timber. Hartley had killed men, and he had seen his friends die. Thousands of miles from those battlefields, across the plains and Rockies, across deserts and the Cascades, he had expected to find peace of spirit. He saw now that he would find no peace, until he had fought for it. . . .

The sun was dipping behind the fir tops of the hills when Hartley took the path through the timber to Parson Dailey's house, where he boarded.

"Who are the Vannings?" Hartley asked that night.

"Unreconstructed Rebels," the parson said heavily. "A bad lot. Avoid them as you would the devil. They care only for drinking and fighting."

"There might be less trouble if their neighbors treated them fairly."

Dailey smiled thinly. "The only way to treat a family of snakes is to bruise their heads under your heel."

"Do they have any children of school age?"

"The youngest boy is eighteen. The Lord help you if he comes to school."

Hartley lay awake that night, thinking about the Vannings—wondering. Parson Dailey was no Hank Bonner. Still, it was something less than sense for a feud like this to be hanging over from the war years.

Hartley didn't see any of the Vannings for more than a week. They lived ten miles up the creek, and came to the settlement only when necessity drove them, or old Enoch's corn liquor prodded them into hunting for a fight. But Hartley heard talk from his pupils, so much talk that his curiosity grew. Everybody who lived within twenty miles of the Corners feared the Vannings; and the rumor spread that the old Union Leaguers would settle the feud bloodily and permanently.

Then old Enoch brought Bud to school. Hartley was hearing little Jane Dailey read, when Enoch and the boy came in. He guessed who they were before old man Vanning opened his mouth.

"You the schoolmarm?" old Enoch boomed.

Anger stirred in Hartley. If Enoch aimed to start trouble, he was beginning the right way. Hartley said: "That will do, Jane." He moved along the aisle to where Vanning and the sullen boy stood. Enoch, red-bearded and buckskin-clad, would have seemed more in place in old Fort Vancouver thirty years before, than slouching now in the doorway of an Oregon log schoolhouse.

"I'm the schoolmaster," Hartley said in a level tone.

"Schoolmaster—schoolmarm. All same thing." Enoch spat a brown puddle on the puncheon floor. "My old woman says this hyar boy needs some book l'arnin'. Now, I don't hold to that. I didn't have none, and my other boys didn't have none, but this hyar's the baby, and the old woman's plumb foolish 'bout him. You do the best you can, Mister. If he don't toe the mark, you lick hell out o' him."

Bud Vanning was a man grown, almost as tall as Hartley, and twenty pounds heavier. He had boasted he could lick any damyankee in the Willamette Valley, and with his brothers urging him on, he'd had a good start toward making his brag good. He laughed now, black eyes ugly, meaty lips curled contemptuously.

"He ain't man enough to lick me, Pap."

Old Enoch smiled tolerantly. "He can try, son. You stay today and see how you make out."

"I'm here to teach," Hartley said grimly. "If this boy doesn't want to learn, he shouldn't be here."

"You can be damned sure I ain't here to learn," Bud snarled.

Enoch moved back to his horse. "Beat it into him. He'll l'arn if you hit him hard enough. That's the way I l'arned my big boys."

Hartley motioned to a seat at the end of a split log bench. "You may sit there, Bud."

"Sure, schoolmarm," Bud said insolently, and sat down, his long legs stretched in front of him.

"You will call me Mr. Hartley."

"Sure." The boy's grin was quick and challenging. *"Mr. Hartley."*

Hartley returned to his desk, feeling the tension in the room, seeing the scared look on the children's faces. Whatever might have been in Enoch's mind, there was only one motive in Bud's—to make all the trouble he could. And Hartley realized that there was but one course of action open to him.

"You don't mind me taking a chaw, schoolmarm?" Bud called.

Hartley wheeled. Bud had taken a long-bladed knife from his pocket and had sliced off a mouthful.

"You will do no chewing in school."

"Aw, hell! Got to have some fun." Bud stuffed the tobacco into his mouth, and slouched lower in the seat. "Bad enough to sit here and have to look at your ugly mug. A chaw might help."

Hartley came back along the aisle. He hated what he had to do, but there was no choice. He was within a step of the boy when Bud drew a long-barreled Colt from his belt.

"Don't make me drill you—" Bud began.

Young Vanning never finished his sentence. Moving with surprising speed for a man as awkward-appearing as he was, Hartley grabbed Bud's wrist and twisted until the boy let the gun go. Hartley laid it on the desk, jerked Bud from the seat and sledged him on the side of the head.

Bud fell face-down. Neil Hartley gripped him by the seat of the pants and his shirt-collar, and shook him vigorously, as a terrier would shake a squirrel. Then he dropped the boy flat and strode back to his desk.

"You have had plenty of time to learn your spelling." Hartley nodded at a row of white-faced children. "Mark, spell *Peloponnesian*."

Bud's notion of making trouble was shaken out of his head. He got up and sat down, and when his gaze locked with Hartley's, he grinned. Hartley grinned back, tension easing in him.

Bud came to the desk when Hartley dismissed school at noon. "You reckon you can teach me anything that'll do me any good?"

"Learning doesn't do anybody any good unless a man makes use of it. Can you read and write?"

"A little. Ma, she taught me, but I can't read good enough. I'd like to know about the furrin countries. Yurrop and Chiny. And Mexico. Pap fought with Doniphan. I want to know how much he lies."

"I'll loan you some books, Bud. If that's the kind of learning you want, it's what I'll teach you."

The boy shifted uneasily. "It was Ma's idee 'bout me coming. Pap and the boys allowed I'd whup you. When they hear what you done to me, they'll be on your tail. Us Vannings hang together. Pap taught us that."

"Don't tell them."

"They'll hear. The Bonner kid will bust a gut getting home to tell his paw, and Bonner'll see Pap hears. Then there'll be hell to pay."

"I'll handle your brothers."

Bud looked at the floor. "There's Pap and five boys beside me. Cass is the oldest. He got wounded fighting with Price. He's plumb proud, Cass is. They'll all jump you, and they'll bust you up. Bonner and his sniveling friends won't help you none."

"No," Hartley said grimly. "I didn't figure on them."

"Can you shoot?"

"Not very well."

"Let's see you have a try at it."

Shrugging, Hartley picked up Bud's pistol and went outside. There had been a day when he was a good shot, but he was nearsighted now, and he knew it was worse than useless to try. He shot twice at a fir stump behind the schoolhouse, the last bullet going wild and taking a piece of hide off the back of Parson Dailey's cow.

"Aw, hell," Bud groaned. "You ain't no good at all."

"I guess not," Hartley admitted. "My eyes are poor."

"You better pack up and git."

"I'll stay, Bud," Hartley said firmly.

From then on, Hartley had no fault to find with Bud's behavior. The boy worked willingly, read everything that Hartley gave him, and he got along with the smaller pupils. But the day of settlement was bound to come, just as Bud had warned. If for no other reason, it would come because Hank Bonner and some the rest taunted old Enoch and the Vanning boys about the way Hartley had handled Bud.

It happened the Saturday following Bud's disciplining. Hartley walked to the post office, the earth gloomy dark even in midafternoon with the giant trees shadowing the trail. He absentmindedly noted the string of horses in front of the saloon, but he saw no significance in their presence until Bonner sullenly handed him his mail and he stepped out of the store.

Old Enoch and Bud were squatting in front of the saloon, the five oldest Vanning boys lounging in the weeds at the edge of the road to Enoch's left. They were each as big as Bud or bigger, and as tough-looking a lot as Hartley had ever seen.

"When you fight one Vanning, you fight them all." Hartley had heard that a dozen times since he had come to the Corners. He glimpsed Bonner's face at a window of the store.

Old Enoch was grinning expectantly under his red beard. Bud looked scared and worried. The older boy chewed and spat and held a sullen silence until Hartley came opposite them. It was the black trouble-scarred one on the end who growled: "The rest of us Vannings want a little book l'arnin', schoolmarm."

It would be Cass Vanning, Hartley guessed. He saw now why folks around the Corners feared the Vannings. He stopped in front of Cass, who had come to his feet, peering at him as he made a quick decision. He couldn't lick the five of them. But there was one thing the Vannings admired. It had worked with Bud. It might work with the rest.

Without a word Hartley swung his fist, a short wicked right to the point of Cass' wide black-bearded jaw that knocked him flat. Hartley picked Cass up, and wheeling, dropped him into the horse-trough and shoved his head under.

"I can handle you boys if you're men enough to come one at a time." Hartley said coldly. "If you're wolves instead of men, you'll come at me in a pack, and maybe you can lick me."

"You're drowning Cass," old Enoch bellowed. "Let him up."

Cass was kicking and snorting and blowing bubbles under Hartley's big hand. Hartley lifted him from the trough and dumped him into the dust. Cass came to his hands and knees, shook his head and choked and spat. His four brothers, held flat-footed by the temerity of Hartley's actions, moved forward now, cursing.

"Don't let 'em, Pap," Bud cried.

Old Enoch rumbled a laugh. "Hold on, boys. The Vannings don't wolfpack any man. Cass just wasn't big enough to do the job."

Enoch was too far away for Hartley to see his face clearly, but he had the impression the old man was grinning at him the way Bud had in the schoolhouse that first morning.

Cass was on his feet now, still choking, water from his soaked clothes making a puddle in the dog fennel at his feet. The other boys had dropped back, still muttering, obeying old Enoch from force of habit.

"I got no use for them that gabble like geese." Old Enoch raised his voice so that Hank Bonner, watching from the store, could hear. "I've got the best piece of land between here and the mountains, and I don't aim to be run off so the goose-gabblers can grab it. Us Vannings don't run for nobody. Reckon you don't neither, Hartley. You won't have no more trouble with us." He started toward his horse. "Let's git for home."

For an instant Cass made no move. His black eyes, fixed on Hartley's face, were unshaded windows opening upon the rushing turbulence of his passion. He turned suddenly, and sloshed to his horse. The other boys followed. The Vannings quit town in a rolling cloud of dust; but Hartley, watching them disappear into the vaulting timber, knew nothing had been settled, that all the boys except Bud would follow Cass instead of old Enoch.

Bud came to school on Monday with a bruised and battered face that was cruel evidence of a beating. "Cass whupped hell out of me 'cause I hollered at Pap to stop the boys,'' Bud told Hartley that night after school. "I ain't big enough to handle Cass yet—but I'm gonna be, one of these days.''

"Is Cass still fighting the war?''

"Naw. He just cain't forget the ducking you gave him.''

Hartley stayed at his desk long after Bud's horse had been swallowed by the timber. He had seen men like Cass Vanning. He had fought with them and against them during the war, big black-tempered men ruled by passion. He understood Hank Bonner too—scheming to use his neighbors' hatred for his own profit, fanning a flame that should have died long ago.

Hartley was still at his desk when the Vannings came.

There was no chance to take Cass alone this time. They moved in like the wolfpack Hartley had called them. . . . They left him on the floor, a sodden bloody mass. Parson Dailey found him there at dusk.

Hartley limped painfully to school the next day, his face as raw as a side of beef. Every move brought misery to him. Bud didn't show up.

Hartley held his silence about what had happened, but the Dailey girl told the others, and the parson told Bonner.

It was Bonner who spread word among the settlers. When Hartley limped home after school, Parson Dailey gravely told him that the Vannings had gone too far, that the settlers wouldn't allow their teacher to be beaten up and let the act go unpunished.

There was no use arguing with Dailey. Bonner was the one, so after supper Hartley saddled his horse and rode through the firs to the store. A dozen men were talking in the back of the room, but Hartley's entrance silenced them.

"You've got no need to call a mob,'' Hartley said directly to Bonner. "I'll take care of my own troubles.''

"We ain't gonna stand for no damned Copperheads beating up our teacher,'' Bonner snarled. "It ain't just your trouble. Might be some of the rest of us next time.''

"I don't know what your plans are, but I'll make you a promise: If you men take the law into your own hands, I'll see that every one of you is punished.''

Hartley limped out, leaving a sullen silence behind him, mounted, and rode back to Dailey's. The parson's horse, he saw, was gone. He went to bed, too tired and sick to think clearly about what was happening.

It was nearly midnight when talking at the door roused Hartley. He heard Mrs. Dailey say, "He's sick," and then Bud's voice, pregnant with urgency: "I've got to see him."

Hartley stood up, swayed until a wave of nausea passed, and put on his clothes. He lurched to the front door. "What is it, Bud?"

"Can you ride?" Bud asked.

"I think so." Hartley clutched the edge of the door. "Why?"

"Bonner and his bunch is fixing to swing Pap. Us Vannings never asked for no help before; but Pap, he sent for you. He figgers if you can't stop 'em, he's a goner."

"You've got five brothers," Mrs. Dailey said angrily.

"They ain't home, ma'am. The Frost kid brought word this afternoon that Bonner's bunch was getting together down the creek, and the boys, they pulled out. Reckon Bonner put the kid up to lying so the boys would be out of the way."

"Go after your brothers," Mrs. Dailey said.

"I don't know where they went. Pap told 'em to stay home, but they just saddled up and rode off without ary a word."

Staring at the boy's tortured face in the yellow lamplight falling through the doorway from the table behind him, Hartley wondered what he could do; but whether he could do anything or not, he had to try. He said: "Help me saddle up, Bud."

"Mr. Hartley, you can't—" Mrs. Dailey began.

Hartley went past her and across the tree-shadowed yard to the barn.

"I got my gun out of your desk," Bud said. "I figgered you wouldn't be doing no shooting."

"Give it to me."

"But you can't hit—"

"If I'm going to help, I'll have to do it my way."

They faced each other in a patch of yellow moonlight in front of the barn, anger high in the boy. Then it faded and he handed the gun to Hartley.

"Now let's get my mare saddled," Hartley said.

They set a fast pace, the trail to the Vanning farm twisting along the bank of the pounding creek. They rode through the settlement, the houses black blots squatting in the clearing. Then they were in the timber, with only now and again a patch of moonlight making a needle-laced pattern on the trail.

Every lift and drop of the saddle was torture to Hartley, but Bud Vanning never knew that. They came, in the ebb-tide hours, into the Vanning clearing. Here was the log barn and house, a scattering of outbuildings, the stubble field partly plowed. And under a great fir in front of the house Hartley saw the milling crowd, and heard Bonner should exultantly: "Let me have the rope, boys. We should have done this the day we heard about Fort Sumter."

"Stay out of sight unless I holler for you," Hartley ordered, and rode directly across the stubble field toward the mob.

Old Enoch Vanning was dangling from the limb when Hartley rode up. "Cut him down," he ordered curtly, Bud's gun lined on Bonner.

Bonner cursed when he saw the gun and who held it. Perhaps because of the way Hartley had handled Cass Vanning, Bonner's slim supply of courage leaked out of him. He let go of the rope. It whined across the limb, and Enoch Vanning sprawled limply on the ground.

"You had best stay out of this, Mr. Hartley," Parson Dailey warned him. "There will be no peace until Enoch Vanning is dead."

"Are you appointed by the Lord to bring death to him?" Hartley asked.

Dailey was silent then, and although Hartley could not see the parson's expression, he felt the shame that rose in him.

"It was you they beat up," Bonner cried wildly. "Old Enoch led the Knights of the Golden Circle during the war. We all knowed they was armed and marching up here at night, drilling and fixing to capture Fort Vancouver. He was a damned traitor; we ought to 'a' stretched his neck then."

"We're building a new state here in the wilderness, Bonner," Hartley said feelingly. "What you do tonight may set a pattern for a hundred communities between the Columbia and the Rogue River. Forget the war, and let Vanning forget it."

They were thinking, these settlers, in a way they hadn't thought before. They backed away from Hartley as if they'd be glad to be gone if they could find a way to save face.

"Vanning's a traitor," yelled Bonner. "What'd *you* do during the war? You must 'a' been a Rebel—"

"I was wounded at the battle of Ball's Bluff," Neil Hartley said slowly. "That was the battle your Senator Baker was killed in. I had learned to know him and respect him. If he stood here tonight, he'd tell you there is an intangible thing called law that is made by the citizens of a republic." He paused, letting them think. Then he added: "Or unmade by those same citizens."

Bonner, under Hartley's gun, searched his cunning for something to say, and could do no better than: "But you're the one the Vannings—"

"And I'm also the one who will kill you or get killed because I believe in that intangible thing called law which is the basis of our life. You're done here now, Bonner. Ride out."

This was the moment, and Neil Hartley had his doubt. He sat there in the moonlight, a tall angular shape, clad with dignity and endowed with a strange and magnificent power.

Then Parson Dailey said humbly: "I'm beholden to you, Hartley, for preventing me from having a hand in something that would have plunged me into a hell of regret for the rest of my life."

Mounting, Dailey rode across the moon-yellowed field to the timber. The others followed. Bonner was the last to go. There was the droop in his shoulders of a defeated man.

Hartley called Bud, and together they carried old Enoch into the house. He had been close to death, and his neck would carry the scar of the rope to the end of his life.

It was dawn when Cass and his brothers rode back into the clearing, tired and bitter with their failure to find the men they sought. Old Enoch, in bed, cursed them for not obeying him, and told them what had happened.

There was no gratitude in Cass' eyes as he stared at Hartley. Bud, standing beside the bed, said: "He held 'em off and scared hell out of Bonner with a gun he couldn't hit a bull with twenty feet away. He can't see good enough to shoot straight."

Then Cass Vanning softened and he held out his hand, for that was the kind of courage he understood. "Mebbe we've been wrong," he admitted grudgingly; and that, Neil Hartley knew, was as far as his pride would let him go.

"You've been set upon so long you think you have to fight everybody," Hartley said. "It'll be different now, if you'll let it."

"Why, hell," Cass said, "all we want is to be let alone." He glanced shamefacedly at old Enoch. "Pap's allus allowed there wasn't no good to come out of book l'arnin'. None of us can read or write but Bud."

"I'll help you on Saturdays, and nobody else need know," Hartley said, and was not surprised at the look of gratitude that came to Cass Vanning's trouble-scarred face.

The Petticoat Brigade

I made up my mind I wanted to be a drummer boy the day we heard about Fort Sumter. Plenty of drummer boys are under twelve. I'd read about the boy who was with George Rogers Clark and how those Virginians carried him on their shoulders when they waded the drowned lands of the Wabash. I could do it if he could.

Of course Oregon was a long ways from Fort Sumter, but I'd have got there. Only Maw said no and Paw said no, and in our family that settled it. Besides, Paw said there'd be plenty of trouble right here at Four Corners.

It was Saturday when we got the news that Paw said, right out of a clear sky, "Bud, if you want to dig some worms, we'll go fishing."

I almost fell down grabbing the shovel. I lit out for the barn. There was a place behind it where the worms got juicy and fat. I turned over a shovelful of dirt and started picking up the worms, all the time thinking it was funny Paw saying we'd go fishing. We had the wheat in and the garden planted, but the hay wasn't ready to cut, but it was more like Paw to say we'd get in a few licks on the winter's wood now that we didn't have any farming to do.

But Paw had been acting kind of funny lately. Worried-like. Sometimes when he'd stop at the end of a furrow to rest the horses, he'd get to pulling at his beard and looking out across the Willamette valley at the Coast Mountains, all hazy blue in the distance. Sometimes he'd forget about me and talk to himself—about rebels and Jeff Davis and the Waldrons who lived in the bottom.

When I got back to the house Paw had the willow poles rigged up. I gave him some of the worms and put a few in my pocket with a little dirt so they'd stay damp and keep wiggling. Maw would raise Cain when she found that dirt in my pocket, but it wasn't every day I got to go fishing with Paw.

We hiked across the pasture back of the house and through the timber down to the creek. Once Paw pointed at a tall slim fir. He said, "Bud, that'd make a good flagpole."

"What in tunket do we want a flagpole for?" I asked. "We don't even have a flag."

"We will." Paw was mighty sober. "It's a good thing for folks to look at the Stars and Stripes once in awhile."

We walked on to the creek. I was thinking this flagpole business was about as crazy as Paw talking to himself.

"You take that hole," I said. "I always get a good trout out of there."

"Thanks, Bud." Paw worried a worm onto the hook. "That pole would be high enough for the Waldrons to see the flag from where they live."

Now that was crazier than ever. The Waldron place was down the hill from us a piece. They'd lived in Kentucky before they came to Oregon, and Paw said they'd owned slaves back there, but they were right good neighbors till all this trouble about States going out of the Union came up.

I'd been with Paw in the store at Four Corners one day when he had an awful argument with Old Man Waldron. They shook their fists and yelled names at each other. Old Man Waldron called Paw a black Republican and a nigger lover, and Paw called the old man a damned dirty rebel and a Copperhead.

It was real exciting for a minute. I'll bet if they'd had their guns there'd have been some shooting. Anyhow, they didn't speak after that, and we quit neighboring with them.

It was hard on Mary Waldron and my brother, Jim. Mary was eighteen and real pretty. Jim was twenty. He was tall and lanky and his muscles was as hard as his splitting wedge. They got that way from making rails. I'd heard that Abe Lincoln was a good wrestler because he'd split rails when he was young, but I'll bet Jim would have given him a run.

Jim and Mary had been going to church and spelling matches together for quite awhile. Rip Bailey liked Mary, too. He was a no-good from down the creek a piece, and I guess Mary didn't have much use for him.

Sometimes Mary and Jim would go walking off through the timber just as if there wasn't anybody in the world but them. Once I saw them coming back when I was fishing. Jim was helping her across the creek when she slipped. I'll bet she did it on purpose. He caught her in his arms and held her there a long time. I watched as hard as I could, figuring I'd see them kiss, but I didn't. I guess it isn't so much to kiss anyhow.

After Paw and Old Man Waldron had their fracas, Paw told Jim he wasn't to see Mary any more. Jim didn't argue. He just said that whatever Paw and the old man did wouldn't make any difference between him and Mary. Paw said it sure did, he wasn't going to have any secesh blood in the family, he allowed.

Jim's kind of bullheaded. He walked off, not saying anything more. Paw started after him, scratching his nose and looking worried. I guess he could see that Jim set a store by Mary.

Well, there we were, aiming to catch a mess of fish for supper, and Paw a million miles away. It did seem to me we had plenty of trouble without Paw putting up a flag for the Waldrons to see. It was bad enough having Jim moping around, his lips frozen up so he couldn't grin. I saw Mary in the store at Four Corners once. Her eyes were all red-puckered and not pretty-bright like they used to be.

I put a worm on my hook and went downstream a piece to another hole. If Paw wanted to go ahead and stew about a flagpole on a good fishing day like this, he could just stew. Me, I was going to get that skilletful of fish.

I didn't even get my worm wet. Somebody was riding down through the timber toward us. Sounded like an army. I was mad enough to throw a rock at him. He'd have the fish scared for miles on both sides of us. I headed back to where Paw was and then this feller came out of the firs and I saw it was Ed Brent from Oregon City.

"Howdy, Ed," Paw said. "What's your hurry?"

"No hurry. Just excited a little, maybe." Ed looked about ready to jump out of the saddle. "What's happened has happened. You heard?"

"No, I haven't heard anything."

Ed was skinny and long-necked, and he had an Adam's apple that bobbed around comical-like when he was excited. It sure was bobbing now. You'd thought he'd just seen a bear.

"The Southerners fired on Fort Sumter, and Lincoln's called for a passel of volunteers."

Paw sat down on a log and began to fill his pipe. "It's war, Ed, and I ain't real surprised. I didn't see no way to stop it with the rebels acting like they've been."

"Oregon won't go out, will it?" Ed asked. "We voted for Lincoln last fall."

"Ed, you know danged well that Breckenridge and Lane came mighty near carrying the state." Paw motioned toward the Waldron place. "What do you think the Waldrons are going to do?" And Rip Bailey and the Copes family and the rest of them? I'm sitting in the middle of the biggest nest of rebels there is in the state of Oregon."

"Then you'd better go easy."

"Go easy?" Paw looked mad. "We can't do that, Ed. Wouldn't surprise me none if we had a war right here like they had in Kansas." Paw lighted his pipe and you could see he was thinking hard. "Somebody's going to make these folks show their colors. If we just flop around like jellyfish, they'll ride right over us and take Oregon out."

Ed shifted in his saddle, looking at Paw uneasy-like. "No sense kicking up trouble when you don't have to."

Paw took the pipe out of his mouth and pointed the stem at Ed. "The thing to do is to kick trouble before it kicks you. Now the Fourth is a mighty good day to make folks think about their country. Maw's going to make a flag and Jim and Bud and me will get a pole up. When the Waldrons and the rest of them see Old Glory flying, we'll soon know what they're fixing to do."

"Yeah, I guess so," Ed said, and rode away, quick-like.

We didn't do any fishing. Paw sat there smoking, and I laid on my back, looking at the sky through the fir needles. I'd heard talk about the Mexican War, but this would be a lot bigger. There'd be bands playing, the fifes squealing and the drums beating and flags waving. There'd be hollering and speeches and whoop-te-do with men marching and crowds on the street and everything.

Stories of Wayne D. Overholser

I just laid there with chills running up and down my backbone. That was when I got the idea for being a drummer boy. I didn't say anything to Paw. He hollered at me that it was time to start the chores. We went back up the hill through the timber and crossed the pasture. I was walking stiff and straight just as if I was beating a drum and marching out there in front of a hundred million men.

I waited until I brought the milk in. Maw was alone in the kitchen. There was always a better chance getting Maw to say yes than Paw, so I started on her. I said just like it was all settled, "I'm going to be a drummer boy in the war."

Maw was pouring milk into some crocks. She almost dropped the bucket. "You ain't going to do nothing of the kind, young man. You'll stay right here and help us."

"I want to do something, Maw. It's no fun just staying here when there's a war on."

"War isn't any fun, Bud." She turned back and finished pouring the milk. She didn't think I saw the tears rolling down her cheeks. "It's bad enough having one boy in the army."

I didn't know what she was talking about, but after supper Paw got us around the kitchen table. He stood back of the lamp, his beard reaching way down on his chest. He looked big and square, like the oak tree in front of the Four Corners store.

"We are living among vipers," Paw said. "Jim, maybe you can see now why I told you not to have anything to do with Mary Waldron. She's a fine girl, but you know there ain't a worse traitor on the Pacific coast than Old Man Waldron."

Jim stiffened, as if something had hurt him inside. I wondered if he had a stomach ache.

Paw gripped the table and looked at me. "Bud, Maw says you're wanting to be a drummer boy. Now that's fine, but we can't spare you. Jim's going back to sign up as soon as we see we won't have any trouble here." He stopped and blew his nose. "Maybe Jim won't live long enough to go back East. It's our job to make every man in this community show whether he's Union or rebel. If we make them do some thinking now, maybe we'll save trouble later on. Come the Fourth, we're going to fly the Stars and Stripes."

Shivers were sashaying up and down my back. It was fine, listening to Paw and watching him, standing there big and stout. Old Man

Waldron had just better not show he was a rebel or he'd get that long nose of his shortened up and spread out some.

I guess Jim didn't think it was so fine. He sat looking at the floor, his big hands folded in front of him, his lips pressed so tight that his mouth looked like a string laid across his face.

Paw went to Oregon City the next day. When he was gone, Jim gave me a folded piece of paper. "You crawl along the rail fence back of the Waldron place," he told me. "Mary will be working in the garden. Don't let nobody see you, but you call her over and give her this."

"Paw'll take the hide off my back if he finds out," I said.

"We won't let him find out."

I got back of that rail fence all right. Of course I read the note. It doesn't say much. Just for Mary to meet Jim along the creek after supper. I waited till Mary was hoeing close to the fence. I said, real low, "Got a note for you, Mary."

She looked over at Old Man Waldron who was cleaning out the stable. Then she straightened up, put her hand to her back, and came over and leaned on the fence. When she put a hand down, I shoved the note between the rails and then scooted for home.

I went to bed that night like I always did, but I didn't go to sleep. I waited till Paw started snoring. There was some scraping around in Jim's room. After while I looked out of the window and saw him legging it across the yard.

I went into Jim's room and found a rope he'd tied to a bed post, one end hanging out of the window. I went down the rope just like he'd done and headed for the creek.

I found them standing beside my favorite fishing hole. There was a big moon in the sky, but it was pretty dark here in the brush along the creek. I dasn't get too close or they'd have heard me. All I could see was a black shadow close to the creek. Just one.

"Everybody's heard about the flag," Mary said. "Father says he won't stand for it flying on the Fourth."

"Paw says he's going to fly it. He brought the cloth from town today, and Maw's going to make the flag. Tomorrow we'll put the pole up."

"There'll be a fight, Jim." Mary was just about crying. "They'll kill your Paw."

"They'll kill me and Maw and Bud, too." Jim said, stony-hard.

"It's so foolish, Jim. The fighting's three thousand miles from here."

"It ain't foolish, Mary. There's a lot of secesh feeling here. It ain't just your dad."

"I know, Jim. People have been coming to the house at night."

"If we don't do something, they'll take Oregon out of the Union. Don't you see, Mary? What Paw's doing ain't foolish at all."

They didn't say anything for the longest time. All I could hear was the creek singing smooth-like where it ran over the log just above the fishing hole. Then Jim said, awful sad, "Maybe we ain't for each other."

"Yes, we are," Mary said, fierce-like. "I'll leave my family if it comes to that. They can't do anything to stop our loving each other."

"I guess we'd better go home," Jim said.

They went right past me. I could've reached out and grabbed Jim's leg if I'd wanted to. I didn't breathe till I couldn't hear them any more. Then I lit out for the house. I had to climb back up that rope before Jim got to his room. I was kind of mad. I hadn't seen them kiss, but kissing never looked like much. I guess Jim thought the same thing.

Next day we put the pole up. Paw fixed a rope so we could raise the flag. Then we got under the pole and lofted it. Jim was on the end, him being the tallest, and pretty soon the butt slid in. Paw tamped some dirt down hard, and that pole was fixed good and solid.

Maw worked on the flag every afternoon, sewing the stripes together and cutting out the stars and putting them on. She said it wasn't a very good job, but Paw allowed it was fine. He said it was what was in your heart that counted, anyhow.

The flag was finished the night before the Fourth. Paw was right proud of it. I guess Maw was, too, the way she looked at it. Then I heard a knock on the door. Jim grabbed up his rifle and Paw slid the hand gun into his belt. He opened the door, and there was Old Man Waldron.

Paw stepped back so he wouldn't be so good a target for somebody out there in the dark. He said, not friendly-like, "What do you want, Eli?"

Old Man Waldron looked at Jim, who had his rifle on the ready. Then he looked at Paw, his eyes hard-sharp. "Samuel, I'm asking you in a spirit of neighborly friendship not to fly that flag tomorrow."

"I'll fly it." That was all Paw said, but he said it in a way that told Old Man Waldron he'd fly it no matter what.

"Then we'll take it down. If you try to stop us, there will be bloodshed." Waldron rubbed his big nose. "If you and your boy want to die foolishly, it's your business, but I hope you'll have enough sense to send your wife and little boy away."

"I'm no little boy," I hollered. "I can shoot straight. If you—"

Paw shook his head for me to keep still. He said, "Eli, my family will stay here. If we have violence, you will start it."

"Then it'll be that way." Old Man Waldron looked at Jim again. "I'm sorry about this. Mary thinks a sight of you." Then he walked off.

Paw shut the door and dropped the bar. He said, "Bud, throw some wood on the fire. We've got to mold up some more bullets."

I heard a rooster crow before I went to sleep that night. It sure did look as if Paw was right when he said we'd have trouble here at Four Corners. I wasn't going to be beating a drum. I was going to pull a trigger. Then maybe I'd be dead.

I wondered what it was like to be dead. I never could forget how Grandma looked when they buried her. All pale and stony-looking. Her eyes closed up tight. I reached over and pulled another quilt over me.

The flag was flying when I came down to breakfast. I stood looking at it quite awhile. The wind was real brisk and the sky was all blue. Not even any smoke from a forest fire. I never had seen anything prettier'n that flag.

"Looks fine, don't it, son?" Paw asked.

"It sure does," I said.

"It's a good flag to live for," Paw said, sober-like, "and it's given some to die for it."

Maw called breakfast then, and we went in. Paw sat at the table so he could watch our lane where it came up the hill from the Waldron place. We didn't eat much. Just kind of pushed the victuals around on our plates.

Pretty soon Paw said, "There goes Old Man Waldron to fetch Rip Bailey and the rest of the rebels."

We watched all morning. We could see a lot of the valley from our house. Seemed as if every man down there in the bottom was on his horse going somewhere. About noon they began riding into the Waldron place.

Maw called us into dinner, but we didn't eat much then, either. Jim shoved his plate back, mumbled something about not being hungry, and walked out.

"I always get sulphur and molasses to cure what ails me," I said.

"It'd take more'n sulphur and molasses to cure what ails him," Maw said. "I don't know that you done right, Paw, telling him he couldn't see Mary no more."

"Jim won't be marrying into a secesh family." Paw's teeth came together with a click. When he did that, there wasn't any use arguing.

I shoved a piece of bread around through my gravy. I was thinking love was a trouble I'd never have any truck with. I hadn't heard Jim laugh out loud for weeks, and I'd seen Mary's eyes that time in the store. Now Jim had lost his appetite. If he couldn't eat, he must just about be done for.

"It'll blow over," Paw said, trying to cheer us up and sounding as if he didn't believe it himself. "Not many hawks in that bunch. Mostly buzzards."

The afternoon went slower than the morning did. Jim puttered around some. Paw fixed up the harness. Maw would stand in the doorway and look down the hill. Then she'd go back into the house. I couldn't find anything to do. Mostly I looked at the flag, or at the Waldron place. I'd never seen so many men since the last Fourth.

I guess there weren't many women, but there were a lot of men standing around in knots. Old Man Waldron would go from one bunch to the next, swinging his arms and shaking a fist in our direction. Rip Bailey was always with him. I sure didn't like Rip. He was big and ugly-mean. I figured he hated Jim because Mary liked Jim the best.

It was about four o'clock when they started up the hill. There must have been twenty of them or more. Old Man Waldron and Rip Bailey were in front. All of them had guns.

"There they come." Paw picked up his long rifle, easy-like, as if he were going grouse hunting. "Maw, you and Bud better get inside."

Maw pulled the shotgun down off the wall. "Sam, I've fought Indians with you and I've fought outlaws. I guess I'm not above shooting a few rebels. Bud, you can go inside."

All of a sudden I was scared. My innards got all knotted up and my mouth was so dry I couldn't spit. Nothing could stop this now. Old Man Waldron would take the flag down or bust trying, and I knew Paw wouldn't back down.

Paw and Maw and Jim stood looking at me. Jim had the hand gun. There was another rifle standing beside the door. "I ain't going inside," I said, and picked up the rifle.

"That's the kind of stuff that made our country," Paw said, proudlike.

We all walked out to the flagpole. I wasn't so scared then. It was better than being a drummer boy.

There was still quite a breeze. We could hear the flag kind of talking above us. I wondered what it was saying. I guess Paw knew, but he didn't tell me.

Nobody opened his mouth till Old Man Waldron and Rip Bailey came through the gate. The rest of them stopped outside the fence.

"We've come in a spirit of friendliness," Waldron said, "and respectfully ask you to take that flag down. Some of your neighbors object to it."

"I can't do that," Paw said. "We have all lived under this flag, and some of us have fought under it. You were with Scott, Eli."

"It ain't my flag now," Old Man Waldron shouted. "I'll be damned if I'll stand here and look at it on a day like this."

"Whatever day it is," Paw said, "that's our flag until Oregon goes out of the Union. If that time ever comes, it will still be my flag. As for today, I'll kill the first man who tries to pull it down."

It stopped them for a while. They stood staring at us, trying to find the courage to charge, I guess. I looked at Paw just a minute. He was standing there with that old Kentucky rifle in his hands, the wind tugging at his beard, big and stout and square like that oak tree in front of the Four Corners store. I felt proud. Mighty proud.

My finger was getting tight on the trigger. I guess Jim noticed it. He said, soft-like, "Ease up, Bud."

I didn't pay any attention. I yelled, "You're a bunch of stinking skunks, or you wouldn't be here. I'm going to shoot you in the belly, Rip Bailey."

One of them laughed. It was kind of a croaking sound. He said, "You want a bullet in your belly, Bailey?"

Bailey cussed a bad word. "I ain't a-scared of a woman and a brat. I'll take Jim. Eli, Sam's your meat. Come on, boys."

Bailey started toward us, Old Man Waldron with him, so mad his cheeks were red. The rest of them came piling through the gate. I put my rifle to my shoulder. If they'd come another step they'd have got it. But they didn't come that step.

I guess none of us ever figured out how the women got there without being seen or heard. Must have been because we were watching each other so hard. Anyway, there they were, Mary Waldron and her mother, riding their horses right between us and the rebel bunch. They'd gone around the hill to the creek and then through the pasture and into our yard.

Old Man Waldron and Rip Bailey stopped short, their feet coming down flat. I never did see anybody as surprised as those two.

"If there's any fighting this day, Eli," Mrs. Waldron said, "it's your womenfolks who'll get shot."

"Get out of the way, Maria," Old Man Waldron croaked.

Mary jumped off her horse and ran to Jim. She turned around when she got to him, and put a hand on his arm. Her voice was clear and sharp so that all those men heard what she said. "You all know this war will be fought in the East and not in Oregon. Jim believes in the Union, so he's going back to enlist. If you want to fight, Rip, why don't you join the Confederate army?"

That just about did it. Rip got red in the face. I guess all of them knew then he wasn't as brave as he was letting on. He spluttered. He stammered. He looked all around. I guess he was trying to find a hole to jump into.

I felt good then. I felt awful good. I yelled, "You didn't give a whoop and a holler about the flag, Rip. You just wanted to get Jim because Mary likes him."

"That's about the size of it," Paw said. "Maybe it's the same with you, Eli. You've been trying to buy my farm. Is this your way of getting it?"

"Hell, I ain't gonna help nobody do their dirty chores," one of the men said. He shouldered his rifle and walked off, and the rest of them began straggling along behind.

Jim stepped off to one side so Mary wasn't beside him and Mrs. Waldron wasn't in front of him. "If this is just between us, Rip, maybe we'd better settle it."

But Rip Bailey wasn't ugly-mean then, and he didn't look so big. If he'd a tail, he'd have curled it right up between his legs. He turned around and walked down the hill.

"I'm staying here, Father," Mary said. "Jim and I are going to be married before he leaves."

Old Man Waldron looked sick. He rubbed his long nose. He looked at Mrs. Waldron. He looked at Mary. Then he looked around and followed Bailey down the hill.

"I'll bring your things, Mary." Mrs. Waldron said. She rode off, leading the horse Mary had ridden, and I could see she was crying.

Paw laughed, soft-like, as if he was kind of relieved. "I guess it was the petticoat brigade that won this fight." He got sober then, and patted Mary on the shoulder. "This is going to be a bad war, busting families up and such, but we're lucky. We've always wanted a girl, and we're mighty glad to get one."

Maw was crying and Mary was crying and Jim looked as if he wanted to cry. Then the women went into the house and Jim trailed along. Paw walked out to the barn, blowing his nose harder than anything.

Me? Well, I looked up at the flag. I understood something that I hadn't before, about the flag and what it means to have it flying. Seemed like being a drummer boy wasn't so important. If the war lasted awhile, I'd be back there with Jim. Fighting for that flag.

I turned around and started for the barn. Then I stopped. There was Jim holding Mary in his arms. They were kissing.

I was kind of disappointed when I went on to where Paw was. I'd been right all the time. Kissing didn't look like so much.

Debt Cancelled

The smart money had been bet against Honest John Travis's being elected governor, but smart money or not, Travis went into office by ten thousand votes. If there had been another election at the end of his first year, he'd have tripled that majority. The politicos who played the angles, like Sheriff Steve Ludlow over in Summit county, couldn't figure it out.

There were two good reasons for Travis's popularity. The state was still young enough for the voters to be proud of a man with Travis's colorful past. He'd been everything from a cowboy to a gun guard on a stage and a lawman in the Black Hills during the gold rush.

The second reason was more important, and one that a man of Steve Ludlow's caliber would never understand. Travis was one of the politicians in the state who deserved the sobriquet "Honest." That was why Travis took the first train for Summit county when he heard that Old Bill Allen was in jail for killing Silver Spur Ord.

It was early afternoon when Travis stepped down from the coach in Sage, the county seat. He went immediately to Judge Ira Weston's office in the courthouse. Weston was talking with the district attorney, Ed Hovey, when Travis stepped into the room. Neither saw him until he said, "Howdy, Ira. Howdy, Ed."

Weston was the first to recognize Travis. He rose and held out his hand. "How are you, Governor?" he asked cordially. "This is almost as surprising as if the President had walked in."

"Not quite, I guess." Travis shook Weston's hand and turned to Hovey.

"You should have warned us you were coming, Governor." Hovey's fat hand gripped Travis's briefly. "Or is this a personal investigation of the political integrity of Summit county?"

"Something like that," Travis said. He took the cigar that Weston offered and walked to the window. They were good men, both of them, if you could say that of men who kept their ears to the political wind. In Summit county Steve Ludlow blew that wind in the direction which suited his interest. "Steve around?"

Neither answered for a moment. Weston made a ceremony of getting his cigar going. Hovey, a pudgy man who was fighting a losing battle with an expanding stomach and wore his vest corset-tight, drew a carefully folded silk handkerchief from his pocket and wiped his forehead. A little smile touched the corners of Travis's lips. He understood the situation here in Summit county, and he knew Steve Ludlow.

"Why, I guess he's in his office," Weston said finally.

"I'd like to see him."

Neither Weston nor Hovey made a move to go after the sheriff. They reversed the former by-play, Hovey fumbling for a cigar and Weston producing a handkerchief and wiping his face. Travis, looking from one to the other, lost his smile.

"I see," Travis said. "You boys think Steve won't want to see me."

"Why, it's just—" Hovey began, and stopped. "I'll fetch him."

"Wait a minute, Ed." Weston moved around his desk to the window. "It's a funny thing, John—ever since Old Bill Allen's been in jail, he's been hollering that you'll get him out. I'm wondering if that's the reason you're here."

"You're guessing well, Ira," Travis murmured.

Weston tongued the cigar to the other side of his mouth. Pink-cheeked and bald, almost as pudgy as Hovey, he made a sharp contrast with stringy John Travis. Weston was not a judge whose decisions could be bought—Travis knew that; but he also knew that both Weston and Hovey were up for election that fall and both liked their jobs.

"You'd be smart to let the local officials handle Old Bill." Weston was watching a man trim the shrubbery around the jail. "Summit county gave you a thousand votes and you can thank Steve Ludlow for it."

Travis didn't argue. What Weston said was true. It was also true that Steve Ludlow had wanted a change in the governor's chair and had considered Travis the lesser of two evils.

"All right, Ira," Travis said mildly. "Steve doesn't want to see me, so we'll forget it. How about bringing Old Bill in?"

"We couldn't do that," Hovey said quickly. "Steve hasn't let him see anyone."

"I see." There was no indication on the governor's high-boned face or in his gray eyes that anger was coming to a boil in him. "You must consider Old Bill a dangerous man."

"He killed Ord," Hovey said. "No doubt about it. Steve figures he'll confess, and that would save the county some money."

"What does Old Bill have to say?"

"Nothing." Hovey pulled at an ear. "Funny thing. He won't say what happened."

"Look, John," Weston said earnestly. "Ord was no good. We all know that, and his cashing in saved Sage from a hell of a fight. What we ought to do is to give Old Bill a medal for beefing him, but the law doesn't read that way about murder. It'll have to take its course. Now why don't you come out to my place this afternoon? I've got a new white-face bull I want you to see. We'll have a good supper and you can take the night train back to the capital."

"I hope to catch that train, and thanks for the invitation." Travis fingered the ash from his cigar. "One of these days I'll take you up. Ed, what happened the day Ord was killed?"

"We were headed for trouble as fast as the devil could take us," the district attorney answered. "Ord's Silver Spur was the biggest saloon in town and the wild bunch hung out there. The last year or so some of the worst toughs in the country drifted in and stayed. Steve didn't want them around, but there wasn't much he could do."

"Old Bill hung out there, too?"

Hovey nodded. "Got to be a regular barfly. Drunk most of the time. His rheumatism was so bad that I guess he was in pain a lot and whisky deadened it. Anyhow, Ord seemed to like him, even gave him a bed in his house and Bill did a few chores around the place to pay for it. None of us have figured out why he plugged Ord. Maybe they got into a row and Bill was drunk."

"What about this trouble you were talking about?"

"Why, it was shaping up to a showdown between Ord's wild bunch and the rest of the town. We've had too many holdups and killings in the last year that are still unsolved. Steve figured it was Ord's outfit, but there wasn't any proof. We couldn't handle it legally, so we organized a Citizen's Protective League and told the toughs they had to get out of town. Ord didn't like it. He closed up the saloon and went to his house. He said they'd fight."

"But the fight didn't come off?"

"No. Ord was killed about four o'clock that afternoon. Steve went out there about five to try to talk Ord and his bunch into leaving. All the toughs were gone, Ord was dead with a slug between his eyes, and Old Bill was sitting in the front room with a forty-five in his fist. He told Steve he killed Ord, but he didn't give any reason. Now he won't talk at all. Just clams up."

"Won't even sign a confession that he killed Ord," the judge said in disgust.

"So he's been cooling his heels in jail," Travis said bluntly, "until Steve gets a confession out of him."

"That's about it," Weston agreed reluctantly. "It isn't right, but I never interfere with the way Steve runs his office."

Travis rose. "Then I guess I will," he said, and started toward the door.

"Where are you going?" Weston demanded.

"To the jail. I'm going to talk to Old Bill."

"Why can't you let it go?" Weston groaned.

"Because the whole thing stinks," Travis said bluntly. "Steve's pulled off some funny things. This is one too many."

"So the governor is personally going to look into it." Steve Ludlow stood in the doorway, a small carefully groomed man with tiny black eyes set astride a sharp nose. "Aren't you out of your ballywick, Honest John?"

Ludlow had put a mild emphasis on the word "honest." Travis had learned long ago to control his temper, but it had been years since he'd had as difficult a time doing it as he did now.

"No, Steve," Travis said finally, his tone even. "The whole state's my ballywick. That includes Summit county."

"Why kick up a dust about Old Bill Allen?" Ludlow asked mildly. "He's just a drunk. Nobody's going to worry about him."

"I will," Travis said. "I knew him in the Black Hills years ago.

What's more important is the fact that he's an American citizen."

"Ideals are strong medicine, John," Ludlow murmured. "Suppose I don't let you see Old Bill?"

"Then I'd know something was wrong," Travis said quickly, "and I'd act accordingly."

Ludlow pulled a pipe from his pocket and tapped it idly against a palm, black eyes pinned on Travis, his smile unreadable. He was a mild-mannered man, sparing in his gestures and soft-voiced, but he was also a shrewd gambler who took long chances only when the stakes warranted it.

"All right, John," Ludlow said at last. "I'll get Old Bill."

Hovey and Weston moved restlessly around the room. Travis stood at the window and watched them with controlled amusement. They hated themselves, Travis thought, for the choice they had made somewhere back along the trail. He didn't think they had any part in Ludlow's political chicanery. It was likely a matter of looking the other way.

Now they were worried, for the next few moments might bring them to the place where they had to choose between the governor and Summit county's political boss, a choice that men of their caliber never liked to make.

It was ten minutes before Ludlow returned with Old Bill Allen. The old man paused in the doorway, cloudy eyes fixed on Travis a moment before he recognized him, and Travis, staring back, felt a sickness crawl into him. This stooped, dirty-bearded man with the whisky-fogged eyes and the hands twisted with rheumatism bore little resemblance to the gutty lawman he had known in the Black Hills.

"Here's your old friend, John," Ludlow said. "I've got a man waiting in my office to see me. I'll be back in a couple of minutes."

Travis waited until he heard Ludlow's steps fade down the hall. Then he swung around the desk and strode to where Old Bill stood, his hand outstretched. "How are you, Bill?"

"John. Damn my eyes if it ain't John Travis."

Old Bill tried to grip Travis's hand, but his fingers didn't function. It was Travis's hand that closed over his.

"Sit down." Travis drew Old Bill across the room and maneuvered him into a chair at the end of the desk. "Been a long time, Bill."

"A hell of a long time. Say, you remember the night in Deadwood when you had to arrest—"

Debt Canceled

"I remember," Travis murmured. "That's why I'm here."

"I knew you'd come. Damned if I didn't." Old Bill threw a scornful look at the district attorney. "I told you he'd come and get me out of this jam, Hovey. Some men don't get too big for their pants. They don't forget their old friends. John's governor, and by hokey—"

"Oh, Bill," Travis cut in. "I wanted to ask you about what really happened when Ord was killed."

"What happened?" Old Bill rubbed a bearded cheek, gaze flicking to the doorway as if expecting to see Ludlow standing there. He brought his eyes to Travis. "I killed him. That's all. Shot him right between the eyes, by damn. Remember that night in Deadwood when I got Ace Morgan—"

"I remember." Travis flipped back the lid of Weston's cigar box and offered one to Old Bill. "Have a smoke on the judge, Bill."

"Sure. Better have something on him before he hangs something on me," Old Bill cackled. He stuffed the cigar into his mouth and fumbled for a match.

Travis said, "Here's a light, Bill," and held a match flame to the cigar.

Satisfaction crept into the old man's face. "Good cigar, Judge. Ain't had a smoke since the sheriff threw me into the jug. Ain't had a drink, neither."

"Now about Ord," Travis said. "Why did you plug him?"

Old Bill took a deep breath. "It was this way, John. Ord kept a bunch of tough hands around him. I knew a lot about what they was doing 'cause I was in the Silver Spur most of my time and I heard 'em talk. Besides, I slept at Ord's place, so I heard more of their scheming out there." Old Bill stared at his twisted hands. "Ord was plumb good to me, John. I ain't worth nothin' no more, but he put up with me and I done a few jobs to kind of pay back."

"He was good to you," Travis murmured, "so you plugged him." He shook his head. "Bill, that doesn't make any sense at all."

Old Bill slumped down in his chair. He stared at the floor for a long moment, and then, raising his head, looked at Hovey from under hooding gray brows. He took another deep breath.

"I guess it don't." He gripped his cigar between thumb and bent fingers and took it from his mouth. "Ord's bunch was robbing stages and holding up banks in other counties and playing hell. Then they'd come back here and Ord would hide 'em out. Give 'em an alibi to boot.

"Got so bad that Hovey and the sheriff and some more got some lawabiding folks together and rigged up a sort of vigilante committee. Only Ord wouldn't pull out like they told him. He was fixing to use his outfit to fight. There'd have been a hell of a lot of killings, John."

Old Bill straightened, shoulders pressed against the back of his chair. "You know what I used to stand for, John. When I ain't too drunk I still stand for the same things. I warned Ord he'd gone too far. I says to him there ain't no sense in getting half the folks in town killed. He'd made his pile and he'd be smart to get out. He says no. He was aiming to hang and rattle. So I plugged him. Right between the eyes, John—hell of a good shot it was."

"No, Bill," Travis said thoughtfully. "That wasn't the way it happened."

"Don't tell us you were there," Hovey said.

"No, but I did have a special agent nosing around. He was in Ord's bunch and he told me how the thing was rigged. Bill, I know exactly what you believed in. That's why I can't think you've thrown in with a thieving coyote like Ludlow."

"Now hold on, John—" Judge Weston began.

"Stay out of this, Ira. Look, Bill—we've beaten around the bush long enough. Some things never change in a man. You can get down and crawl to Steve Ludlow when he whistles. You can act like a whipped pup because he's been paying for your drinks and grub, but you're not a whipped pup inside. You hate yourself because the pride you used to have is still in you. You think it's gone but it isn't. You've drowned it with whisky—that's all. When you get sober it's there again. That's why you kept going back to Ord's saloon to get drunk."

Ludlow was in the doorway then, the mask of courtesy gone from his face. "That's enough, Travis," he snarled. "You wanted to hear Bill tell what happened. You heard. Now he's going back to the jug."

"Don't make a move, Ludlow." Travis laid a .45 on the desk beside Old Bill. "I'm cleaning house today, and Summit county's had a damned dirty house for a long time. Look at him, Bill. A small-time crook who bought your help with whisky, and you're ashamed of yourself for giving it to him. Ace Morgan and his outfit were men, Bill. Bank robbers and killers, sure, but they didn't make any bones about what they were. They didn't hide behind a sheriff's star."

"So help me, Travis—" Ludlow bellowed.

Debt Canceled

"Shut up, Ludlow! I'll tell you what happened, Bill. You were out there in Ord's house all right. You'd been telling Ludlow what he wanted to know about Ord so he could make the toughs dig up for protection. Ludlow had so much hollering on his hands he had to clean things up, but Ord wouldn't go. He told Ludlow he'd let it out how he'd been paying for protection, so Ludlow had to kill him to shut him up. He got you drunk and put a bullet between Ord's eyes."

"Ord was dead when I got there," Ludlow cut in. "Your yarn—"

"I told you to shut up, Ludlow. Listen, Bill. He left. Then he went back. He pretended to find the body so he could lay it onto you. There was nothing to hold the tough bunch together when Ord cashed in, so they rode out. That left Ludlow sitting pretty again."

"You don't have any proof, Travis," Ludlow raged.

"It isn't a question of proof, Bill." Travis shoved the gun at Old Bill. "It's a question of how much man you've got left in you. There was plenty when you gave me a hand against Ace Morgan's bunch. I'm betting there's plenty in you now. All you had to do was to get the whisky worked out of your carcass."

Old Bill put a hand on the gun butt and jerked it back. "I'm no good any more, John," he muttered. "Can't hang onto a gun."

"You didn't kill Ord, but you know Ludlow did," Travis pressed. "You were sober enough to see what went on, weren't you? Ludlow made some promises about getting you off if you'd sit in jail awhile. He hasn't done it, Bill. He never will. He'll see you swing. Look at him, Bill. Guilty as hell. You've seen men hanging from a rope. He's got a loop ready."

It happened then exactly as John Travis wanted it to happen. Old Bill grabbed the gun, almost lost it, fumbled with it while he tried to cock it. Then he had the hammer back, an ominous sound breaking into the pool of quiet, a sound that cracked Steve Ludlow. That, too, was what John Travis had counted on. Ludlow jerked his gun from its holster.

Travis's gun thundered the same instant Old Bill's did, but Bill's slug went wild through the doorway. It was Travis's bullet that made the little black hole between Steve Ludlow's black eyes.

Old Bill was still shaking from relief after they'd taken Ludlow's body across the street to the undertaker's, but he managed to crow,

"Got him dead-center, John. Crookeder'n any sidewinder you ever seen. I should o' got him a long time ago, but I didn't think I could shoot that straight."

"You're a good man yet, Bill." Travis drew a handful of gold coins from his pocket. "Sometimes it takes the public a long time to get around to rewarding the men who make the law mean something, but generally it does after a while. This came through the other day for killing Ace Morgan. I made the trip to give it to you personally."

Old Bill seemed to have something in his eyes. He rubbed them with his knuckles, choked, and shook his head. "I'm sure beholden, John. I, I . . .."

"Forget it." Travis looked at Hovey. "I guess there's no charge against Bill now, is there?"

"No," the district attorney said.

"I think you've got some rewards coming, Bill. I'll see that you get them. Let the booze alone." He turned to Weston. "Ira, if that invitation—"

"Still good, Governor," Weston said briskly.

That night Travis and Judge Weston stood beside the loading platform of the depot, the locomotive whistle a distant sound.

"I guess Ed and I had about as much backbone as a jellyfish," Weston said apologetically, "but if we'd made a move against Steve—"

"I know," Travis murmured. They'd both be better men with Steve Ludlow gone.

"If you had a secret agent in here, why didn't you take his evidence and turn it over to Hovey?"

"He didn't have any real proof. Besides, he'd have been worthless for any other jobs if he'd appeared in court." Travis smiled a little then. "There's another thing, too, Ira. I doubt if the legal machinery of Summit county would have held up against Steve."

The judge went "Harumph," and scraped a toe across the cinders. "I don't know why you thought Old Bill would try to use that gun, or how you knew it was Steve instead of Bill."

"If you'd used your head," Travis said, unable to keep the scorn out of his voice, "you'd have known that Bill couldn't shoot fast enough or straight enough to have drilled Ord. I wanted you to see him try to use an iron so you'd know he couldn't have done it."

"But he's been a drunken bum ever since he's been in Sage—"

"He was one of the guttiest lawmen I ever knew when he was in Deadwood," Travis cut in, "and he had the most pride. The trouble was he got stove up so he couldn't pack a star. He lost his savings in some bad investments, and he got to brooding about the rotten deal he'd got. That's why he's been a bum here, but I knew that if I could stir some of his old pride, he'd make a try. He'll be a different man now, Ira."

The judge went "Harumph" again. "Hovey and I will see a few more rewards get paid."

The train was there then, the headlight tunneling the darkness. "So long," Travis said, and swung aboard.

He dropped into a seat, shoulders slack, suddenly very tired. A governor couldn't go around doing jobs like this, but thinking back to that smoky night in Deadwood when Ace Morgan and his bunch had gone down before his and Bill Allen's guns, he felt only satisfaction that he had been able to do what he had today. In the book of his past he could write, *Debt canceled*.

The Hero

Jimmy Bonner had never understood why his folks didn't like Cousin Knapp. He hadn't seen Knapp for three years, but he remembered him as if it had been only last week. Six feet two, Cousin Knapp was, and as straight as the barrel of Jimmy's .22 except for his legs which were bowed enough for you to throw a beer keg between them. Cousin Knapp often said that himself.

And his clothes! That was what Jimmy remembered the best. Green silk shirt. Orange neckerchief. Cream-colored Stetson banded with a rattlesnake skin. Expensive spike-heeled boots. A spotted calf-hide vest. And two pearl-handled guns corded down on his thighs. Cousin Knapp was a sight to make your eyes pop out, and Jimmy's had popped all the time Knapp had been in Bowstring.

It wasn't that Jimmy's folks *said* they didn't like Knapp. Jimmy could tell by the way they acted. Like his mother sitting down and crying after Knapp had ridden out of town, and his dad patting her on the back and muttering, "Danged bragging fool! Mortgaged his horse to buy those duds, or I miss my guess." And his mother stopping her crying long enough to say, "John, I'd have gone crazy if I'd listened to him another five minutes."

That had been three years ago. The only times they'd heard from Knapp since then had been at Christmas when he'd write long letters filled with exciting stories of his bear hunts and gun fights and his narrow escapes when he'd ridden as deputy beside the sheriff after bank robbers.

Jimmy's dad always read the letters and then threw them away, saying something like, "Knapp's the only Bonner I know of who's long on wind and short on guts." Jimmy's mother never even read them. But she did read the letter that came on the last day of July, and she immediately started to cry. It was addressed to Jimmy, and was very short for one of Knapp's letters.

Dear Jimmy,

I know you'll be tickled to here Im coming to sea you agen. Ill make this a little letter so I can tell you all thats happened. Beelieve me Iv had some hare raisin times since I wrote last. Ill reach the Hat Crick brig Satirday noon. You meat me there, Jimmy. Well ride into town and blow Bowstring up. Yessir, well blow it up proper.

Cousin Knapp.

Jimmy couldn't see anything to get upset about, but his dad did when he got home from the bank. "Been saving his money for three years to have another blowout." He threw the letter into the fireplace. "Well, Ann, we'll have to grin and bear it."

"I'll take my .22 when I go to meet him," Jimmy said.

"No, you won't," his mother said flatly. "You aren't even going."

That was when Jimmy felt like crying. He probably would have if his father hadn't said, "Now let's not be hasty, Ann. Might be a good idea to let Jimmy go. Just keep your .22 at home, son."

A quick look passed between his mother and father that Jimmy didn't understand. His mother took a long breath. "Go out and water Sandy," she told him.

"I watered him this morning," Jimmy protested.

"It's a hot day. He might be thirsty again."

Jimmy went out through the back door, steps lagging. He stopped to pick up a marble and heard his father say, "The only reason Knapp's coming back is to let Jimmy worship him, but Jimmy's old enough now to see through him."

Jimmy went on to the barn and untied Sandy. He thought about it all the way to the trough and back, but he couldn't see any sense to what his father had said. He couldn't see through Cousin Knapp no matter how big he got. Not a big-boned, hard-muscled man like Cousin Knapp.

Jimmy was waiting on the Hat Creek bridge half an hour before noon. Knapp was there right on time, dressed just like Jimmy remembered except that this time he had a fine saddle and he was forking the most beautiful bay gelding Jimmy had ever seen.

"Say, it's sure good to see you, Jimmy boy," Knapp boomed when he came up. He held out a big calloused hand. "Why, you've grown a foot, haven't you?"

"Almost," Jimmy said.

Knapp pulled his bay in beside Sandy and they hit a good pace for Bowstring, Knapp riding high and handsome in his saddle. Jimmy kept looking at him out of the corner of his eyes. There was something about Cousin Knapp that wasn't just the way he'd remembered him. Jimmy couldn't tell what it was except that Knapp reminded him a little of a cowboy actor in a play he'd seen last winter.

"Well, sir, I've sure had a time since I was here," Knapp said in his loud voice. "Been mining above Cripple Crick a piece, and I struck it." He slapped a heavy sack tied to his saddlehorn. "See that, Jimmy? Gold. Yessir, gold. I sold that claim for ten thousand dollars. Now I'm gonna buy me the best danged outfit in the country. You know of any, Jimmy?"

"Old man Paris'll sell his spread," Jimmy said. "It's up the creek about three miles. Want to see it?"

"Not today. We'll just ride into town and have ourselves a time. Still like gumdrops, Jimmy?"

"Sure."

"Well, we'll get some. We sure will. Nothing's too good for you, Jimmy."

"I've got a .22. Maybe we could do some shooting. You reckon your six-gun can outshoot my rifle?"

"Why, sure. There's no rifle on the western slope that can shoot as good as these here Colts."

"Let's try it when we get home."

Knapp cleared his throat and looked down the road. "Well, to tell you the truth, my eyes kind of hurt today. Been on the trail a long time. Sun and dust. You know how it is. Kind of makes you squint."

"Sure," Jimmy said, and let it go, but he was disappointed. He'd

been thinking about a match with Cousin Knapp ever since his father
had suggested it the night before, but maybe Knapp's eyes would feel
better in the morning.

Everybody looked at them when they rode into town and dismounted in front of Henry Paul's Mercantile. The sheriff was standing in front of his office and Doc Peters was just climbing down from
his buggy. Miss Tollard—that was Jimmy's teacher—was coming out
of the Mercantile. They all stopped and looked, and the sheriff
grinned as if he'd just thought of a joke.

There was a stranger on the street who looked at Cousin Knapp,
too, a little dark-eyed man who wore a black stubble and was dusty as
if he'd just come in from a long ride.

Knapp slapped the sack. "Wonder if I ought to put that gold in
your pa's bank?"

"He's still open," Jimmy said.

Knapp considered. "Maybe I'll just keep it on me. You know, ten
thousand is a lot of money to put into a bank. George might not want
to be responsible for it."

"He wouldn't care. Why, the Bar Z sold a herd the other day, and
dad said old Henry Diggs brought in twenty thousand dollars."

"Well, that's all right for them that lives here." Knapp slapped the
sack again. "Trouble is, I'm not real well known hereabouts, so it
might be better if I kept the cash on me. I want to look at some big
outfits tomorrow and when I see something I want, I'll buy it right
then. That's the way I'm made."

The dark-eyed stranger moved across the street and stood at the
end of the hitch pole rolling a cigarette. The sheriff came up and held
out his hand. "How are you, Knapp? Fine horse you're riding."

Knapp shook the lawman's hand with long pumplike strokes.
"That he is, sheriff. Finest animal I could find in South Park. I just
struck it rich above Cripple Creek a piece. I sold my claim for ten
thousand dollars and I'm hunting a place to light." He looked at
Jimmy as if thunderstruck. "Say, I forgot all about them gumdrops.
Now you go in and get a big sack. Tell that Henry to give you good
measure or I'll come in and mop the floor up with him. Yessir, I'll mop
the floor up good."

Knapp made a ceremony out of digging a dime out of his pocket and handed it to Jimmy with a flourish. Jimmy turned into the store, hearing the sheriff say, "I reckon you can find something hereabouts for ten thousand, Knapp."

When Jimmy came back, Knapp was standing alone beside the horses. The little dark-eyed man was still at the end of the hitch pole, a quizzical look on his knobby face. Jimmy held out the sack and Knapp helped himself.

"Thank you, Jimmy. You're as generous as you always were. Well, let's get along to the old homestead. I don't reckon I'll be riding any this afternoon. Time enough tomorrow."

They mounted and rode away, the dark-eyed man watching them until they were out of sight around the locust trees on the corner.

"Did you see that fellow standing at the end of the hitchrack?" Jimmy asked his cousin.

"Sure. What about him?"

"I dunno. Didn't look like the fellers you see around here. Kind o' mean-looking."

"Well, if he bothers you any, just let me know. I'll mop up the street with him. Yessir, just let him make a move, and I'll mop up the street with him."

When they reached the house, Jimmy said, "I'll put your horse away, Knapp. You go on in."

"Thank you, Jimmy. I'll sure do that." Knapp swung down and untied his sack. "I'll keep this with me. I don't reckon anything ever gets stolen in Bowstring, but there's no sense taking chances. A man don't come to ten thousand dollars every day. No sir!"

"I never saw that much before," Jimmy said. "I'd sure hang onto it."

"I aim to." Knapp turned toward the house. "You come on in when you get done with the horses. I want to tell you about the time me and the Cripple Creek marshal gunned down the Horrible Gang when they came out of the bank."

When Jimmy finished in the barn and went into the house, Knapp was at the table popping pieces of steak into his mouth and telling Jimmy's mother about his strike and his sack of gold.

"You'd better take it to the bank," Mrs. Bonner said. "We never keep that much money in the house."

Knapp took time to put down his fork and pat his gun butts. "Don't you worry none, Annie. I'll shoot the pants off anybody that comes sneaking around here. Yessir, I'll shoot their pants off an inch at a time."

Mrs. Bonner set a plate on the table. "Here's your supper, Jimmy." She gave him a pat on the back, and walked out of the kitchen.

"What's the matter with your ma?" Knapp asked. "She looks downright puny."

"Dunno. She was all right when I left this morning."

"Excitement, I guess. Shouldn't have sprung the news on her I'd hit it lucky, I guess. Women are mighty funny animals, Jimmy. Yessir, mighty funny. I was engaged once, but it was sure a mistake. She busted it. . . . I mean I saw it wasn't gonna go, so I got my ring back from her. Sure a good thing I did 'cause she married another feller the next week."

Food put a brake on Cousin Knapp's tongue for a time, but after the peach pie was gone, three-fourths of it down Knapp's throat, he moved into full speed again. There was the tale of a bear hunt on Pike's Peak after he'd related the finish of the Horrible Gang. Then the yarn about the time he'd dived into the Royal Gorge from the rim and saved a beautiful girl from being battered to pieces on the rocks.

It was almost dusk when Jimmy's folks came in. His mother started supper and Jimmy had to cut some wood. He didn't know until he got outside that his ears were humming. He fed and watered the horses. Then his mother reminded him he hadn't gathered the eggs. By the time he came in, supper was ready and his father was holding his head as if he had a headache.

Supper was a little boring to Jimmy because Knapp, having eaten a late dinner, wasn't very hungry and he used the time to tell the stories he'd told Jimmy in the afternoon.

Jimmy's mother kept going into the kitchen for this or that, and when the meal was finished, she said she guessed she'd leave the dishes. Mr. Bonner said they had a date to play cards at Henry Paul's place, and they'd have to go or they'd be late.

"You sleep in the room at the head of the stairs, Knapp," Mrs. Bonner said. "The same one you had the last time."

"I remember." Knapp gave way to the luxury of a yawn, and Mr.

Bonner took advantage of the moment of silence to say, "Jimmy, you've had quite a ride going to meet Knapp. There'll be plenty of time tomorrow to talk, so you'd better go to bed."

Say, that reminds me of an old fellow in Cañon City who went to bed and discovered a cougar between the blankets. He let out a holler they heard plumb down to Pueblo and yelled for me. I came in with both guns a-smoking. . . ."

"You get to bed right now, Jimmy," Mr. Bonner shouted, and fled.

"And I shot that lion right between the eyes, but something went wrong. That animal's head must have been made of solid bone because the bullet bounced off and slapped into the ceiling. There wasn't nothing to do but go it hand to hand. I had a knife in my belt and I managed to pull it out while I choked the animal with my left hand. There he was, a-snarling and a-growling and a-spitting. He had teeth six inches long. Never saw the like of it. I plunged my knife into his chest, but I might as well have saved myself the trouble 'cause he was dead. I'd choked him to death."

"I guess I'll go to bed," Jimmy said. "You going to sleep with your money?"

"Yessir, I'll keep it right beside my head. Or maybe I'll use it for a pillow. Imagine me using ten thousand dollars for a pillow, me, Knapp Bonner."

"Yeah, imagine it," Jimmy said. "Well, guess I'll go to bed."

Jimmy laid awake a long time staring at a black ceiling. The Horrible Gang. Bear hunting on Pike's Peak. Jumping into the Royal Gorge. Choking cougars. He rubbed his eyes. It seemed as if the room was filled with spitting, scratching, howling monsters. He had never been so tired before in his life, and all he'd done was to listen to Knapp and ride to Hat Creek and back. He'd ridden to Hat Creek lots of times and it had never made him tired before. He dropped off to sleep and woke in a cold sweat. Something was wrong!

Jimmy lay there, his heart pounding. At first he thought he'd had a dream about the Horrible Gang. Then he heard Cousin Knapp say, "Don't kill me. You can have the sack."

"Damn you, I ought to shoot you between the eyes," a man's voice growled. "Nothing but pennies in that sack. And them two guns! Pearl handles and as worthless as a kid's toy."

Jimmy knew he wasn't having a dream. Cousin Knapp was cornered. Jimmy tiptoed toward the door, expecting to hear Knapp jump out of bed and beat the man to death. But nothing happened. The man was cursing Knapp in a cold, deliberate tone for having pennies instead of the gold he'd bragged about.

"I'm gonna have a look around the house now that I'm here," the man said. "This is the banker's house, ain't it?"

"Sure," Knapp quavered. "You'll probably find a lot of diamonds and jewels and things."

Something was wrong! Really wrong, or Cousin Knapp would have handled the situation before now. Jimmy picked up his .22 and slipped down the hall. The door of Knapp's room was wide open, lamplight spilling into the hall and across the head of the stairs.

"You'd better be right," the man was saying, "or I'll skin you alive. Making me risk my neck just on account of your brags."

Then Jimmy was in the doorway, the hammer of his .22 back. He said, "Hook the moon, mister," in a tough voice the way Cousin Knapp had talked when he'd finished off the Horrible Gang and had them cornered in the Bucket of Red Blood Saloon.

The man wheeled toward the door and stopped. It was the dark-eyed little stranger who had been watching Cousin Knapp from the end of the hitch pole that afternoon.

"Take it easy, kid," the man whispered. "Don't squeeze that trigger no harder."

"You're coming with me," Jimmy ordered. "I don't care if I haven't got anything but my pajamas on. I'm taking you to the sheriff."

The dark-eyed little man had his back to Knapp. He was watching Jimmy, eyes glued on the muzzle of the boy's .22. That was when Knapp crawled out of bed, picked up the water pitcher on the stand and hit the little man on the head. The man went down and out in a splatter of broken crockery and water, and Knapp was on top of him in a dead faint.

There was a lot of commotion after that. Mr. Bonner ran in with the sheriff when Jimmy yelled, and both of them laughed fit to kill when the dark-eyed little man came to and hollered about not knowing there was a Billy the Kid in the house. The sheriff carted the man off to jail and Mr. Bonner was downstairs with Mrs. Bonner when Knapp came around.

He sat on the bed, as groggy as if he'd been the one who got hit on the head.

"Why did he keep saying you had pennies instead of gold in that sack?" Jimmy asked.

With great dignity Knapp got up and started dressing. "The damned fool was drunk, Jimmy. That's why he couldn't tell copper from gold. A man should never be drunk when he tries a holdup. If he hadn't been, I never could have sneaked up on him and knocked him out with a single blow of my fist. It reminds me of the time. . . ."

"You hit him with the pitcher," Jimmy said, pointing to the broken crockery on the floor.

"I must have knocked it off when I got out of bed. No, I hit him with my fist." Knapp buckled on his gun belt and picked up his sack. "It reminds me of the fist fight I had in Cheyenne last winter with Iron Chin McGinnity. I hit him once, just once, and when they picked up his head in the alley, they found his chin had been splintered clean up into his eyes."

Knapp walked down the stairs, a very dignified man. When he came into the living room, he said slowly, "George, I am not a fool. There has been skulduggery in this household, and don't try to lie out of it. You hired that man to invade your own house. I shall take the hint."

"Good-by," Mrs. Bonner said.

Knapp walked out as if he hadn't heard. The door had hardly closed when Mr. Bonner started to laugh. He fell into a chair and slapped his leg and laughed until he cried. Jimmy, watching from the head of the stairs, didn't understand. There were several things he didn't understand. Like why the dark eyed little man couldn't tell the difference between gold and copper. He hadn't looked drunk and he hadn't acted drunk. And Knapp saying Mr. Bonner had hired him to invade his own house.

"Go back to bed, sweetheart," his mother called up to him. "I'm sure that's all the excitement for tonight."

Then Mr. Bonner quit laughing. He looked up the stairs and there was pride in his eyes. He said, "Jimmy, you and I ought to take a trip."

"Where?"

"Where would you like to go?"

Jimmy considered. "Well, I'd like to see the Royal Gorge. I want to see how far Cousin Knapp jumped when he saved that beautiful girl from being smashed to death on the rocks."

Mr. Bonner choked and looked at his wife and finally managed, "Why sure, Jimmy. Sure."

"Go on to bed now," Mrs. Bonner said.

Jimmy went back along the hall to his room, walking slowly because he was thinking about the trip to the Royal Gorge. There was a growing suspicion in his mind that Cousin Knapp was a liar. When he saw how deep the Gorge was, he'd know.

The Steadfast

When disguised by the darkness of a prairie night, Gunlock seemed a pleasant place with its one wide street and the pools of yellow light spilling out across the dust from Clem York's hotel and saloon. But the sunrise drew away the disguise. Then Gunlock could be seen for what it was, a huddle of buildings dropped here among the empty miles, an evil, almost deserted, town with broken hitch rails and walks that had more splintered boards than sound ones, with cobwebbed windows and doors that hung askew from bent hinges.

Each morning Dave Lowrie viewed Gunlock with distaste as he walked from his house at the east end of town to his livery stable. He always had the weird feeling he was looking at something that should have been a corpse but stubbornly refused to become one.

There was something painful about seeing Gunlock this way, for he had been here when it was a brawling trail town; he had seen the settlers come filled with hope and leave with no hope at all, humbled by drought and hard times. He had seen his father die here in front of Clem York's hotel, shot in the back by parties unknown, or so the coroner's jury had said.

Almost every morning Dave met Marshal Arno Slade on the street, a toothpick gripped between his strong white teeth, the sun gleaming on his large gold star. The meeting had become an anticipated drama laden with dynamite that never exploded.

This morning Slade was standing in his usual position, the slanted sunlight cutting sharply across his bold face. Dave glanced at the gold star, thinking of his father, Ben Lowrie, who had been Gunlock's

Marshal through the boom years when it had been a tough town. A small star with doubtful silver plating had been good enough for him.

Dave's gray eyes lifted to the Marshal's cynical black ones and held there. There was a gun on Dave's hip, the same .44 his father had worn for so many years. Now Dave's hand dropped to the worn butt as it always did when he met Slade, for the man was unpredictable and dangerous.

Slade said, "Lowrie."

Dave stopped, saying nothing. He suspected, as everyone in Gunlock suspected, that Arno Slade had killed his father. From the day Ben Lowrie had died, Dave had known that the time would come when he would kill Slade, but he had waited until he had proof of the man's guilt. Now, meeting the Marshal's cool, malicious stare, he wondered if his two years of waiting had been a mistake. There were those in Gunlock who said it was.

"A man came through last night," Slade said. "He wanted a fresh horse."

Dave nodded, a prickle running down his spine. Perhaps Slade had grown tired of the waiting.

"You wouldn't let him have one," Slade pressed. "Why?"

"He didn't have any money."

"He offered to trade."

Dave shrugged. "His animal was dead on his feet."

Slade jerked the toothpick from his mouth. "Don't be such a damned fool, Lowrie. We all make our living the same way. This fellow was headed for the strip the same as a hundred other men have. He needed that horse."

"Why didn't you let him have one?"

"I did. I've got his horse in my barn now. Come over and get him and fetch me one of yours. I ain't no horse trader. You are. You can doctor him up and trade him off to the next man who comes through."

"If you traded, you're a horse trader," Dave said evenly. "That don't mean I'm taking him off your hands."

"You come and get him," Slade said flatly. "Fetch me that black gelding of yours."

"You giving me orders?" Dave asked.

"That's exactly what I'm doing."

"Then you can go to hell. I'm not Clem York or Fred Dunham."
Dave started toward his livery. Slade said, "Lowrie."

Dave swung back. "Now what?"

"Clem does a good business with his hotel and saloon. Fred ain't doing so bad in his store, neither. You know why?"

"I know all right, but I'm satisfied."

"You won't be long if you don't accommodate the boys who come through. There won't be nothing left of Gunlock, neither. They talk when they get together in the strip. They know they can lay over here. Get a drink and a meal. A room if they want it. If they don't have the *dinero* on 'em, they get it and send it back. You could have asked a hundred dollars' boot and you'd have had it in a week."

"I don't do business that way," Dave said, and started for his livery again.

"Damn you, Lowrie," Slade said darkly. "You won't stay here long if Judge Patterson decides to move you out."

Dave went on, and when he reached the archway of his stable, he looked back and saw that Slade had disappeared. Judge Patterson was probably having his breakfast and listening to Slade's angry report.

Dave picked up a fork and began cleaning out the stalls. Judge Patterson had controlled Gunlock from the day Arno Slade had pinned on his gold-plated star. That was one of the things which kept Dave from forcing the issue with Slade. Killing him would actually settle nothing unless Patterson was dealt with at the same time, and that was a difficult matter. The Judge ran the bank, a soft-spoken man who was well liked. Even Annie Wallen, one of the first settlers, couldn't believe that Patterson had any part in making Gunlock the outlaw haven it had become.

Dave was finishing the last stall when June Wallen came down the runway to him. She said, "Grandma wants you, Dave."

Startled, Dave wheeled, wanting to shout at her never to sneak up on him again. He didn't. Nobody shouted at June Wallen. She was the one lovely thing in an ugly town. At eighteen she was a mature woman who was repelled by the wickedness around her and withdrew from it, held here only because of her loyalty to her grandmother.

Every hardcase who drifted through Gunlock and saw June stopped long enough to woo her. Arno Slade asked her to marry him on the average of once a week, and even Judge Patterson in his mild-mannered way had let her know she could have him the minute she said the word. She treated them all alike, holding them off with cool disdain, although sometimes she looked at Dave in a way that made him think she had a higher regard for him than for the others.

Now, looking at her slim figure in a bright print dress, her soft-lipped pliant mouth, her brown hair pinned in a high crown on her head, he thought that this girl was at least partly responsible for his remaining in Gunlock.

He said, "You're as pretty as the morning, June. Makes me feel good just to look at you."

"Grandma wants to see you," June said sharply. "Come on."

"I don't know that I'm gonna run every time. . . ."

"Dave, will you come on! She's in a tizzy."

"I guess there's nothing that needs doing around here that can't wait." He leaned the fork against the wall and walked down the runway beside her. "Ain't Annie in a tizzy most of the time?"

"She isn't well, Dave," June said gravely. "She wants to see things changed before she dies."

"What will you do when she dies?"

"Get out of here," the girl said dully. "Go to Denver, I guess."

They walked in silence then, Dave thinking about what June had said. Towns died when their people left, and nothing remained but empty buildings for spiders and mice, empty buildings with their windows gone. The wind would howl around the eaves and dust would drift through the open doorways. Then the buildings would disappear and grass would grow in the street, hiding the scar the town had once laid upon the face of the prairie. That would be Gunlock's fate, a thought that brought a vague disturbance to Dave.

Annie Wallen sat in her rocking chair on the porch. When Dave and June came up, she rapped her cane on the railing, calling, "Is that the fastest you can move, Dave Lowrie?"

He dropped down on the porch and leaned against a post. "I'll do anything for you, Annie, except run." He winked at June. "I'll even marry your granddaughter."

Blushing, the girl glanced at her grandmother. Annie motioned to the door.

"Go get them dishes done. What's the matter with you? You haven't got time to stand around and listen to this blatherskite's soft talk."

June fled, her cheeks scarlet. Dave said hotly, "Some day I'm going to tell June your bite ain't as bad as your bark. You keep her scared half to death."

"Scared? Ha! You don't know June. And you don't need to josh about marrying her unless you mean it."

Dave had lifted tobacco and paper from his pocket. Now he looked at the old woman, fingers clutching the makings, his eyes searching her wrinkled face.

He said, "Annie, you're as crusty as hell, but you wouldn't say that unless I had a chance with June, would you?"

"Why don't you ask her? I'd like to see your face when you do. Yes sir, I would." She tapped her cane on the railing again. "Well, I didn't call you over here to gab about June. When are you going to clean this town up?"

Dave rolled his smoke then, not looking at her. She was old and she was sick, and it was understandable that, as June had said, she wanted to see things changed. Still, she had no right to prod him into something before he had the proof he needed.

Firing his cigarette, he tossed the match into the yard. He said, "You ain't one to beat around the bush, Annie. Speak your piece."

She scowled at him, her cane tapping steadily on the railing. Her white hair was pulled into a tight knot on the back of her head. Now she lifted a hand to touch a brown mole on her cheek. Looking at her, Dave thought of something he had not thought of before. In a way she was like Gunlock; she simply refused to die.

"I will," Annie said. "For two years now you and Arno Slade have been walking around on your tiptoes like a couple of dogs wanting to tear into each other and lacking the guts to do it. You know he shot your pappy. What's the matter with you?"

"It ain't just a matter of guts," he said irritably. "Slade's fronting for somebody else."

"Who?"

"Patterson."

"Hogwash. You don't know that." She waved her cane at him. "Now look here, Dave Lowrie. We made this town, me and your pappy and Jake Bendix and some more. Come in covered wagons from the Arkansas. Followed the Santa Fe Trail till we left the river. Fought Comanches once. I lost my son in that ruckus. I ain't crying over him. I never did and I never will. It's part of the price he paid for wanting to have a hand in making a new country. It might have been me or your pappy or Jake."

She looked northward across the low, rolling hills, a mottled green with the sun making alternate patches of light and shadow upon them.

"It was a purty sight when we got here. A mighty purty sight. Right off we saw this was the place to build our town. We knew we could raise wheat as good as they could in Kansas, but likewise we knew we'd have to fight cattlemen who claimed this range. We did, too. We knew there'd be times when we'd go hungry. There'd be sickness and we didn't have no doctor. Some of us would die. Your ma was one of them. Typhoid. So did June's mother. Scarlet fever. But that was part of the price, too. We done the best we could, Dave, and we made a town."

She brought her eyes to him and she was very old and tired. "Your father died for the same thing the rest of them did. Right from the first he was cut out to be a lawman same as I was cut out to be the cook in the hotel. Same as Jake Bendix had ink in his veins and started the *Herald*. Well, Dave, we had cattle going up the trail right here beside Gunlock. Then the settlers came in, folks like we was who wanted to raise wheat. They knew they could because we had, but they didn't have the kind of backbones we did and they fizzled out."

She pounded her cane on the railing. "Damn it, Dave, can't you see what this town was made of? Our blood. Our sweat and our hopes. Sure there was bad years, but we stayed and most of us lived. Now we've had rain again and the settlers'll come back. If Gunlock's a decent town, they'll trade here. If Arno Slade goes on running it for outlaws, it'll die."

Dave's cigarette had gone cold in his mouth. Annie Wallen had told him nothing new, but he had learned something just sitting here and watching her. Her spirit had kept her alive, the same spirit that had kept Gunlock from going back to the prairies. That spirit was the difference between those who had come and failed, and those who had made the town in the first place and stayed.

He said, "As long as Patterson . . ."

"Oh, shut up," she said testily. "Maybe you're right about him, but it's Slade that's given this place the name it has. Who's to blame for letting him stay? You! That's who. Now don't get your mad up. Ben told me a dozen times you had every quality a lawman needed, but what have you done? You've been satisfied to run a little old livery stable, a job anybody could do who can fork hay into a manger and manure out of a stall. Ben Lowrie wouldn't have been satisfied with that. He was the same caliber man as Bat Masterson and the rest who've kept the lid on out here. There ought to be a monument to Ben. The *best* kind he could have would be a Gunlock that'll be here a hundred years from now."

Dave rose and tossed his half-smoked cigarette into the yard. He had felt this. Everything Annie had said. It had been bottled up inside him, a smoldering fire he had tried to smother. Now it blazed up, and then died down, for he was remembering things his father had said when he'd taught him the use of a gun, about the responsibilities a man faced when he became deadly fast with a gun.

"Well, Dave," Annie threw at him. "Are you going to run Slade out of town?"

"He wouldn't run," Dave said somberly, "and I can't pull a gun on him until I know he killed Dad."

She snorted. "You think Slade's going to come around and tell you he shot Ben?"

"Dad was shot in the back," Dave said dully. "No one saw him do it."

"I know," Annie said in a milder tone. "It's made me crazy, I guess, just sitting here and watching Slade and knowing how it's going to be when the settlers come in again. We'll see wheat raised all over the country. There'll be a town. It just won't be Gunlock."

Dave wiped a hand across his face, puzzled by this sudden change in her. It wasn't like Annie Wallen to back up after she had started something.

"I guess it won't," he said, and stepped down from the porch.

She drew her shawl more tightly around her shoulders, tears running down her cheeks. "Dave," she said, "will you run over to Jake's office and fetch me the paper? It ought to be off the press by now."

In all the years he had known Annie Wallen, he had never seen her cry. He looked away, embarrassed. It would have been all right to have seen tears on any woman's face but Annie's.

He said, "I'll see," and walked rapidly away.

She was a little crazy, Dave told himself as he moved along the street to the print shop. Jake Bendix was crazy, too. Ben had been the same when he was alive. They were hipped about this town they'd made. They'd had their dreams, but now, after twenty years, their dreams had still remained only dreams.

Then resentment was in Dave, a bitter resentment that cut like acid in his blood stream. Annie had said he was to blame for Slade's giving Gunlock the name it had. That wasn't true, and it wasn't right for Annie to say it. He had been only twenty-one when his father had been killed, a kid barely old enough to vote. The older men were to blame, men like Clem York and Fred Dunham who had bowed before Judge Patterson's will.

There was something else, too, and as Dave thought about it, his resentment grew, for he knew he could do nothing more than he had. Ben Lowrie had been no part of a braggart. Quiet, conscientious, colorless, a brave man who did his job as he saw it. To Dave he had been the greatest man in the world. Often, as dusk flowed across the prairie, the two of them had sat smoking on the front porch and talked. It had been mostly about one basic conflict in life, the battle between right and wrong. As Ben had seen it, the struggle between law and lawlessness was part of that basic conflict, but he had continually sounded one warning note.

"Some men who are fast with a gun get the notion they're God," Ben had said. "Whenever a man, and it don't make no difference whether he's got a star on his shirt or not, gets the notion that he's got the right to take his gun and settle with another man on a personal basis, he's wrong, just plumb wrong."

That had been back of Dave's waiting. When the settlement came with Arno Slade, it must come with Judge Patterson, too, but he was determined it would not be on the issue of personal vengeance.

Dave walked slowly, wondering what Ben would have done if he were alive and making the decision. They were interwoven into one pattern, his father's death and Gunlock's becoming an outlaw haven. In some way, although Dave had never been sure how, Judge Patterson was making money out of the thing Arno Slade had done to

Gunlock. That was the reason Ben Lowrie had died. Still, it was only Dave's explanation, and if he set out to punish Slade and Patterson without proof, he would be playing God and Ben would have said it was wrong.

Dave was picking his way along the splintered walk in front of Fred Dunham's store when he heard the first yell of pain. It made only a faint impression on his consciousness, so deeply was he buried in his thoughts, but the second brought him to a stop. He stood motionless for an instant, not sure where the sound came from, then decided it must have originated in Jake Bendix's print shop. He ran past the vacant building that stood beside Dunham's store and turned into Bendix's place.

He saw at once he had guessed right. Arno Slade and Judge Patterson were standing at Bendix's desk. The old editor was slumped over in his swivel chair, blood from a cut streaming down his face.

As Dave came to a flat-footed stop, Slade raised his fist and struck the old man, shouting, "If it wasn't Lowrie's idea, whose was it?"

Patterson, a small man beside Slade, tugged at the Marshal's coat tail, crying, "That's enough, Arno. That's enough."

"He'll talk," Slade raged. "I tell you he'll talk," and raised his fist again.

"Don't do it," Dave called.

Slade and Patterson wheeled away from the desk. Slade must have recognized Dave's voice, for he pulled gun as he turned. Dave had no choice; no time to think about what he should do. His response was the natural reaction that a man makes when he is prompted by the instinct of self-preservation, but it was the training that Ben Lowrie had given him, not instinct, that saved his life.

Dave drew his gun and fired while Slade was still turning toward him and lifting gun from leather. Slade lurched with the impact of the slug, his own shot going wild. He took one staggering step and fell. Patterson let out a strange cry that sounded like the bleat of a sheep, yanked a gun out from under his coat, and went down under Dave's second bullet.

Bendix rose, holding a handkerchief to his battered face. He said, "You use a gun just like Ben did. Annie said it would be that way."

Dave stared at the dead men, suddenly cold and trembling a little. He looked at the smoking gun in his hand and then at the dead men again, not understanding this or what Annie Wallen had to do with it.

Picking up a paper from his desk, Bendix brought it to Dave. Men poured in from the street, Clem York and Fred Dunham and some more, gaping at Dave and the two bodies and throwing questions at Bendix.

Dave glanced at the newspaper, still not understanding. In the center of the front page was a black box holding the words:

ARNO SLADE HAS TWENTY-FOUR HOURS TO LIVE UNLESS HE LEAVES TOWN

"They pulled on Dave," Bendix was saying. "He shot both of them in self-defense."

"I didn't think the boy was that fast," Clem York said, as if this was beyond belief. "You were right about him, Jake."

"Dave, you didn't know," Bendix said, "but Annie and me wanted you to have the star after Ben was killed. Patterson held out for Slade, saying you was too young." He motioned toward the men who had come in. "They agreed with Patterson."

"And lived to regret it," Fred Dunham said.

Dave jabbed a long finger at the newspaper. "What is this?"

"Annie's notion," Bendix said. "We were pretty sure Slade was ready to bust. He's been scared for two years that you'd jump him. He didn't have the guts to jump you, and another back-shooting job would have been one too many. Annie said she'd get you over here just about the time Slade always came in for his paper. Naturally Slade jumped to the conclusion you were warning him to get out, and when he saw you, he blew up like we figured he would." Bendix's bruised lips shaped a grin. "We timed it just right, looks like."

Suddenly Dave was aware that he still held his gun. He dropped it into his holster, saying, "Patterson didn't have to . . ."

"Yes, he had to make his try," Bendix cut in. "He sank or swam with Slade. You see, he was buying stolen money from the boys who came through here, giving them fifty cents on the dollar, and then sending it to California where it could safely be put into circulation. I knew about it, but there wasn't anything I could do with Slade packing the star. Now you'd better take that paper over to Annie."

As Dave turned, Clem York said, "You'll take the Marshal's job, won't you, Dave?"

"I'll take it," Dave said, and walked back to Annie Wallen's house.

She was still sitting in her rocking chair when Dave came up and handed her the newspaper. He said, "It's finished. Patterson, too."

"Well then, I was wrong about him." She folded the paper, her eyes fixed on his face. "Dave, I made you risk your life. I would have taken your place if I could, but it had to be you. All of us have some talents, and you were the only one who had the right talent for this job. If you had died, I would never have forgiven myself. But you were Ben's son—I knew you wouldn't."

He dropped a hand to the butt of his .44, thinking of the things his father had told him about the responsibilities a man had who was fast with a gun. Annie Wallen and Jake Bendix might have been wrong, but the job was done. Tomorrow was another day and Gunlock would be a different town, but the important thing was that he had not done something for which he need be ashamed.

"We made Gunlock," Annie was saying, "but it's up to the new generation to keep it going." She motioned to the door. "June's making a cake. Go tell her she's got no call to hate Gunlock. It'll be a good town for her to raise her children—hers and yours."

She heard his steps fade as he walked through the house. She was still sitting there, her eyes on the low hills when a settler's wagon appeared on the horizon.

"The first," she said softly. "They'll come, hundreds of them. That one's like the first robin in the spring. Ben Lowrie has got his monument, the kind he'd like."

The Patriarch of Gunsight Flat

The sins of man are many. He will kill. He will take that which belongs to others—money and cattle and all that can be turned into money. Aye, and other things: a good name—a woman's virtue—a man's home—a friend. And who can say with certainty that murder is a greater crime than thievery?

Dave Cray was hitching up when Gramp hobbled out of the cabin and came across the trodden earth of the yard. Sometimes Dave wondered if he hated the old man. The years had made his hair white, had scarred his gaunt face with deep lines. They had brought rheumatism to his gnarled and twisted muscles until there were days when he could not walk. But Gramp didn't hate nor speak ill of anybody.

No, it wasn't that Gramp had ever done anything wrong. It was just that he'd brought Dave out here to Gunsight Flat to dry up with the wind. There'd come a day when Dave's bones would whiten under a hammering sun set in a brassy sky. A million years from now somebody would dig them up like the Gable kids had dug those queer-looking bones out of the sand dunes to the north, bones that must have gone through uncharted eons since some misty day when creatures that were no longer here walked the earth.

"Don't lose your head with Solly," Gramp said in the same even tone he used whether it was a good day or a bad day, whether the rheumatism was giving him its special brand of hell or had for the moment forgotten him.

"I ain't making no promises," Dave replied, climbing into the buckboard.

"You got Luke's list?"

"I've got it."

Dave spoke to the team and wheeled out of the yard, keeping his gaze ahead on the twin tracks that cut straight north through the sagebrush. He didn't hate the old man. He knew that. You couldn't hate a man who had waited for death with the uncomplaining fortitude Gramp had. It was just that Dave Cray's life would have been different if Gramp hadn't settled here. . . .

There were the early treasured years in the Willamette valley with its people and cities. There was Dave's gem box of memories: the valley in spring and the smell of its rich life-swelling earth; the first lamb tongue; Indian summer days when the Cascades were blurred by smoky distance; the cries of other children as they played tag through a July twilight, the thrill of the game itself, and his first kiss when he had caught Ruthie Norton back of the big oak.

Dave had been twelve when the news of Lee's surrender came to Oregon. That was when Gramp sold the place. "Ain't much sense in going west—just fall into the Pacific. We'll go the other way, and I aim to keep on believing what I believe."

So they had gone east—over the Cascades, through the Douglas firs and then the pines on the east slope, around the lava flows that an enraged nature had spewed out upon the earth like the fiery vomit of an animated prehistoric gargoyle.

Across the Deschutes—the Crooked River—the John Day: searching, always searching, while the empty miles twisted behind in trackless solitude. Rimrock and sage and pine forest—or pine forest and sage and rimrock. No reception committee, unless it might be a marauding handful of Snake Indians. No band to blare out a brassy welcome. . . . Only the lonely miles.

Then Gramp found it: Gunsight Flat, an emerald in a gray sage setting—pines in the near-by mountains—a crystal-clear creek—fish—antelope—deer—bear—and hay land in the flat that would never want water, for water was always there.

Dave, watching Gramp, knew this was the end of the search. The twisting, seeking tracks would go no farther. But the empty miles were there, all around them, running away in any direction as far as Dave could see and on beyond into the unmeasured distance.

"We won't starve," Gramp had said. "Fish and game a plenty. A fine land to become a man in." He pulled at his beard that had been black then, and a glint was in his eyes that comes only to a man when he feels the ultimate in satisfaction. "A land where a man can think what seems fitting to think."

They had gone back the next summer for more horses and stock, for seed and tools. It was the last time they had seen the Willamette valley. Others had come: Luke Petty, Fred Gable and his cabinful of kids, Jared Frisbie, loud-talking Abe Mack, and more and more, until the whole flat was taken.

Then came Smiling Jim Solly with his wagons and cattle and his fine riding buckaroos; and there was pigtailed Ann Solly, riding a bay mare up at the head of the column alongside Smiling Jim. Seeing her that first time, Dave thought her corn-yellow hair was as fine as real silk, as beautiful as gold in the sun.

Aye, the sins of man are many. . . . Standing with the thief and the murderer is the one who says his daughter shall not see the man she loves. If they run away together, he will follow them and hang the man and black-snake his girl and bring her back. Smiling Jim Solly would have done exactly that—and kept his smile through all of it.

"Don't lose your head with Solly," Gramp had said.

Well, maybe Dave wouldn't lose his head, but he'd kill Smiling Jim Solly. Ann wouldn't hate him for it. . . .

The buckboard left the sage flat and climbed the bald face of the rimrock by a twisting route, dropped over, and came down to Solly's store. There was no money in Gunsight Flat except what Solly had brought, but there was a deal of swapping. Solly had cattle and winter shelter, but he had no hay land. The Flatters, as they were called, had hay. Every autumn, wagons rumbled into Solly's canyon with the hay and built credit for the Flatters at the store.

Only this winter it would be different, for Solly had steadily built a carry-over of hay until now he wouldn't need any for another year. Dave, his eyes sweeping the long row of round weather-browned stacks, choked with the fury of his anger. Smiling Jim Solly would look at you and say you could buy his sugar and salt and coffee and dried peaches if you had money. That was the way it had been with Jared Frisbie and loud-talking Abe Mack—the week before, when they had come.

As Dave tied his team in front of the store he saw Ann working in her yard. He grinned; he wanted to yell; he wanted to get up on the buckboard seat and holler like a rooster when a hen comes off the nest with fifteen chicks. Smiling Jim Solly could laugh in your face and say he'd starve you to death if you didn't sell to him, but he couldn't keep his girl from loving one of the Flatters he despised.

Dave picked up a rock and weighted down the letter he'd written the night before to Ann. Smiling Jim Solly was slick, but he wasn't as slick as his daughter and one Dave Cray. Solly would raise Cain if he ever found out. Dave's jaw set stubbornly. Let him find out. It had to come to a showdown sometime.

Smiling Jim Solly was in the back of the store, one of his long cigars tilted at a cocky angle between his teeth. Half a dozen buckaroos squatted on the floor or sat on a counter, listening and laughing to the big tale Solly was telling. He was a bragger, Smiling Jim was. He liked to talk, and he liked to hear his audience laugh.

There were some Flatters over there, too. Jared Frisbie and Abe Mack were helping themselves out of the cracker barrel, only Abe wasn't as loud as usual. The only racket he made was when Solly finished his story. Then Abe laughed louder than any other two men in the store.

Dave stood there in the door, half turned so he could watch Ann run across to his buckboard and get his note. It was the way they always worked it. If Dave stepped out of the doorway, Ann knew her father was watching.

As soon as Ann had the letter and had slipped it inside the bosom of her dress, Dave stalked into the store. Smiling Jim saw him, all right, but he didn't pay any attention. He tilted his cigar a little higher and started on another windy.

There were several things crowding Dave, but mostly it was Abe Mack and Jared Frisbie coming back after the way they'd been turned down cold last week. It was worse standing there filling their bellies with Solly's crackers. But it was a hell of a lot worse for Abe to laugh like that at Solly's sorry jokes.

"Here's some things Gramp wants." Dave shoved a ragged corner of paper under Solly's nose. "Likewise there's Luke Petty's list."

Solly looked mad because Dave had butted into his yarn. He chewed on his cigar a minute. His mouth was still smiling, but his eyes weren't. He said, "Got any money?"

"No, but we've got hay."

"You know damned well I ain't taking no hay."

"How do you expect us to eat?"

"Eat your hay, if you've got so much."

They laughed—especially Abe Mack. Funny about that laugh: it sounded like a mule's bray. The Flatters eating hay might be funny to Solly's buckaroos; but it wasn't funny to a Flatter, and Abe was a Flatter.

"Maybe you're horse enough to eat hay, Solly," Dave said evenly, "but we ain't. You don't need to get so smart about not taking any hay, neither. There's gonna be another year."

"By that time you Flatters will be starved out, and you'll sell your places to me like I've been asking you to for the last five years."

"Then you're nothing but a thief."

When a man was rich like Smiling Jim Solly and had the power and dignity that money gave him, and when he liked to have other folks bow and scrape around, you didn't call him a thief—not more than once. Solly wasn't smiling. Nobody was laughing. It was the first time Dave had seen Solly when he wasn't smiling.

"You're a brave man or a fool," Solly said slowly. "Either way I'm telling you something you'd better listen to. Get out of this country and don't never come back."

Dave laughed. So Smiling Jim was going to run him out of the country! Suddenly everybody was still. Nobody else had laughed. Dave took a long breath. He said, "Solly, what would you do if your hay burned up?"

He shocked them. Seems it's all right for a man like Jim Solly to make threats and talk tough, but the little fellows like Dave Cray weren't supposed to do that.

They had forgotten to breathe. Everybody but Abe Mack, who took an extra-deep breath—the way a man does when an idea has crawled up his spinal cord into his brain.

"You threatening me?" Solly asked.

"No. I'm just giving you something to chew on along with that cigar. I reckon big talk can blow both ways."

Solly laughed. "Only I wasn't making big talk, kid. I'm just telling you that if you stay in these parts you're likely to meet up with an accident."

They all laughed then, all but Dave. The laughs were a little shaky, as if it wasn't real funny but they knew Solly expected them to laugh. Abe Mack's was the biggest and loudest.

Dave said: "I'm sure gonna run, Solly. I'm gonna run like hell." He picked Abe Mack up, turned him over, and dropped him headfirst into the cracker barrel. Then he walked out.

Ann wasn't in sight when Dave stepped into the buckboard. That was the way it should be. She'd come. He turned the team and whelled up the grade to the top of the rim. He was a little uneasy about what Gramp would say when he heard the way things had gone.

A dozen times since Smiling Jim Solly had come to the canyon, Gramp had said: "He's a bad one. You can't trust a man who smiles all the time. There'll come a day when we'll have to have it out; and if we don't handle it right there'll be some shooting."

Dave hadn't handled it right. Uneasiness deepened in him. He felt he shouldn't have called Solly a thief. It was up to Dave now to fight or run, and he didn't want to do either. Not till Gramp said it was time.

He turned off the road when he reached the plateau above the rim and followed it until he came to a cluster of junipers. There he waited—and presently Ann came, as he knew she would.

Looking at Ann was like seeing a million stars flash across a sky that was gloomy black a moment before. When he kissed her he forgot his uneasiness, he forgot about the empty miles and the lonely years, forgot the childhood memories that had been his treasury. He even forgot that Smiling Jim Solly was her father.

Then she was motionless in his arms, head on his chest, and his heart was pounding with great hammering thuds. He was remembering things now, the things that he had forgotten a moment before.

"It can't be this way," he said. "Turn your horse loose. He'll go back."

"I can't."

What he saw in her brown eyes frightened him. He had seen something like that in a doe's eyes when she was badly hurt. He said more roughly than he intended to: "You don't owe him anything. You owe it to yourself—and to me!"

She drew his arms away from her and walked to the rim. The wheel ruts of the road were like tiny threads laid through the sage. The flat lay below her, the dots that were houses, the brown haystacks squatting in the grass stubble.

"No, I don't owe him anything," she said, "but I have seen him kill men. I know the pride that is in him, and I know what it will do. I couldn't stand it if he killed you."

She mounted and rode away. That was the end of it. The stars were gone. It was a black sky again, gloomy black, and the years lay ahead like the twin tracks through the sage. Only they didn't end here in the flat. Somewhere out there, beyond the horizon, lay Dave Cray's destiny. It wasn't here.

Ann Solly was gone. Dave would never look back again; there was nothing to hold him now. Gramp would be dead soon. There was a world to see, a distant world that waited out there beyond where the twin tracks disappeared in a sea of sage.

But he didn't go that day. Gramp listened to what had happened in the store. He packed his pipe and lighted it, eyes narrowed with feeling, face lines as deep as irregular furrows plowed across a brown and aged field. But there was no reproof.

"It's been a good place to live," Gramp said at last, "but I knowed, the day Jim Solly drove his herd across the flat, that we'd have to fight. I've been hoping we'd get it settled afore you had to plant me. Saddle up, Dave. Tell the folks to meet here tomorrow night."

Dave rode that day, uneasiness biting at him again. He couldn't leave today—nor tomorrow. He'd have to wait until he'd buried Gramp up there on the rim, a spot he'd picked out years before. It was a gossamer bond, but it held him as no clanking chain or jail bars could have held him.

He told them all, and they said they'd come. Smiling Jim Solly would have to get up in the morning if he wanted their places. It'd take more than a year to starve them out. They'd got along before he'd started his store. They'd sent their own freight wagons to the Dalles, and they'd do it again. Dave didn't have the heart to tell them that they had had money in those days, and didn't now. They had hay, but they couldn't haul hay across those unmarked miles, and nobody would buy it if they did.

Even loud-talking Abe Mack listened, a grin on his lips that was meant to be friendly; but his eyes had a way of touching Dave's face and sliding off like the slimy trail that marks a snail's passing.

"I'll be there," Mack promised. "Solly ain't gonna push us off this flat."

They were there, with the sun still showing a red arc above the western horizon, the promise of tomorrow a shining brightness above the edge of the earth.

They hadn't brought their women, for this was men's business. Nor had they brought their guns. First there would be the talk. Then the fighting if it had to come. But there was no talking yet. They respectfully waited for Gramp to start it. All but Abe Mack, who had much to say whether anybody listened or not.

Then Gramp got up from where he'd been sitting under a poplar, a poplar he'd planted the second year he'd come to the flat. He knocked the dottle from his pipe into the palm of his hand. They stopped their chatter. Even Abe Mack braked his tongue to silence.

"We all came here for our own reasons," Gramp said in his even-toned voice. "That ain't of no importance. What is important is that we put a part of our hearts, aye, our souls, into what we've made home. When folks do that, they don't move off 'cause Smiling Jim Solly gets it into his head to have what is ours.

"Trouble is, Solly's smart. He knows it's too late in the year to get wagons to the Dalles and back. Besides, we ain't got money. Now I've been thinking about this ever since Dave came back from the store yesterday, and I can't see no way out. Come spring, most of us will be riding over to the store with our tails dragging. We'll be begging Solly to give us anything he feels like for our places."

It was true. What would life be without coffee, or tobacco, or salt? They had always stocked those things in the fall when Solly's wagons got in from the Dalles. It was late summer now, and they were out. There was no hope except from the shelves of Jim Solly's store.

"We can steal from him," Fred Gable said. "He's fixing to steal from us."

"You reckon a winter's supply of coffee is enough to pay your kids for the loss of their pappy?" Gramp asked. "That ain't the way, Fred."

They were silent then. They knew that Gramp was right. They looked at one another, a hopelessness spreading among them like a psychic plague. The sun was almost gone now, just a red slash along the horizon. The glitter of the sunset had spread to be echoed by clouds low in the east. The deep purple and dusk began building below the rimrock. It seemed to move in now, as it always did when the day had spun its allotted thread.

They were still silent when they heard the thunder of hoofs on the road between them and Solly's store. They fell back, edging toward their horses, thinking of their women at home, of the guns they did not have.

"Don't nobody go," Gramp said. "Solly's a patient man. He won't be pushing—not yet."

It was Ann. Dave recognized her before the others, bent low on her horse's neck, riding as only a girl raised in the saddle can ride.

She came thundering into the yard and pulled up, dust rolling around her. She coughed and stepped down into Dave's arms. She coughed again, and he led her out of the dust.

There was no telling what they thought. Even Gramp stared at her with cold eyes. They didn't know, and Dave didn't tell them—not then. He waited, like the others—not knowing and, like them, a little scared.

"Somebody burned our stacks," she said. "Dad's coming with his men."

They stood like chiseled granite, thinking of this and what it meant, but mostly they thought about what Smiling Jim Solly would do and what this gave him a right to do. But to Dave Cray it meant something else. It meant that Ann had at last cut loose. She was giving to him what a woman owed to the man she loved. Suddenly the golden childhood memories were gone. This was his life. This was his home. Here was his destiny. His arm tightened around her to hold this thing that was his.

"Thank you, Ann," Gramp said. "Does he know you're here?"

"No."

Dave had never told Gramp about him and Ann, but Gramp saw it now. He had a way of knowing things like that.

"Go inside, girl," Gramp said. "I think the way has been shown us."

She went without question. They waited while that last trace of the sun was lost to sight and the scarlet began to fade in the west, while purple slid out across the flat from the rimrock. They heard the horses. "A dozen," Luke Petty said. "We ain't got a weepon amongst us, Gramp. What have you got inside?"

"The weepons I've got inside will stay there," Gramp said, more sternly than he usually spoke. "This ain't the night for fighting."

They shuffled uneasily, and Mack muttered; but they stayed until Smiling Jim Solly came out of the dusk, a dozen buckaroos fanning out on both sides, guns cased on their hips.

"My stacks were burned today," Smiling Jim Solly said coldly. "Nobody was home but Ann. She was in the store, so she didn't see who done it. Rest of us was north on Cold Creek, but I don't have to have anybody tell me. Cray, you asked me yesterday what I'd do if my stacks burned. You denying you fired 'em?"

"*I* didn't do it!" Dave shouted. "It'd be like you to fire 'em yourself—just to blame it onto me."

Solly's cold smile broke now into a raking laugh. "No, I wouldn't do that, Cray. I told you yesterday to get out of the country. I reckon you're fixing to, but first you had to fire my stacks so I'd buy your crop this year."

Dave, staring at the man, knew that was the way it would look to anyone. He said: "I didn't do it, Solly. Gramp knows I was here all day."

Solly lashed them with his raking laugh again. "So you think I'd believe the old coot? Not me, Cray. I knew about this meeting you was having, and I'm guessing you figgered you'd boost the price on me. All right. I'll make a deal, but I'll make it my way: I'll buy your places, and I'll pay you a fair price—but you're turning in this year's crop for nothing, to pay for what Cray burned."

"Hell, Solly, you can't do that!" Abe Mack yelled. "We've got to have stuff out of your store this winter."

It was plain enough to Dave. Jared Frisbie, who had been in the store with Mack the day before, must have had the same thought, for he said in cold fury: "Abe heard Dave ask Solly what he'd do if his hay burned. . . . You knew Solly would jump Dave, didn't you, Abe?"

"How would I know?" Mack cried, and backed away.

"How did you hear about this meeting, Solly?" Gramp asked.

"Mack told me," Solly said. "He told me he saw Cray riding over the rim early this morning."

"You got a limb that'll hold Mack's carcass?" Fred Gable bellowed. "We don't want the likes of him around."

"There will be no act of that kind," Gramp said sternly. "Mack, be out of the country by morning. You've got no family to hold you.

What you did was bad enough, but putting it off on Dave was worse. Git, now!"

Mack left in haste and without dignity. Solly said darkly: "Don't make no difference who done it. Mack was a Flatter. You'll make that hay good."

"You can have Mack's hay," Gramp said quietly, "but you'll pay the rest of us. I wouldn't be surprised if you put Mack up to burning your hay just to give you an excuse for shoving us off the flat. I know what you are, Solly. You came after the rest of us were here. You came after we'd made it safe for your money and your cattle, all the time thinking you'd work it around to own the land that's ours. We'll never go, Solly. If you murder us, our blood will be on your shoulders. It will be in your dreams and in your soul."

"I ain't worried about my dreams," Solly said contemptuously.

"We've had our dreams, Solly, dreams about our homes. You had money to hire your work done. We had our two hands. Maybe we won't live to see the day, but it will come when a million people live in this country. A million people with hands and faith. Your kind can live with us if they want to. If they don't, they'll have to go like Abe Mack went."

"You're a fool, old man," Solly raged. "I ain't worrying about the million people. I'm worrying about the hay I've got to have to get me through the winter."

"You'll have it for a fair price. You'll be fair with us, Solly, because you've got to live with us the same as we've got to live with you. You think your money gives you the power to ride us down. That makes you a fool. Your money can't even buy you the thing you want more than anything else in the world."

There was silence with only the breathing of thirty men rasping into the stillness. Then Smiling Jim Solly, who had lost his smile a moment before, asked: "What do you mean?"

"Ann!" Gramp called.

She came out of the cabin and across the yard until she stood beside Dave. Her hand sought his. She held her head high, proud and defiant.

"Tell him why you're here, girl," Gramp said.

"Go home," Solly said through gritted teeth.

"It's not my home now. I'm staying here."

"You see how it is, Solly," Gramp said. "All the money and power and pride in hell can't buy your girl's love, and it can't keep her away from the man she loves. We understand that, Solly, but you don't. You'll have to work for her love if you ever have it."

Aye, the sins of man are many, and there must be compensation for them. There must be life, as there is death; there must be love, as there is hate. Smiling Jim Solly shriveled in the eyes of those who looked at him. Dignity garbed Gramp like a cloak, but there was no dignity about Solly. He turned his horse and rode away, his men lining out behind him.

"You can go home and sleep well tonight," Gramp said. "That was the only way anybody could touch Jim Solly."

Then it was just Dave and Ann and Gramp, and the sound of horses' hoofs dying across the flat. There would come a day when the empty miles would not be empty, when train whistles and the shrill scream of whirring saws slicing pine into lumber would cut the high thin air. There would be people and cities; there would be the echo of children's laughter. There must be compensation, the companionship of tomorrow to replace the loneliness of yesterday, the goodness of the Gramps to balance the sins of the Jim Sollys. It takes time to understand these things: time and human dignity and a willingness to understand.

And Dave Cray did understand. It was a fine land to become a man in—a land where a man could think what it seemed fitting to think.

High-Grade

Rawson stood by the window in Dorothy Hardifer's hotel room, his eyes on the dusty, wind-swept street below him. He knew he should leave, but he hesitated, vaguely hoping that something would happen or that a new idea would show him a way out. Then he was ashamed, for he was a practical man who made it a rule to solve his problems instead of depending upon miracles which never happened.

He glanced at Dorothy, sitting there in a rocking chair. She smiled and asked, "What time is it, Paul?"

He looked at his watch. "Ten till five," he said, and wondered how she could be composed when so much depended upon what happened in these next few hours.

She rose and crossed the room to him. "Are they still in the Casino?"

"Still there," he said.

"They'll be pulling out in a few minutes," she said. "Dad won't make a row about it tonight."

He wondered how she could be so sure of it, but if anybody knew Steve Hardifer, it was his daughter Dorothy. Rawson shoved his hands into his pockets and stared down at the street, deserted except for the line of Star Cross horses racked in front of the Casino. This was like grabbing a handful of fog, he thought, or being smothered under a ton of feathers. There wasn't anything he could get his teeth into that held the slightest promise.

He glanced at the girl again, a little irritated by her calmness. But she was always this way. He had never seen her lose her temper or heard her say a harsh word, and he constantly marveled over the way she handled her father.

She must have sensed that Rawson was worrying, for she said, "The stage won't be here for half an hour. They'll be gone before then. They've still got some things to do before they start for the mesa."

Well, maybe she knew, but actually it didn't make much difference. If it wasn't settled tonight, it would have to be tomorrow, or the next day, or the day after. He wished this was something simple, like facing a killer in the street, or throwing a drunk into jail to cool off, or tracking a horse thief.

Those were things he could do and had done often. He was serving his second term as sheriff and he had established his reputation. No one questioned his courage, least of all Dorothy. The thing that worried him was his feeling of helplessness.

He couldn't do anything when no crime had been committed. At the same time he couldn't wait until there was trouble, for then his course of action would be clear and he'd drive a wedge between Dorothy and himself that would separate them forever. Steve Hardifer had consented to their marriage only last week and the date was set for the fifteenth of next month, just after fall roundup. It had taken Dorothy a year to wangle that consent from her father.

The swing doors of the Casino were flung open and the Star Cross crew filed out, Steve Hardifer in front, walking in the straight-up, arrogant way that was characteristic of him. In that same instant Burnham left the lobby of the hotel and crossed the street, moving directly toward Hardifer, who had stopped beside his black gelding.

"I told you they'd be pulling out," Dorothy said.

"I've got to get down there," Rawson said.

"Wait," Dorothy caught his arm. "I want you to fetch Cameron up here as soon as he gets to town."

Surprised, he looked at her, feeling the tight grip of her fingers. She was a small girl just turned twenty, blond and pretty and utterly feminine. She suited him perfectly all the way down to her number-three boots. He was always aware of her strength, but it was not the domineering, bull strength of her father. Dorothy's strength was that of fine steel which went into a surgeon's scalpel.

"No," he said. "This is my job."

"Paul, let's get one thing clear. I've got some notions about a wife's obligations to her husband." She hesitated, and then added, "I mean, there are a few situations that a woman can handle better than a man."

He couldn't keep the irritation out of his voice when he said, "You're not my wife yet."

"But I'm going to be." She crinkled her nose at him. "If you want me."

"Of course I want you." She had a way with him just as she did with her father, and because he didn't want to make an issue out of it now, he said, "All right, I'll fetch him up, but I don't see—"

"There's one thing I haven't told you. My mother knew Cameron back in Lennox County before she moved out to Colorado with Dad. I remember her talking about him after he became famous. Nobody ever thought he'd amount to anything."

"He hasn't."

"Well, he's famous, anyhow. Now before you bring him up, just mention that it's awfully dangerous to go hunting on Dolan Mesa."

"That won't stop him, with Burnham giving him a big spiel about the elk he's got staked out for him."

"Of course it won't stop him. Just mention it."

He nodded. "All right," he said, and crossed the room to the door.

"Paul."

He looked back. "I said I'd do it, although I'm blessed if I know why. Just because it's you, I guess."

Her smile was quick and genuine. "I like that, Paul, but I was going to say something else. Don't lose your temper down there."

"I'll hog-tie it," he said, and left the room.

When he reached the boardwalk in front of the hotel, he saw that Burnham and Hardifer were still talking, Hardifer's crew a solid mass behind him. Rawson glanced at the long banner stretched across the street, scowling at it: WELCOME GRIZZLY BILL!

That was the town for you. Every businessman in Long's City would bow and scrape around in front of Grizzly Bill Cameron because they stood to make a little money, and all the time they knew there wasn't a bigger fake in the country than Cameron. He'd made a fortune out of his traveling rodeo show and now he was coming here to spend a little of it.

Rawson moved along the boardwalk to his office and stood in front of it, a slight, prematurely gray man, the late-afternoon sunlight shining on his star. He stood motionless, watching Hardifer and Burnham, who were talking loudly and waving their arms.

Rawson glanced at his watch. It was after five. If Hardifer was going to leave town before the stage got here, he'd better start.

Suddenly Hardifer wheeled toward his black, calling, "Let's ride, boys. No use augering with an idiot." He mounted and spun his horse and rode directly at Burnham, who swore and jumped aside to avoid being run down.

"You ain't bluffing me," Burnham shouted, shaking his fist at Hardifer.

"You know me better than to think I'm bluffing," Hardifer said, and rode down the street, his crew falling in behind him.

Hardifer was opposite the jail before he saw Rawson. He nodded, his square face dark with his fury, then he seemed to think of something and turned his big black toward Rawson and pulled up.

"I've made it clear to Burnham," Hardifer said. "We're starting the roundup in the morning, and we'll be on Dolan Mesa most of a month. Them steers have been up there all summer and they'll be plumb spooky."

Rawson knew that, and Hardifer knew that he knew it. Rawson said, "I reckon they will."

"Well then, it's up to you. If Burnham brings that dude Cameron up there and starts shooting around, they'll stampede our gather and we don't aim to do our work over again. We ain't got time. I've contracted to have five hundred head of steers in Denver on the tenth and I aim to keep my contract."

That wasn't news, either. Rawson said, "Well?"

Hardifer scowled. He sat his saddle the same way he walked, straight up and arrogant, and Rawson thought, as he had many times, that it was too bad a man couldn't pick his father-in-law. If he could, Steve Hardifer would be his last choice, but when he married Dorothy, he got Hardifer whether he liked it or not.

"It's clear enough to me," Hardifer said. "Your job is to keep Cameron off the mesa."

"You've got yourself tangled up in your own twine, Steve," Rawson said. "My job is to enforce the law, and the way I read the book, there's no law saying Burnham can't guide a hunting party on Dolan Mesa."

"Then I'll write a new book," Hardifer said.

"Not in this county, you won't."

Hardifer glanced up at the second story of the hotel, an instinctive act that admitted he knew Dorothy was watching. He gripped the saddle horn and leaned slightly forward, laying his gaze again on Rawson's face.

"I'll make this clear, Paul," he said. "Real clear. If Burnham fetches Cameron up there, they'll guzzle a lot of whisky and do some crazy shooting. Now this is what I want to make clear. If they stampede our gather, I'll hang 'em to the first limb I find."

"Then I'll come after you and you'll get a hanging, a legal one."

Scanlon, the Star Cross foreman, swore softly. He said, "Rawson is a mighty little man to be making that kind of talk. Why don't I get down and show him how little he is?"

"You know why," Hardifer said grudgingly. "You wouldn't lay a hand on him and he'd make sausage out of you. I don't want you stove up. We've got work to do tomorrow."

Hardifer cracked steel to his black and left town at a gallop, the crew lining out behind him. Rawson watched them go, a sense of satisfaction warming him. It was the first time Hardifer had ever complimented him, and it would probably be the last time, but coming under these circumstances, it was something a man could take pride in.

Boot heels cracked against the boards of the walk behind Rawson. Turning, he saw Burnham coming toward him. The guide said:

"Throwing his weight around, ain't he? Who does he think he is?"

"He's Steve Hardifer," Rawson said, "and he knows it."

"What are you going to do?"

"Nothing. It's you who had better do something. If you've got a lick of sense, you'll take Cameron hunting somewhere else. Up Troublesome. Or Buck Creek. There's plenty of good hunting in this country that ain't on the mesa."

Burnham's face was hard set. "I know the mesa like the palm of my hand. I know where Cameron can get his elk the first day and a bear the second day. I don't know Troublesome or the Buck Creek country half as well."

"Steve's right," Rawson said. "Star Cross has used the mesa for summer graze as long as I can remember."

"So he's right, is he?" Burnham shouted. "I should have expected that, you marrying the girl. I suppose that from now on the sheriff's office and Star Cross are the same thing."

Rawson laid his eyes on the guide's face. "Say that over, slow-like."

Burnham backed up. "All right, all right. I was wrong, but I'm taking Cameron's party to Dolan Mesa."

"It ain't worth getting killed over."

"Hardifer was just talking."

"You know better."

"He knows what you'd do."

"But it won't stop him. You know that, too."

Burnham's lips tightened. "I'm not backing down, Paul."

They heard the stage coming in from the east, and Burnham wheeled and ran back to stand in front of the hotel, waving his hat and yelling, "Welcome to Long's City, Grizzly Bill." Men boiled out of doorways along Main Street, taking up the cry.

Watching the scene sourly, Rawson told himself that this was exactly the way he had known it would go. All the talk had changed nothing. Time was like the current of a river, moving with tragic certainty, and he could neither dam it nor divert it.

The stagecoach, piled high with luggage, thundered down Main Street to the roar of the crowd. The driver laid his silk out over the horses, cracking it with pistol sharpness; he wheeled in from the middle of the street to stop in front of the hotel door with minute exactness, brakes squealing.

He yelled, "I fetched him, boys, I fetched Grizzly Bill."

The mayor opened the coach door and held out his hand. "Welcome, Grizzly Bill. This is the biggest day in Long City's glorious history."

Bill Cameron shook the mayor's hand and stepped down. He was a big, impressive man dressed in softly tanned buckskin and wearing a wide-brimmed Stetson. He lifted it and waved it above his head, shouting, "I am honored, gentlemen, I am honored and deeply touched."

He might have been opening his rodeo show, Rawson thought. It was sham, plain, unadulterated sham, and it made Rawson a little sick. Everything about Cameron was phony: his buckskin suit with the long fringe, his flaring black mustache and pointed beard, the pearl-handled Colt that was belted around his middle. He had built his reputation on reams of carefully written publicity and his appearance, the only real assets he had.

They crowded around him, Burnham and the townsmen, shaking hands and telling Cameron that this was the biggest thing that had ever happened to Long's City. Others got out of the coach, his personal publicity man, who had a knack for getting his employer in the headlines from coast to coast, and the rest, who were glory seekers, satisfied to bask in the light of the great man's presence.

Cameron's baggage was handed down from the coach top and the rear boot: gun cases, valises, a couple of trunks, and boxes of ammunition. They were piled in front of the lobby door, and Burnham motioned for a man to take them inside.

"Gentlemen," Cameron said solemnly, "this has been a long, dry ride. The drinks are on me."

"Right across the street," Burnham said, and led the way into the Casino, Cameron keeping step with him, long fringe swaying as he walked.

Rawson waited until the street was cleared, for this was not a thing that could be hurried. The coach wheeled past Rawson, the driver raising a hand in greeting and Rawson nodding back. Then he crossed to the Casino and went in.

Men formed a solid line along the bar. Cameron lifted a glass and poured a drink, saying, "The best for everybody, bartender. I always say that good whisky makes for a good shooting eye."

He raised his glass, nodding and smiling. Rawson hesitated until the drinks were downed, then he moved directly toward Cameron and pushed in between him and Burnham.

He held out his hand, saying, "I'm the sheriff, Paul Rawson. I want to add my welcome to the others."

"The sheriff," Cameron said, each word coming out of him in an explosion of sound. "I'm not being arrested, am I?" He laughed as if it were quite a joke.

A weak titter ran along the bar. All of them but Cameron and his party knew that being arrested by Paul Rawson was not a joke. Burnham jabbed Rawson in the back with an elbow, but Rawson didn't turn.

He said, "No arrest, Mr. Cameron, but I have a message."

"Grizzly Bill, if you don't mind," Cameron said. "You know, I got my nickname right here in Colorado. Up the Poudre, it was. Burnham, if I don't see a grizzly on this trip, it will be all right with me. I was lucky that time."

He paused to let them know it had been skill and courage and not luck. "I ran smack-dab into that bear on the trail, twenty feet tall he must have been. He looked that big to me, anyhow. Drooling for Cameron meat, he was, his mouth open and his red tongue hanging out. My gun jammed, the only time in my life, so I had to fight him with my knife and I killed him."

The mayor shuddered. "It must have been terrible, Bill."

"Terrible." Cameron poured another drink. "Yes sir, it was terrible. I got clawed up something awful. Just me and that there grizzly, fighting it out, man to man. Or bear to man I should say. I was laid up for six months after that."

"It took a brave man to fight that way," the mayor said, properly awed. "And a courageous one."

Rawson struggled against his threatening grin. A courageous man was not the same as a brave one, according to the mayor. Well, the mayor wouldn't know. The last time Rawson had needed a posse, the mayor had been sick.

"I said I had a message," Rawson said. "I've always heard that there were two things Grizzly Bill could not turn down."

Cameron stared at him, puzzled. "What are they?"

"Good whisky and a pretty girl."

Cameron laughed and slapped the bar. "You're right. Well, it must be a pretty girl because the whisky is at hand. Who is she, Sheriff?"

"An admirer who has been looking forward to your visit."

"Well," Cameron crowed, "let's not keep her waiting."

"Later—" Burnham began.

"Now," Cameron said firmly. "Excuse me, gentlemen."

Cameron turned to the batwings and walked out. Rawson winked at Burnham and followed Cameron, catching up with him on the walk.

He said, "She lives on a ranch, but she's staying in town tonight just to meet you."

"Why," Cameron said expansively, "that's fine, mighty fine. I'll see that she gets an elk head with the biggest set of antlers in Colorado."

"She'll like that," Rawson said. "There's one thing I wanted to tell you. Burnham plans to take you hunting on Dolan Mesa, but I advise against it. Star Cross is starting roundup tomorrow, and that makes it dangerous."

Cameron looked at him as if insulted. "Danger is a word I never use," he said.

"I just wanted to tell you," Rawson said. "As a matter of fact, it's more than dangerous. It's suicide."

"If you brought me out here to talk—"

"I didn't," Rawson said, opening the lobby door. "She's waiting upstairs."

Some of the exuberance went out of Cameron. He was glumly silent as he followed Rawson up the stairs and along the hall to Dorothy's room.

Rawson knocked on the door, and when she opened it, he said, "This is Grizzly Bill Cameron. Mr. Cameron, Miss Hardifer."

She held out her hand, giving Cameron a quick, warm smile. "This is a real pleasure. Come in, Mr. Cameron."

He swept his hat from his head in a grand gesture and took her hand, good nature flowing through him again. "My pleasure, Miss Hardifer. The sheriff said a pretty girl wanted to see me, but he didn't say she was as beautiful as a wildflower, unsullied by the touch of human hands."

Dorothy moved back across the room to her bureau. Cameron stepped in and Rawson closed the door.

Dorothy said, "I had a very serious reason for wanting to see you, Mr. Cameron, a reason that only a woman would have."

Cameron glowed with pride: he stroked his sweeping mustache, nodding as if this was understandable.

"A woman is God's most glorious creature, Miss Hardifer. I am complimented."

She faced him, standing straightbacked in much the way her father habitually stood, her face severe. "You misunderstand me, Mr. Cameron. Because I am a woman, I have an understanding and a sympathy for a bereaved widow. You are married, aren't you, Mr. Cameron?"

His hand dropped to his side; he stood so still that the fringe along his legs hung motionless. "I don't savvy this," he said. "What was your reason for having me—"

"I asked if you were married."

"Yes." He swallowed. "My wife is on our ranch near Omaha."
Dorothy picked up a sheet of paper and a pencil from the bureau.
"Will you give me her name and address?" she asked.

"Ma'am, I don't think—"

"Your wife's name and address, please. I'll write to her as soon as
it's over, and I'll take the responsibility of sending the body home."

Cameron's mouth sagged open. "What body?"

"Yours. If you go hunting on Dolan Mesa, you'll be killed. The Star
Cross outfit is starting fall roundup in the morning and they won't
permit any hunting up there till it's finished. You see, I've lived here
most of my life and I understand these people. I just want to be sure
that everything is taken care of."

"You're talking about murder," Cameron whispered. "The
sheriff—"

"That's right," Rawson said, "but I can't save your life after you're
killed, Cameron."

"It would be a shame if the great Grizzly Bear Cameron died with so
little glory," Dorothy said with contempt. "My mother knew you in
Lennox County. She's told me about you. You'll remember Ann
Ollinger—"

Without another word Cameron wheeled and stalked out, slam-
ming the door. Dorothy laughed softly.

"I told you, Paul."

"You don't know if it'll work."

"It'll work," she said, "although I'm not sure it's because he's
afraid of getting killed. I think it's more probable that his pride
couldn't stand for me telling about my mother. You see, he courted
her, but there was another fellow in love with her. He braced Cameron
and made him leave the country. My mother said everybody laughed
about how he ran for ten miles before he stopped."

"Was it your dad?"

She shook her head. "That was before the Hardifers came to Lennox County. Mother never told him about it. I think she'd forgotten it
until she read in the paper about Cameron's show."

Dorothy moved to the window. "Cameron didn't wait long. Burnham's on his way over here."

"I'll talk to him," Rawson said, and left the room.

He waited at the head of the stairs until Burnham reached the foot.
He asked, "What's biting you?"

Burnham stopped and stared up at Rawson, his face turkey-red.

"What did you say to make that fool back out?"

"Did he back out?"

"You know he did," Burnham shouted. "He's going over on the Grand River. I lost a thousand dollars just like that. I'm going to cut you down to size, Rawson."

"I'm waiting," Rawson said.

Burnham swallowed, then wheeled and stalked out. Rawson returned to Dorothy's room, grinning a little.

He said, "It worked all right, but I dunno. I don't think you'll have both me and your dad after the way I talked to him while ago."

"Oh yes I will, " Dorothy said. "You're the only man in the county who could talk that way and stay healthy."

Rawson shoved his hands into his pockets, both relieved and irritated by the way this had gone. He said, "There's two ways of looking at a wife's obligation to her husband, your way and my way. I don't know why I—"

"Oh, Paul." She came to him quickly and, putting her arms around him, kissed him. "All I did was to give you a hand."

"Don't look that way to me," he said.

"Then you'd better look again. You settled this yourself."

"How?"

"By the way you stood up to Dad. And Burnham walking out just now. It's the way you've lived every day since you first put on the star."

"It's the way I like to look at it," he said, "but why were you so sure it would be this way?"

"It's just another notion of mine. Like having a piece of ore assayed. If it's high-grade, it's always high-grade, but if it's just old country rock, it'll stay country rock even when you dress it up in buckskin."

She tilted her face again, inviting his kiss. "You're high-grade, my friend."

Winchester Wedding

Jake Erdman, who had taught our school about as long as I'd been sheriff, used to say he was going to write a book about Mountain County and call it *The Decline and Fall of a Typical American Community*. The decline started with the Panic of 1893 and the silver trouble, which plagued most of Colorado, but we really fell when Eli Hoven dropped his loop over the neck of every man, woman, and child in Mountain County.

Jake explained that in most ways we weren't typical—not in location or industry, and we weren't the average kind of people—but according to Jake, those weren't the important elements. The big thing was that we reacted typically when times were hard. We got scared, so we took to leaning on Eli. After that Eli became what Jake called a benevolent despot, but Jake wasn't altogether right. The way I saw it, Eli was long on the despot part and short on the benevolent.

"We've traded our guts for a mess of pottage," Jake would say. "That's why we're typical. The whole country's following the same path."

Jake never got around to writing the book for the simple reason that he wanted his mess of pottage the same as the rest of us did. If he did an honest job of book writing, he'd have lost his teaching job the minute Eli finished reading the first chapter. Then Rance Collins moved to Mountain County and fell in love with Eli's little girl, Bunny, and we had what Jake called a moral revolution. After that Jake quit talking about his book.

At one time Mountain County had been prosperous, with the silver mines running full blast. After they shut down, more than half our people moved out and the rest of us found something else to do. I was elected sheriff, and Jake got the teaching job. The bank closed down, and Ben Nelson, who was the cashier, went to work in Eli's store.

Ranching took the place of mining as our chief industry. We had a few sawmills that kept operating, although the national forest had been set up and we had one of Teddy Roosevelt's rangers telling the sawmill boys what trees they could cut and what they couldn't. We built up a little tourist business with some Eastern greenhorns who rode the train to Gunnison and took the stage to Mountain City. They'd fish for two, three weeks and pull out, leaving a few gold eagles around that we wouldn't have had without them.

We finally got lined out, but there were a few years after the panic when it was touch and go. That was how Eli got his loop on us. You see, he had the store and most of the money that was still in the county; so those of us who got credit had enough to eat. The rest left. It didn't take Eli long to separate the sheep from the goats. He doted on us sheep, and he sure hated the goats.

I don't aim to make out that Eli was exactly mean, but on the other hand he wasn't good. Physically he was an ugly little man with a head too big for a fellow his size; mentally he had a gift for picking people who were good risks, and he was the savingest man I ever knew.

His wife died when Bunny was small, and he raised the child, doing a better job than you'd expect. We all liked her, but we felt sorry for her too. She never had any money to throw around carelesslike, and she didn't have pretty clothes, although she was a good dressmaker, and if Eli had let her have the cloth to work on, she'd have rigged herself up real attractive.

Eli carried a few bolts of silk and organdy, and I've seen Bunny feel the cloth the way you'd fondle your pet kitten, but she kept on wearing calico and gingham. And as for food, well, it was a crying shame. Eli claimed he had stomach trouble, but Doc Bartle said it was just his stingy soul that hurt. Anyhow, Bunny cooked mostly vegetables, which she raised in her garden, or fish she caught in the river, and maybe venison she would fetch in herself, come fall.

When Bunny got hungry for meat, old Eli would just hand her a rifle and a few shells. Shortly thereafter, there'd be meat on the table, because Bunny could shoot the ears off a cottontail at two hundred yards. It's a good thing Bunny was such a crack shot—if she wasn't, she'd have been on a vegetable diet for life.

Eli didn't have a real friend in the county. Like a lot of men I've known, he was vain and egotistical, so to stay on his good side, we pretended we were his friends; and we were careful not to cross him. When it came to the turkey shoot at Thanksgiving, we always saw that he won. He was a good shot, so maybe he would have anyhow, but the point is none of us tried to beat him.

If Eli knew how it was, he never let on. He seemed satisfied with the bowing and scraping we gave him instead of the honest friendship most men wanted. As he got older, he was tougher and tougher on Bunny so she never had a good time, and every year he seemed to get smaller and his head bigger. I mean that both literally and figuratively.

Proud? Hell no, we weren't proud of ourselves, but we couldn't be blamed much, either. None of us had saved anything for a rainy day, and we all remembered how tough it was right after the panic when we'd have starved if it hadn't been for Eli, so we went on year after year, fawning over Eli and cussing him behind his back and cussing ourselves too. It was like Jake said. We'd traded our guts for a mess of pottage.

By the time Rance Collins moved to Mountain City, I'd been sheriff for almost twenty years. Most of the time it was a lazy man's job, just sitting around the office in the courthouse and drawing my pay, but once in a while during the summer, some of our greenhorns got drunk, and I'd have to throw one of them into the jug to sober him up.

I liked my job well enough to do my share of the kowtowing to Eli. If I'd beaten him out of the turkey at Thanksgiving, for instance, he'd remember come election. He'd have passed the word along that Mountain County needed a new sheriff, and I'd have been out of a job.

That's the way it was when Rance Collins rode in one spring and bought Clawhammer, a run-down little spread a couple of miles downstream from town. We liked him right off, which is a compliment on account of we were kind of clannish and he was the first outsider to settle among us for five years or more.

Rance was young; maybe twenty-five, big and red-faced because the sun seemed to scorch his skin instead of tan it. He was a working fool, and by fall he had Clawhammer neat as a pin, the corrals rebuilt, a new roof on his house, fences repaired, and every calf branded and earmarked.

He started off with a little money. None of us knew how much, but we did hear he'd paid cash for the ranch. The trouble was he wouldn't have any steers to market for a couple of years, so he asked Eli for credit and Eli gave it to him. At the time he hadn't shown he was as independent as a hog on ice because he'd been as busy as a tongue-tied drummer.

Somewhere along the line, he'd started shining up to Bunny, unbeknownst to Eli. She worked in the store on Saturdays, so he must have seen her the first week he'd come to the valley. After that I guess he saw her along the river, because Bunny's favorite fishing hole was just above the Clawhammer buildings.

Come fall, our greenhorn fishermen cleared out and roundup was finished and school started. Then we found out how things stacked up. Jake had a basket social every year along in October to raise money for the school library. It was a shindig we all looked forward to, the same as we looked forward to the turkey shoot. Rance was on hand, decked out like a Christmas tree in a fancy green shirt and polished black boots and a brand new stetson he'd just bought from Eli.

I was the auctioneer, and I started things off holding Bunny's pretty basket up for everybody to see and talking big and handsome about the goodies that were in it. I thought Eli would bid fifty cents the way he always did and folks would let it go at that, but this time it was different.

Bunny must have described her basket to Rance. Anyhow, he yelled, "Five dollars" before Eli could open his face. He got it. Eli looked sick, but he'd have been sicker if he'd raised that bid. I knocked the basket off to Rance, and the next thing I knew Eli was gone.

We had a good time that evening, the best I could remember. We danced until after midnight with Jake sawing away on his fiddle. You see, Eli always kind of held us back when he was there. I guess he didn't approve of all that energy going to waste. He never would dance. He'd just sit there on a bench along the wall and scowl, his lips drawn up tight like the strings on his purse.

Usually Bunny sat beside Eli, wearing her best gingham dress, her blond hair curled up nice and pretty and her blue eyes staring at the floor. We had a few young bucks who wanted to dance with her, but they were scared of Eli.

If Bunny danced at all, it was with me or Doc Bartle or Eli's clerk, Ben Nelson, all of us fifty or more and married up good and tight. That way Eli didn't have to worry about losing his housekeeper and Saturday clerk.

That night it was different. You know how it is when the sun breaks through heavy clouds after you've had a solid week of rain. Rance had every dance with Bunny. It was nice to watch them. Bunny had stars in her eyes and a smile on her lips, and all you had to do was look at her and see she was in love.

The next morning we woke up with a hangover. I was sitting in my office worrying about it when Doc Bartle and Jake Erdman came in. They sat down and looked at me, and I looked at them, and it was like a wake.

Pretty soon Jake said, "Fear is the strongest human emotion. When you tie it up with economic power, it's unbeatable."

I knew he was thinking about his wife and kids and that Eli was going to blame him. He'd blame me too for letting Rance bid Bunny's basket in. I had a wife and kids too. And Doc? Well, everybody in the county owed him money, and it would be like Eli to tell folks not to pay him. Doc was the best friend Rance had in the valley.

Doc lit his pipe and asked gloomily, "How cowardly can people get?"

"If you want an answer to that question," I said, "just look at us."

"What we need is a revolution," Jake said. "Tar and feathers would look good on Eli."

"Cop that," I told him. "I'd have to stop it and I wouldn't want to."

Doc stared at the ceiling and puffed away on his pipe. He said thoughtfully, "Maybe Eli will get sick. Then I'll say, 'Eli, when you get a little milk of human kindness in your blood stream, I'll tend to you. Otherwise you'll die.' "

Crazy talk, and we all knew it. We sat there thinking about it and hating Eli and hating ourselves and not knowing what to do. After a while Ben Nelson, who had been delivering groceries, came in and sat down. From the expression on his face I judged he'd been helping himself to Eli's vinegar jug.

"How's the great man?" I asked.

"The great man is wild enough to bite a dog," Ben said. "Bunny came in a while ago and looked like she'd been crying all night." Ben swallowed. "Boys, I'd fix everything if I'd kill Eli. Bunny would inherit the store, I'd still have my job, and she could hitch up with Rance."

From anybody else that kind of talk would have sounded crazy, but not from Ben. He loved Bunny because he didn't have any girls of his own and he'd wanted a daughter as long as I could remember. When she was little, he used to snitch a piece of hoarhound or peppermint out of the glass case for her. Then Eli would give him hell and make Ben pay for it out of his wages.

"Morally we're with you," Jake said gloomily, "but logically it won't do, on account of we wouldn't want to be on the jury that hung you."

Ben walked out, looking as if he wanted to cry. Jake got up and kicked one of my chairs across the room. He said, "It's coming. I can feel it just like my right knee gets rheumatism before a rain."

"Feel what?"

"Trouble. Rance is the one who'll shoot Eli. It would be dogslaughter, wouldn't it, Sheriff? That isn't a crime."

"When the dog who gets shot walks like a man, it's manslaughter," I said. "Might even be murder when the lawyers get done with it."

"Let's go see Rance," Doc said.

"I've got to go study up my Monday lessons," Jake said, and walked out.

Doc cussed until he was out of breath. "That damned Jake is worse than the rest of us. He's taught those lessons for twenty years."

"I'll go," I said, and right away wished I hadn't said it, because I knew how it would be. Eli would start separating the sheep from the goats again, and I didn't cotton to the idea of being included among the goats.

Doc and I found Rance painting his kitchen and singing *Rescue the Perishing* in a deep bass voice that made him a good candidate for the preacher's choir the next time we had a meeting in Mountain City. Rance waved the paint brush at us and said to come in. He'd warm up the coffee as soon as he got to the corner.

"Don't bother," Doc said. "We just came to sit and gab."

We sat down and watched him paint for a couple of minutes. He seemed as happy as if he had good sense. When he reached the corner, he laid his brush across the paint can and went over to the stove and stirred up the fire.

"You've got to drink some of my coffee," Rance said. "I make the best coffee in Mountain County. When I marry Bunny, I'm going to teach her how."

Doc looked sick enough to take one of his own pills. I didn't feel good either. I said, "Rance, what do you think Eli will do when you mention marrying Bunny?"

He set the coffee pot on the front of the stove and turned around. "Why, he'll get madder'n a cat with a passel of pups, but it won't make no difference. Bunny's twenty-one. She loves me, I love her, and getting married is the natural fate for a woman, especially a pretty one like Bunny."

"Sure, sure," Doc said, "only Eli won't like the notion of losing his housekeeper, gardener, fisherwoman, meat provider, and free clerk on Saturday. He'll whack off your credit."

Rance laughed. I liked his laugh. It came from way down in his belly and had a good bass quality like his singing voice. He said, "Gents, that threat don't scare me like it does the rest of you."

"So you've got money," I said.

He shook his head. "Everything I've got is sunk right here in this spread. I'll need credit until I raise a herd of steers to drive to Gunnison, but I'm damned if I'll let a dried-up old goat like Eli buffalo me."

Fine talk, I thought, coming from a young buck who was in love and didn't know Eli very well. I said, "Will Bunny marry you regardless of her pa?"

Rance gave me a straight look. "None of you know what she's been up against. She'd marry me even if she didn't love me. She's got to the boiling point. If I hadn't showed up, I guess she'd be fixing to run away."

You made a mistake bidding in that basket last night," Doc said. "You got his supper. He won't overlook it."

Rance fetched some cups from the pantry and filled them with coffee. "Of course me and Bunny would rather have the old boy's blessing than to buck him." He looked at Doc and then at me. "Gents, I don't mean no offense, but I'll tell you right plain out. There's more cowards in Mountain County in proportion to the total population than anywhere else in Colorado."

"Guilty," I said.

"Which same is funny," Rance said, "on account of folks tell me you're a good sheriff. Take going over to Bill Godkins' ranch when them two greenhorns got drunk and started busting up the place. You packed 'em off to jail single-handed. No coward would do that."

"I'm guilty too," Doc said.

"Which is even funnier," Rance said. "I heard about you going up to the Big Star mine last spring—when the snow slides were running—and fetching that miner to town who had a busted leg. Why, I'd be scared to death to get up there at timberline at a time like that."

We drank our coffee, which was strong enough to take the lining out of our stomachs, and we didn't say anything. Sure, we had courage of a sort when conditions were right, but that didn't mean we weren't scared of Eli.

"I'm gonna ask Eli for Bunny's hand," Rance said. "Won't do any good, but I'll ask him."

"Just make trouble," I said.

"He likes to show off his power. Wants folks to bow and scrape. That it?" When we nodded, Rance went on. "You've got into the habit of letting Eli boss you. That's a habit I aim to bust."

"If somebody else started a store," I began.

"Or a bank so folks could borrow," Doc began.

"No sense dreaming," Rance said. "No, I aim to do this right in front of everybody. Maybe he could be persuaded to leave the county. That's the only way Bunny and me would be happy. Eli would rig up something to get between us if he was around."

"How are you going to cook up a miracle like that?" Doc asked.

"I've got to think on it," Rance answered. "The turkey shoot comes off in about three weeks, don't it?"

"Four," I said, "but—"

"Just how good a shot is Eli?" Rance asked.

"Good enough to put three bullets in the bull's eyes," I said. "It hasn't been exactly a gift, him winning every time."

Rance got up and started painting. "This year he won't win."

"How good a shot are you?" Doc asked.

Rance laughed. "Well sir, I couldn't hit the side of a barn with a load of buckshot."

Doc and I left then. Later on we heard from Ben Nelson that Rance asked for Bunny's hand and Eli ordered him out of the store. That night after closing time, Eli came to my house.

"Collins misrepresented his financial status," Eli said. "He can't pay his bill. I want you to throw him into jail."

Eli had never tried to make his own code of laws before, and by trying it now, he put me on solid ground. I said, "Eli, there's no law on the books that says I can arrest a man because he hasn't paid a store bill. Besides, Rance is good for it and you know it."

I guess he was surprised. He blinked and scratched his big chin and then he said, "You refuse to arrest Collins?"

"Unless he commits a crime."

"Very well," Eli said. "I'm warning you now. This is your last term as sheriff of this county."

I was pretty uneasy for the next few weeks, and on the day of the turkey shoot I was more than uneasy. Doc and Jake and I always made up the committee that handled the shindig. We got the turkey, a big tom we bought from Bill Godkins, who raised them, and we had this fellow in a crate for everybody to admire. He was the best bird we ever had.

Everybody in the county was on hand for the affair. We put the targets up at the end of the vacant lot on the east side of the courthouse, and we passed out the cards that gave folks their order for shooting. We always rigged it for Eli to shoot first, a matter of expediency so everybody would know how good they could shoot and still not beat Eli.

The profit went to Jake's school library fund the same as the basket social. That satisfied Eli because Jake didn't have to use school money to buy library books and that helped keep the taxes down.

This time it was different. I guess Rance had done a little talking. The crowd was the same size as usual, but the feeling wasn't the same. A sort of electric expectancy was in the air. You know, the way it is when a big storm is blowing up.

As far as Eli was concerned, it was just another turkey shoot. At least he didn't let on that he knew anything was up. He ignored Rance, who was walking around and talking to folks he knew. He even ignored Bunny, who was there wearing a heavy coat and overshoes because we'd had a little snow the night before.

We started at two, the way we always did. Eli put his three bullets in the bull's eye, as good as ever except that one wasn't dead center. It went on down the line with Jake, collecting the targets as soon as a man shot. Each time he announced that Eli's record was still the best.

Rance was the last man in line. When it was his turn, he asked, "Sheriff, is there a rule which says you can't let somebody else shoot for you?"

I didn't have the slightest notion what he was getting at. I looked at Doc and Doc looked at Jake and they both nodded. I said, "It's your privilege."

Eli was standing on the sidewalk, impatient for it to be finished. He said sharply, "This is very irregular, gentlemen. I don't see—"

"Have you any objection to your daughter shooting against you?" Rance asked.

Well, that about knocked us down on our faces. Bunny never had taken part in the turkey shoot before. For the first time in the years I'd known Eli, I could see he was shaken. He mumbled, "No, I haven't any objections."

With a grand flourish Rance handed his Winchester to Bunny. He said, "Get us a turkey for our first Thanksgiving dinner, honey."

She gave him a big smile when she took the rifle. She didn't look at her father; she just stepped up to the line and blazed away, and the second she was done she handed the Winchester back to Rance.

Jake took a look at the target. He said in a hollow voice, "Bunny wins the turkey. All three of her shots were dead center."

When I looked around, Rance had the rifle at his side. He didn't make any threats, but all you had to do was to look at him and you'd swear you were looking right into the face of death. Eli saw it too.

I expected Rance to give Eli a cussing, tell him he'd blow his head off if he didn't give them his blessing, but all he said was, "The preacher will be in Mountain City tonight to marry me and Bunny. Will you come to the wedding?"

I didn't hear what Eli said, but I saw what he did.

Eli still had his Winchester, and what happened then was exactly what Rance figured would happen. At least I have a hunch that's the way it was, and if I'm right, it made any courage Doc and I had look mighty puny. Rance turned around and started walking toward Bunny. Eli threw his Winchester to his shoulder and lined it on Rance's back.

I tried to yell, but nothing came of it. Doc was close to Eli. He grabbed the rifle and threw it twenty feet over his shoulder, then he got hold of Eli and shook him. Doc's a big man, and for a few seconds Eli was busy moving in several directions at the same time. When I finally got Doc quieted down, Eli had the look of a man who had been standing on his head for about an hour.

I said, "That was attempted murder, Eli. You'll get twenty years, and if it hadn't been for Doc, you'd got a rope."

By that time Eli realized what he had done, and he was hoping a hole would open up and swallow him. Rance and Bunny came up. Bunny looked scared and upset, but Rance was as calm as you please. He said, "I'd hate for my kids to know their grandpa spent his last twenty years in the pen."

"So would I," Bunny said in a shaky voice.

"I'll tell you what, Sheriff," Rance said. "I think Eli is going to come to the wedding. Then I think he's going to sell his store and retire to Florida."

I guess it was the first time in his life that Eli really knew what it was to be without friends, even Bunny. She'd swap him for Rance any old day and figure it was a good trade. Eli could see that, and likewise he could see that nothing he did would change Bunny or get her back.

"Yes," Eli said. "That's what I'm going to do."

A lot of things have happened since then, all good. Ben Nelson is happy because he's running the store for the man who bought it from Eli. Every time Bunny comes in with her three daughters, Ben fixes them up with hoarhound candy.

Jake's happy because he says Bunny's girls are the smartest kids he ever had in school. Doc's happy because he delivered every one of Bunny's babies, and delivering babies is the thing he likes about his business. I'm happy because I keep on running for sheriff and I keep getting elected. I suppose Eli's happy staying warn down there in Florida, if a man like him ever is happy. And as for Bunny and Rance, I guess they're about the happiest people in the world.

Well, Jake's started to talk about writing another book. He's going to call it, *The Birth and Growth of a Family of Girls Who Wouldn't Be Here If It Wasn't for the Annual Turkey Shoot in Mountain City.*

We still have that turkey shoot. Bunny wins every year with all hands trying their level best to beat her. Rance lines his girls up, and they yell like crazy when Jake announces the winner. Jake claims it's a sign of the times. He says women are about to have their day.

Outlaw's Wife

Jim Barnes and Duke Tribble rode into Sentinel late on an August afternoon, the air hot and heavy with dust and faintly scented by the pines that grew on the ridges above town. No change, Jim saw, no change at all. Not that he had expected any. It was just that he'd been in a dozen towns that looked much the same as Sentinel, isolated, cow-country towns without even a decent road for the stage to come in on.

The point was that Jim, seeing Sentinel for the first time in nine years, hoped that it wouldn't look exactly as he remembered it. He had grown up here, so to him Sentinel wasn't like any other town. But now he saw that his memory had been accurate. Sentinel did not have a single distinguishing characteristic.

Jim said, "The courthouse is at the end of the block. The sheriff's office is there."

Tribble nodded, his lips curled a little at the corners as much as to say that he wasn't blind and where the hell would the sheriff's office be if not in the courthouse. Funny how a man is burdened by the past, Jim thought, as they rode slowly between the false fronts, little bursts of dust exploding with each downstroke of a hoof into the street.

A man's own past and the past of others he had called friends, tangled like a knotted string so there seemed to be no patterns at all. You could go crazy trying to straighten it all out. To make it worse, the present got twisted up with the past. That was where you got your tail in a crack. To make it still worse, you got loaded up with Duke Tribble.

They stopped in front of the courthouse and tied at the hitch rail, shadowed by the big locust trees that formed a square around the building and the little jail in the back. Jim remembered when the trees had been planted. He'd been six, maybe seven. One of the things a kid remembers because they'd made quite a ceremony out of it; speeches and singing and the band playing and all. A long time ago, but he remembered.

They kept step along the boardwalk to the front door, neither saying anything. You didn't talk much to Duke Tribble because Tribble wasn't a talkative man. Not unless you just liked to hear yourself talk. Besides, talk seemed to irritate Tribble. A lot of things irritated Tribble.

"Sam's office is in the back," Jim said as they went in. "I'll ask the questions."

Apparently Tribble didn't hear. It was often that way. Tribble just ignored you. They tramped down the corridor, spurs jingling. Jim glanced at Tribble, his long, dour face burned to a dark mahogany by wind and sun, the expressionless gray eyes, the jutting jaw that gave an odd, shoved-forward look to the lower part of his face.

Something hit Jim then, something right in the pit of his stomach that hurt like hell. This was his last job. He'd get his resignation in the mail before he left Sentinel. It had been all right when he'd worked alone, or with a man who was a little bit human, but to hell with it when they saddled him with Duke Tribble.

Sam Fenton was still here, although it was after five. Jim said, "Howdy, Sam," and paused in the doorway, Tribble looking over his shoulder.

Fenton glanced up, his face blank for a moment. He'd changed, Jim thought, even if the town hadn't. But maybe a town never changed unless it had a fire or a flood. It was the people who changed with the years. The kids grew up and the older ones got older.

Sam Fenton was old, too old to be packing a star, but he'd been a good sheriff and he'd have his job as long as he wanted it. Nothing much ever happened in Sentinel. Or if it did, all Fenton had to do was to holler and he'd have a dozen young bucks to do his riding and shooting for him. He had friends, Sam Fenton did, and that made him about the richest man in the county.

"I'll be damned." Fenton got up from his swivel chair. "Jim Barnes. I didn't know you, boy. It's been a long time."

Fenton was pleased to see him and that pleased Jim. It made coming back worth while, even if he had a dirty stinking job to do and he was stuck with Duke Tribble. Jim crossed to Fenton and held out his hand. "Yeah, a long time, Sam."

Fenton's red face crinkled with a smile. Jim had never seen his face take the dark, saddle-brown tan that was typical of those who spent the bulk of their time outside. Every spring it got kind of scorched and stayed that way all summer.

The sheriff gave Jim's hand a hard grip, glancing briefly at Tribble and bringing his gaze back to Jim's face. He said, "Heard a lot about you, boy. You know how it is, even in a country like this that don't have many people. I guess we just like to talk about a local fellow who goes out and gets famous."

This was wasted time for Tribble. There were moments when he had all the patience in the world and others when he had none. He had none now. He stalked to the desk and handed his credentials to Fenton.

"Duke Tribble, special agent for the governor," Tribble said. "We want your cooperation, but if we don't get it, we'll work alone. I want to make that plain, first thing."

That was like Tribble. He'd kick a pup in the ribs if the pup got in his way. He wouldn't walk around. The old irritation was in Jim. It wasn't enough to be burdened by the past and the present. There was the future, too, and Jim didn't like what he saw coming.

Plenty of folks over in Salem thought Tribble was a good man. Lot of guts. No nerves. A record that didn't hold a single failure. But there was one thing they didn't know. Tribble had a heart the size of a peanut. Or maybe no heart at all.

Fenton handed Tribble's credentials back and looked at Jim, not smiling now. "You, too?"

Jim nodded. "I've had this job for about six months."

"Thought you were still deputy for the Crook County sheriff." Fenton dropped into his chair, and picking up his cracked briar pipe from the desk, began to fill it. "Well, sit down."

"We'll stand," Tribble said. "We want to know where the Moray woman lives."

Sure, Jim thought, I was going to ask the questions, but when the time came, Tribble took the play. He was younger by a few months, but he'd been on this job for three years and he figured it gave him the bulge.

"We want Ted Moray," Jim said. "We figured Addie might know where he was."

Tribble made a sound. "Cut it plain, Barnes. We'll talk to the Moray woman. If she won't tell us anything, we'll watch her place. He'll show, sooner or later, and we'll nab him."

"Addie's been back a couple of years." Fenton lighted his pipe, not looking at either of them. "A good girl, Addie is. Ted fooled her. Turned out bad and she finally left him."

Tribble made that sound again. A sort of snort loaded with contempt. A superior man, was Duke Tribble. All you had to do was to ask him. Smarter than anyone else. Faster with a gun. Tougher, too. Well, maybe he was. Jim hadn't found out yet, but he'd known a few who had bucked Tribble. They were buried here and there around over the state.

"There's one thing in our business you can count on," Tribble said. "A woman who marries an outlaw ain't a good woman."

"You've got it figured, ain't you?" Fenton leaned back in his swivel chair, staring through the smoke at the ceiling. "I've heard of you. Hard, they say. Well, obsidian's hard, but it chips. Real brittle."

Tribble walked around the desk and stopped a pace from Fenton. "Save your lectures for them that'll listen. Where does the Moray woman live?"

He had a way, Tribble did. He could scare the pants off most men when he talked that way. There were times when it helped. Get a tough boy who wouldn't talk and Tribble's way was good. But Fenton went on smoking and looking at the ceiling.

"Funny thing about Addie," Fenton said. "Folks hereabouts like her. Nobody holds it against her because she married Ted. She's taught our school for two winters. She loves kids. We used to have a man teacher who whaled the pudding out of the big boys and they gave him hell, but Addie, she just talks easy like, and damned if they don't jump when she hollers."

"We'll find out where she lives," Tribble said, and wheeled toward the door.

"Wait." Fenton rose. "Tribble, you wanted it cut plain. All right, that's just what I'll do. Addie lives in a white house at the south end of town, last place on your left. She lives alone. Go talk to her and then let her alone. Ted won't be there. Never will."

"We got a tip he's back in the state," Tribble said, "and his wife's the only thing that'd fetch him back. That's why we're here."

Tribble walked out. Fenton laid his eyes on Jim's face. They weren't friendly now. He said, "The preacher says God creates every man. If that's right, He sure ought to be ashamed of some of 'em."

"Maybe He is," Jim said, and left the office.

They mounted and rode on down the street. Quite a homecoming, Jim thought. You travel with a man like Tribble and you get his smell on you. Well, folks would know, folks who used to like Jim Barnes. Now they'd be ashamed they'd ever known him.

"You and Moray were good friends at one time, weren't you?" Tribble asked.

Jim was surprised that Tribble knew. He said, "Sort of. We both rode for the Star K east of town."

"You knew his wife, too."

"We went to school together."

Jim hoped that was all Tribble knew. But there was more to it, a lot more Tribble would find out if he stayed around Sentinel. Jim had been in love with Addie. They'd been kids, the three of them, Addie just seventeen. She'd gone with one and then the other and wound up getting engaged to Ted.

That was why Jim had left the country. He'd show her, he'd told himself, show her what a man could do when he set out to do it. Addie would kick herself for marrying the wrong man. Chances were she had, but she hadn't known what was in Ted Moray any more than Jim had. A good cowhand nine years ago, but that was before he'd married Addie. Maybe that was the trouble. Maybe he'd wanted more for his wife than thirty a month would buy.

There was a blank spot after that. All Jim knew was that they'd left the state and nobody had caught up with Ted. Jim hadn't heard anything about Addie until a year or so ago when somebody who had known Jim in Sentinel stopped in Crook County and mentioned that Addie was back. Alone.

They rode past the old Rome house, the picket fence broken down and the yard grown up in weeds. Al Rome had gone broke and left Sentinel with his family. Jim had heard that from someone, too. Boom or bust, that was the way Rome had always lived.

Prices had been down the last year Jim was in Sentinel. He remembered Al Rome saying, "They can't go no lower, so they've got to come up." He'd taken a shot at the moon, slapping a second mortgage on his spread and his town house, gone over into the John Day country and bought a herd of young stuff. He'd shot the moon, all right, but he'd missed. Prices did go lower.

Hard to tell where Al Rome was now, but wherever it was, he'd be shooting for the moon again. He was made that way. Maybe it was the same with Ted Moray. He'd loved Addie so much he'd wanted her to have the best. Well, you couldn't blame him. Not when you'd loved Addie yourself.

Addie's house was next to the Rome place. You knew somebody was living there just as you knew the Rome house was vacant: the grass cut, flowers blooming, a garden in back, somebody who took pride in living there.

As they dismounted, Tribble said, "I'll do the talking, Barnes. You're too soft."

Tribble took a hitch on his belt, eyes meeting Jim's. He was hungry for trouble; he lived for it the way some men live for power. Or money. Back of that hunger was Tribble's pride. He wasn't quite sure his reputation was greater than Jim's. He wasn't even sure he was faster with a gun, but sooner or later he'd find out.

"Maybe you're wrong about how soft I am," Jim said.

"I know your record," Tribble said, and opening the gate in the picket fence, went up the path to the front door, Jim following.

Addie opened the door to Tribble's knock. Jim stood back a few feet, satisfied for the moment to look at her. Nine years he'd been gone. She'd been seventeen then. So she'd be twenty-six now. She looked older. There were lines around her eyes that shouldn't be there, a few gray hairs sprinkled through the black ones, but she was still Addie and to Jim she was the prettiest girl in the world. No, she was a woman now, and that was the big difference in her.

Tribble said in his overbearing way, "You're Mrs. Moray?"

Her dark eyes touched Jim's face, turned to Tribble's, and then swung back to Jim's as if brought there by some magnetic power. She cried, "Jim," and pushing past Tribble, held out both hands to Jim. "Why didn't you tell me who you were instead of just standing there and looking at me?"

He took her hands and looked down at her.

"I just wanted to look," he said. "It's been a long time."

"You just wanted to find out if I'd know you." She laughed. "You ought to be ashamed of yourself."

Her laugh was the same laugh he remembered. He had always liked the sound of it, and he had felt better just by hearing it even when his luck was sour. Then he was stirred by old memories, and the knowledge came to him that he had been like Ted Moray when he had been younger. And Al Rome. He hadn't been afraid to take a shot at the moon. Now some of the old recklessness was in him again.

He winked at her. "Sure, I'm ashamed."

Tribble said brusquely. "We're here to ask about your husband. If you want to see our credentials—"

"No." Her hands dropped to her sides, the laughter gone out of her. "Come in."

She swung around and walked into her living-room. Tribble followed, not bothering to take off his hat. Jim stood awkwardly inside the door, his hat held at his side, and he wished he was a hundred miles away. It had been wrong, coming back this way.

"We understand your husband—" Tribble began.

"You don't understand anything." Addie sat down in a rocking chair and motioned toward a horsehair sofa. "Sit down and maybe I can make you understand."

Tribble remained standing. "Don't play games with us, ma'am. We have information that your husband is back in the state and we want him. We think he's here now, or he will be if he ain't. You'll be all right if you cooperate. If not, you'll be in trouble."

He cut it plain, Duke Tribble did. And hard. Most women would have been scared. Not Addie. She looked at him, hating him, then slowly her eyes came to Jim. "Is that you talking, too, Jim?"

"I—"

"Shut up." Tribble didn't turn his head. "It's both of us."

"You've changed, Jim," Addie said.

He knew what she meant. She didn't have to spell it out. He had learned caution. You didn't stay alive if you didn't. And you learned to get along with the man you were forced to work with. All right, he'd changed. There had been a time when he'd have grabbed Tribble by the seat of the pants and thrown him out of the house.

"Will you tell us—" Tribble began.

"No." Addie folded her hands on her lap and she met Tribble's gaze and she matched his toughness with hers. "I don't know you, but I know your kind. Ted made one mistake. It was men like you who kept him from forgetting that mistake."

"He's wanted," Tribble said, and walked out of the house.

Jim hesitated, wanting to tell her he hadn't really changed, not in the things that counted. Now that he had seen her again, he knew why he hadn't married. She had been in his mind all this time. He should have stayed in Sentinel, should have kept her from marrying Ted Moray.

"Don't waste your time here, Jim," she said in a tight, hard voice. "Go after somebody you can get. That's how men like you make your reputation. I know all about it."

He went out into the late afternoon sunlight. No use, he thought. Maybe she still loved Ted. Or maybe not. No matter. She had him pegged just as she had Duke Tribble pegged. She didn't understand because she'd been on the other side of the fence. Well, he didn't know about her side. But why should he? Why should a bank robber have a side?

Tribble gave him his flat-lipped grin. It was as close as he ever came to laughing. He asked, "Want to get out?"

Sure, he wanted to get out. He wanted to kick Duke Tribble in the teeth. He wanted to kill him. And he wanted Addie. But you didn't say those things to Duke Tribble. Not unless you were ready to back them up.

"No," Jim said.

Tribble's face had the look of a mean dog that was chasing a little one. He said, "I figure Moray's in that house right now. She's hiding a man."

"How do you know?"

"Plain enough if you had an eye in your head, but hell, you wouldn't look when it's a woman you used to be sweet on. You still are. Don't tell me different."

"Nobody tells you anything, Duke."

"That's right," Tribble said. "Well, there's a pair of men's boots and a gun belt over a chair in one corner of the room. They'd be Moray's wouldn't they?"

"Maybe."

"Call it maybe if you want to," Tribble said harshly. "I don't. I could have taken him when I was in there, but since I don't have a warrant, it's easier to wait." He nodded at the Rome house. "I'll watch from over there. He's boogery, so he'll make a run for it."

"I'll get something to eat and be back," Jim said.

"Not till morning," Tribble said. "I'll take care of this."

"You haven't eaten since—"

"I'll make out," Tribble said curtly.

They rode back up the street, and when they were out of sight of Addie's house, Tribble cut around a corner and started down an alley. Jim went on to the livery stable and left his horse, then stepped into the Top Notch Café and ordered supper.

Ted might be in the house, Jim thought. If he were, Tribble wanted to make the arrest by himself. Jim's steak came and he ate mechanically, wondering what he ought to do and whether Tribble would wait until Ted showed. If he didn't, Addie would give him trouble.

Tribble wouldn't be above killing a woman in what he called "line of duty." That was it, Jim thought, all wrapped up in a nutshell. What Tribble and Jim called "line of duty" were two different things.

Sam Fenton came in and took the stool beside Jim. He called to the counterman. "Coffee." Then he said in a low tone, "You're riding in bad company."

"Damned bad," Jim agreed.

The coffee came, but Fenton let it cool in front of him. "Why did you come back, Jim?"

"Orders."

"You didn't have to take 'em."

"Yeah, I could have resigned."

Fenton gave him a sharp look. "You don't belong in this game, not playing Tribble's rules, anyhow. Maybe you came back to see Addie. Or maybe to show us what a hell of a tough hand you turned out to be."

"You guess."

Fenton drank his coffee and put the cup down. "Maybe you've forgotten, Jim, but we're a little clannish hereabouts. We like to stomp our own snakes, and likewise we take care of our own. Addie's suffered enough."

"Tribble thinks Ted's in the house. Is he?"

"No."

You could take that for the truth, or take it for a lie. But lying didn't fit Sam Fenton. If a man was wanted by the law, he'd go after him. But you couldn't be sure. Not real sure, because Fenton resented interference.

"Did Addie really love Ted?" Jim asked.

Fenton gave him another sharp look. "Why?"

"I was wondering if she'd protect him. Don't seem like she would after leaving him."

Fenton nudged his cup back and forth with his thumb. "I think she loved him at one time, but love's a funny thing. Kind of like a tender plant. Can't stand too much cold or too much sun."

"What are you trying to say, Sam?"

"She strung along with him as long as she could. He wasn't any good when it got down to cases. She tried to straighten him up, but the law kept hounding him and he didn't have the guts it took." Fenton shrugged. "Finally she came home. But Ted loved her, Jim, although you might say he got her by default, you pulling out like you done."

Jim's face was red when he slid off the stool and tossed a silver dollar on the counter. He said, "Thanks."

"You deserved it. What are you gonna do now?"

"Dunno." Jim picked up his change. "Could Tribble get a warrant to search Addie's house?"

"No."

Jim went into the street. The sun was almost down now, the heat of the day still lingering between the false fronts. He rolled a smoke, still not knowing what he should do. Then Fenton came out of the café. He asked, "Why is the governor interested in Ted?"

"Personal with some politician," Jim answered. "Ted robbed the wrong bank. When they got the tip he was back in the state, they wanted him."

"Figuring I wouldn't arrest him," Fenton said sourly.

Jim walked away. Fenton caught up with him. "I need a deputy, Jim. I won't run for office again. The right deputy wouldn't have no trouble getting elected."

"The right deputy?"

Fenton nodded. "One who savvies this county."

Jim threw his cigarette away and moved south along the boardwalk.

He knew what Fenton meant. The right deputy! You didn't use Tribble's rules to enforce the law in Sentinel. In the past Jim hadn't, either. There was an intangible element Tribble didn't recognize. Call it compassion maybe. Or just human decency. With Tribble nothing counted but his record. If somebody like Addie got hurt, well, it didn't matter.

Jim moved through a patch of shadow made by the poplar trees that lined the street. He shouldn't have come back, but he was here and he had to do something. For Addie. As Fenton had said, she'd suffered enough. She could have taken the easy way and told them to search the house, but she had her share of stubbornness and Tribble had botched it the way he'd talked to her.

The Rome house was just ahead. Talking to Tribble was a waste of breath. He probably knew he couldn't get a search warrant. His patience would hold him for awhile, but only a short time.

Jim swore softly as he moved around the Rome house, wading through the knee-high weeds. A bullet would stop Tribble. It was the only thing that would, but it would have to be from a faster gun than Tribble's, and Jim wasn't sure his was.

Then he saw Tribble, watching Addie's house from the corner of the Rome barn. Tribble glanced at him, scowling. "Couldn't stay away, could you?"

"I've been thinking—" Jim began.

"Save your wind," Tribble said impatiently. "The Moray woman's got a horse in her barn, a roan gelding that's been ridden hard. That enough for you?"

"No. What I—"

Tribble stiffened. "Take a look, bucko. Maybe you'll believe what you see."

A lamp had been lighted in one of Addie's bedrooms. The shade was up and now a man was silhouetted against the lamp. In that instant it flashed through Jim's mind what Tribble would do and he knew at once what he had to do regardless of the identity of the man in Addie's house.

"You ain't going in after him," Jim said. "Not with Addie in the house."

Tribble made a slow turn to face Jim, the light still strong enough to show the hard set of his face, the flat-lipped grin that was a sort of grimace because it so utterly lacked humor. He said, "I didn't want you along in the first place, Barnes. I knew you were too soft for a job like this, knew it when we left the Columbia."

"You ain't going in after him," Jim said again.

"Wait till dark," Tribble said, "and let him slip between my fingers. I ain't that loco, mister. Stay out of my way."

"I'm in your way, Duke," Jim said. "I'll take your iron."

Tribble went for his gun. He had wanted to find out how fast Jim was and now he found out. Jim was too fast. Not much difference in their draws, but enough. Jim's shot made a great racket, and Tribble, his gun unfired, took one step forward and went down on his face.

The back door of Addie's house banged shut. A man ran across the yard to the barn. Jim stood there, staring down at Tribble's body, wet with the sweat that suddenly broke through his pores. He heard someone come up; he heard a great sigh, and then Sam Fenton said, "I wasn't sure you could do it."

"Or had the guts to try," Jim said.

"I wasn't sure of that, either."

"A man ran out of Addie's house to the barn. If it's Ted—"

"Go see," Fenton said.

Jim swung around and ran across the back of the Rome lot; he jumped the fence and reached the barn just as the man who had been in the house finished tightening the cinch on the roan gelding. He looked at Jim, and in the thin light inside the barn, Jim saw it wasn't Ted Moray. He was young, almost a kid.

"Who are you?"

"Harrison. Fred Harrison. I had to get out. I wasn't going to fetch no trouble to Mrs. Moray. Ted wouldn't have wanted me to."

"Where is Ted?"

"Dead. That's what I came to tell Mrs. Moray. I fetched a few of his things. He got into a fight in Burns and was shot. We made it into the Blue Mountains where we hid out. He died two days ago." The boy swallowed. "He was my friend."

He said a lot in those last four words. Maybe Ted wasn't much good, but he wasn't all bad, not if this Fred Harrison could call him his friend, and maybe it was that part of him which had held Addie as long as it had.

Jim turned and left the barn. He knew what would have happened if Tribble had found the kid in the barn. He'd have shot him before he found out it wasn't Ted Moray. The idea that he could be mistaken was a thought which had always been foreign to Duke Tribble.

Fenton was waiting outside. Jim said, "You knew Ted was dead." When Fenton nodded, Jim asked, "Why didn't you tell me?"

"No need to. I aimed to stop Tribble. Besides, I wanted to find out something about you." Fenton motioned toward the house. "Addie will want to see you."

"I've got something to do first," Jim said. "Sam, I wasn't sure about wanting to stay here, but I am now, if I'm the right kind of deputy—"

"You are," Fenton said, smiling. "What is it you have to do?"

"Get a hotel room. I'm going to write out my resignation when I send in my report."

Jim walked down the alley toward town, and when he thought of Duke Tribble, there was no regret in him.

Smart

We came down off Big Mesa early Monday morning, Barney Nolan, Babe Dode, and I—Jimmy Ryan. Our object—to rob the bank at
Three Forks.

Barney was the leader, so he rode in front where the leader should.
Babe was in the middle, I brought up the tail. I couldn't help looking
at Barney's back; he was the kind you just naturally looked at. I guess
he'd have been a leader no matter where he was or what he was doing.
He was big and tough and mean, and he was smart—real smart, the
way he looked ahead and planned everything out and all that.

He rode his saddle as if he were made for it. He had a .30–.30 in the
boot and he packed two guns on his hips. I'd heard of men who
carried two guns, but he was the only one I had ever seen who actually
did it. Any way you looked at him, he was quite a man, Barney was.

Babe was different. He was just a big, fat nothing. The only thing
he was good for was to do what Barney told him and I'll admit he was
good for that. He never questioned an order. If Barney had told him to
go stand on his head in the marshal's parlor at midnight, Friday the
thirteenth, Babe would have done it. But Barney wouldn't have given
a foolish order like that. Like I said, he was smart. That was the whole
thing about Barney. I guess he was about the smartest gent I ever ran
into.

The plan was to hit Three Forks just at noon when the marshal
always stepped into Dolan's Bar for a drink before he went home to
dinner. Barney picked Monday to do the job because Monday was
usually a quiet day, the chances being good that we wouldn't run into
cowhands from the ranches that were strung up and down Three
Forks Valley.

Barney had stayed in town most of the weeks we'd been holed up in that cave on Big Mesa. That is, Babe and I holed up while Barney had himself a time. It didn't bother Babe, being Barney's Number One yes man the way he was, but it bothered the hell out of me, especially since I was the leading candidate for getting my hide perforated with lead.

At twenty minutes to twelve, we pulled up at the edge of town and stepped down. We watered our horses and Barney took a good, long look at his gun. I didn't know why because the only one likely to be using a gun was me, good old Jimmy Ryan, nineteen my last birthday, and too young to die. In my opinion, that is—not Barney's. Somewhere along the line I got the notion that the only reason he had picked me up when they rode through Meeker was to have a man handy to throw to the wolves.

Barney got back on his horse and had Babe check his watch to be sure they were together. Then he asked, "You're sure you know what to do?"

"Sure," Babe said. "We wait fifteen minutes. If you ain't showed up by then, we'll know there ain't no cowhands around and we'll come on in. Jimmy stops at Dolan's Bar and I go on to the bank where you'll be."

"That's it," Barney said.

He'd have ridden off then if I hadn't said, "Barney."

He looked down at me, kind of as if he figured I was a fool to have got into this deal in the first place and a bigger one for staying. I was and knew it, but I'd give my word and wasn't about to crawl out now and let Barney think I was yellow.

"Well?" Barney asked.

He looked exactly the way I had always pictured Blackbeard the Pirate, face covered by a heavy black beard like it was. He wore a flat-topped Stetson that he kept pulled down. His brown eyes were squinted half shut because the sunlight was sharp. He gave his hat a yank to settle it tighter. I could see he was impatient, but he needed me and he wasn't giving me any excuse to get off the hook.

"Suppose I get into trouble when I jump the marshal?" I asked. "Just supposing?"

"I've told you a dozen times and now I'll tell you for the last time," Barney said. "You won't get into no trouble. None of us will have trouble unless there's some cowboys on hand. If there is, we ride out, quick and peaceful. This thing will go slicker'n goose grease 'cause there ain't a fighting man in this burg—and that's counting the marshal."

He rode off, fast because I'd used up a couple of minutes when he should have been riding. I sat down and put my back against a cottonwood and rolled a smoke. He hadn't answered my question.

That's another way he was smart. He never had answered the question. That was why I asked it the thirteenth time. If I got into trouble, Barney and Babe wouldn't be coming back for me. That was plain. But I still wasn't backing out. If I got into trouble, I'd handle it.

I suppose any smart man looks ahead. Same with a woman, I expect. It sure was the trouble with Annie Peck. She'd been way too good at looking ahead. That was how I got hooked up with Barney Logan and Babe Dode.

I'd been going with Annie for a couple of years, figuring on marrying her all that time. I thought she'd been figuring the same with me. We had an understanding that seemed plain enough. I had a steady job riding for the Box A and I'd been saving all I could so we'd start married life with a little spread of our own. I had about two hundred dollars in the bank, and I'd done without a lot of things to put it there. But it wasn't enough to suit Annie. The night before I left Meeker she told me she wouldn't marry a man who hadn't at least one thousand dollars. Then she gave me my walking papers.

"Two hundred dollars in two years," she said scornfully, as if it were two cents. "Jimmy Ryan, if you think I'm going to wait ten years for you, you're crazier than I thought."

"I figured we were in love," I said. "I thought. . . ."

"Then you can just quit thinking!" she snapped. "Takes more than love to live on if you're married to a cowboy making thirty bucks a month."

I couldn't see anything to do but walk out, which was what I did.

A new man had come from Denver to work in the bank and he'd been shining up to Annie. It didn't take any brains to figure out she didn't want to discourage him by having me clutter up her parlor when he came calling. So I guess Annie was smart the same way Barney Logan was. In looking ahead, I mean.

I finished my cigarette and tossed the stub into the creek. Babe

Dode looked at his watch. "He ain't showed," Babe said, "so I guess it's time to ride."

I got into the saddle and we moseyed down the road that became Three Forks' Main Street, just taking it easy so we wouldn't attract any attention, but I sure didn't have my mind on my business. Thinking of Annie, I couldn't think about anything else. She was little and cute—a decided blonde, and the way she kissed made a feller think tomorrow was Fourth of July with fireworks and everything.

After she tied the can to my tail I swore I'd dig up the thousand dollars she claimed a man had to have to marry her. I was just about drunk enough to tackle a bank myself when Barney and Babe showed up, riding south from Wyoming. They bent an ear to my troubles, agreed about women and said I was a chowder-headed chump to stick around Meeker with Annie sticking her nose in the air every time she walked past me.

"Better ride along with us," Barney said. "There's plenty of big deals that three men can handle but two can't."

This was the big deal he had in mind, I guess. I was to jump the marshal and work him into a fight. Call him a few names—anything to attract a crowd while Barney and Babe knocked the bank over.

Barney hadn't seen me pull a gun, but it was plain enough he didn't care whether I was fast or not. It amounted to the same thing whichever way it worked out. Any kind of excitement that would create a diversion was all Barney wanted.

Barney had been around town enough to size everything up. He said the marshal was a young buck not much older than I was. Had a wife and a baby, and the only reason he carried the star was because no one else wanted it, this being a gone-to-seed town not paying enough to keep a good man. According to Barney, the marshal was just a bluff, the kind who wore a great, sweeping mustache to make him look older and fiercer than he was.

"A gent of his caliber likes to play big," Barney said. "I know the kind. He struts around town wearing a shiny star. He's got a deep voice that sounds like God talking. Every noon he stops at Dolan's Bar, has one drink and talks a few minutes before he goes home. That's when you'll brace him."

By the time we got to Dolan's Bar, I pretty well had Annie out of my mind and this show-off marshal in. I stopped and got off my horse in the middle of the street while Babe Dode rode on toward the bank. Barney was already there, leaning against the wall with a cigar in his mouth.

I waited until I saw Babe step out of his saddle. I was looking up and down the street as if I was trying to see someone, which I was. The marshal must have got here ahead of me. I pulled my gun and banged away at the sign in front of the saloon, putting a hole right in the middle of the o in Dolan.

A man was going into the saloon when I fired. He fell flat on his belly in front of the batwings just as two men ran outside to see what the shooting was about. They walked right down his back. As soon as they got off him, he crawled inside. The two who had come out took a look at me as if they weren't sure whether they liked what they saw or not.

"Is the marshal inside?" I asked.

All the one guy could do was swallow. The other one wet his lips and finally managed to nod.

"Send him out," I ordered. "I got something to say to him, something that'll burn his ears all the way down to his heels."

Town men on the street began working toward me. They wanted to see what was going on but they didn't want to get close enough to have any part in the trouble. Barney was right about that bunch. Some came barging out of the saloon and walked away fast until they figured they were out of danger, then twisted around to watch. There wasn't a fighting man in the bunch.

I waited two, three minutes, standing so I could see the front of the bank. By that time a dozen or more jaspers were in the street watching me. I still had my gun in my hand. Waving it at the batwings I yelled, "Where'n hell is that marshal?"

He came out then, blinking as the sunlight hit him. He was exactly the way Barney had described him, a kid pretending he was plumb growed up. Takes more than a mustache, gun, star, wife, and baby to make a real man. He stood there in front of the saloon looking at me and not knowing what to say or do. Anybody could see that he was having a hard time keeping his feet where they were.

"You wanted to see me?"

All I wanted was to use up time. If I pushed him too hard, he might go for his gun. Then I'd have to kill him and I didn't want that. I said,

"Yeah, I wanted to see you. Look up there at that sign. I put that hole there. What are you going to do about it?"

The marshal stepped off a piece and squinted up at the sign. Then he looked at me, grinning as if he thought it was a kid antic. He said, "Well, that's fair shooting, sonny, but what makes you think I'm going to do anything about it?"

Calling me sonny made me sore. "Your job, ain't it?" I said, throwing the words at him fast.

He shook his head. "You're a drifter, I figure. Keep on drifting and we'll all be happy."

I said, "You're just a wet-nosed kid packin' a piece of tin. I don't like star packers. I don't like you in particular."

"I'm sorry about that," the marshal said. "I was in hopes you'd like me."

Somebody snickered. I turned part way around and threw a shot that kicked up some dust in front of the gent who had done the snickering. "This kid with the tin star ain't funny," I said. "Now if you think he is, start laughing, big and loud."

The fellow was wearing a green eyeshade and cut-off black stockings up to his elbows. His face turned almost as green as his eyeshade. He backed up some, spluttering, "I didn't think he was funny. He's not a bit funny."

I turned back to the marshal. He didn't look half as scared as I had been thinking. He didn't look scared at all. I waved my gun some more, feeling like a fool, and said, "Go roll your hoop."

I had been figuring on holstering my gun and inviting him to make his play, but that didn't look so good to me now. Barney had this huckleberry sized up wrong. He'd go for his gun if he had a fair chance, and one of us would be toted off on a shutter, which was exactly what Barney wanted.

So I made a spiel about lawmen being crawling things which ought to stay under rocks instead of getting out into the sunlight and I kept waving my gun. Then Barney and Babe came out of the bank, Barney carrying a gunny sack that looked pretty heavy. They mounted and rode out of town, so slick nobody but me even noticed.

It was time for me to do likewise. A man can sit on a deal like this about so long, and then some fool is bound to get himself killed. I stepped into the saddle, still hanging onto my gun.

"I'll be sloping along, Marshal," I told him. "Just wanted to see if
you had any guts and it looks like you have."

I cracked steel to my horse and took off at a run, not holstering my
gun until I was past the last house. I looked around once and saw the
whole bunch, including the marshal, standing in the street staring
after me like I was loco.

I got to where we'd left the fresh horses ahead of Barney and Babe.
They had farther to go than I had, having to cross the creek and circle
back on the other side. I changed my saddle to my sorrel, the horse I'd
ridden out of Meeker, and waited.

After a while they rode in, their horses all lathered up and mighty
near dead. "Why didn't you plug that marshal?" Barney yelled as
they swung down.

"Didn't need to," I yelled back. "Kept him busy, didn't I? You
didn't have no trouble getting out of town."

Barney changed the saddle, so mad he was red clean around on the
back of his neck. "You should have killed him. He got a posse together and he's on our tail. Better run those crowbaits across the
creek."

Maybe he was sore because I was still alive, three-way split instead
of a two-way. But I was sore, too. I'd done all I was supposed to and
there was no sense getting his tail up. I hadn't heard any horses. I had
a hunch he was lying about a posse being after us. But I ran the three
horses we'd been riding across the creek and up the bank the way
Barney had said, then I followed him and Babe, keeping in the water
the way we had agreed.

Any posse on our tail would probably lose some time following the
tracks of the horses we'd run across the creek, then they'd have to
come back and work up and down it until they found where we came
out. That would take time. Meanwhile we'd be back on Big Mesa
holed up in the cave. Or maybe keep on going if it got dark enough. I
wasn't sure how we'd play it.

Funny thing, now that I thought about it. Barney hadn't ever said
what we were going to do after we got the dinero. I grabbed onto the
same notion I'd had before, only this time it was more than a notion.
Barney'd figured I'd be kicking my life out on Three Forks' Main
Street. Now they had me on their hands.

By the time we got to the cave, I knew what I was going to do. I said,

"Divvy up. I'm riding one way and you can take another. I don't want to see either one of you again."

"Suits me," Barney said.

He glanced over at Babe and I could see they figured I was dead sure enough. When we went into the cave, Barney said: "Take all you want of the grub, Jimmy. I'll split the dinero and we'll ride. We ain't got much time."

If I had gone on past Barney to the pile of grub like they figured me to, I'd have been plugged in the back. I took three steps, then turned fast, pulling my gun as I came around. Caught him right in the act. He was looking at me, gun half out of leather.

If I'd waited another second, he'd have got me cold turkey. Way it was, I got him. He tried to hurry his draw when I started to turn, but I was too fast, nailing him in the mouth, the slug angling up into his brain. He never got off a shot. Neither did Babe Dode who made a try for me when he saw what had happened, but he was way too slow. He caught two slugs in the brisket, and that tied everything up neat and pretty.

I picked up the gunny sack and looked inside. Some loose greenbacks, gold, and silver, and half a dozen buckskin sacks that were filled and heavy enough to contain lead. I tied the gunny sack and started toward my horse, thinking I'd high-tail off the mesa and keep on going. Wasn't even going to be a two split now. It was all mine.

It hit me just as I was tying the sack behind the cantle. There was Barney Nolan, smart as all hell, figuring things out so careful like, a piece of dead meat. That was where being smart had got him.

If he hadn't been so smart, picking me up in Meeker and tolling me into Three Forks to get killed, he wouldn't be where he was right now. What kind of a sucker would *I* be, taking off on the owlhoot! I wasn't in trouble yet, but I sure would be if I took this bank money.

I headed back to town. When I got to the place where we'd changed horses I found the posse, six men including the marshal. They was floundering around, not knowing up from down, going round in circles.

I had my gun in one hand and the gunny sack in the other. I said, "The gents you want are back there in a cave." I jerked my thumb in the general direction. "Except I've got what you're huntin' right here. Leastwise I found it on them."

The marshal looked me over kind of puzzled. "That looks like the stuff we lost from the bank."

"I figured so," I said, "them bags being marked." I knew I couldn't let on to knowing anything about the robbery. I said, "I was camped in this cave when two gents rode up. Guess they figured I'd blab. Anyhow they tried to kill me." I waggled the gunny sack in front of the marshal. "How much reward is there for bringing them in?"

"About five hundred," the marshal said. "Hand it over."

"Look," I said, "I could have gone over the hill with it but I didn't. Now I sure don't aim to lose the reward."

"All right," he said. "I'll ride into town with you. The rest of you boys go look in that cave. Fetch me back whatever you find."

He nodded at me. "Put your iron up. We'll get along fine if you keep a civil tongue in your head. When we get to town, you can turn the dinero in and pick up the reward. Fortunately them fellers in the bank were knocked out. There's no killing to answer for."

We started back down the creek. I put my gun in the holster and took a good look at this kid with the star. "Wouldn't have bothered me none if there had been a killing," I said.

He grinned under that big, sweeping mustache of his. "Think not?" he said. "After that hoorawing you gave me in town?"

He had it figured out, I guessed. I was kind of uneasy even though I knew he couldn't prove anything.

"From the description the bank fellows gave me," this tinbadge went on, "the two robbers are worth two-fifty apiece. I'm guessing the big one to be Barney Nolan. Other's probably Babe Dode. He used to ride with Nolan. Nolan's been hanging around some. I been watching him, but I sure wasn't watching him at the right time." He looked me over. "You made yourself a quick thousand bucks. I'm gonna let you collect it and git outa town. I got nothing against you except them names, but I'll tell you one thing: Keep your nose clean from now on."

"I aim to," I said. "What's your handle, Marshal?"

He said with a chuckle, "Brazos Sam Jones."

I'd have flopped right out of my saddle if I hadn't grabbed onto the horn. No wonder Barney didn't expect me to show up alive. Brazos Sam Jones was just about the best marshal in Colorado. The main thing was he had the fastest draw in the country. If it had come to a showdown between him and me I'd be as dead as Barney Nolan and Babe Dode.

I had to stay in Three Forks a while to get my money. I didn't get over the shakes all the time I was there. I rode back to Meeker with the thousand dollars in my pocket and bought that spread up on White River that I wanted. It wasn't a big outfit and I was into it up to my ears, but I figured with any luck I'd make out.

Somewhere along the line that day I heard that the bank fellow who had been shining up to Annie Peck had quit town. Seemed a wife and three kids had showed. After making eyes the way he had at Annie, I guess he figured he'd better light a shuck out of there.

News gets around pretty fast in a town like Meeker. Annie must have heard about me buying the ranch. When I came out of the courthouse, the deal all wrapped up, she was waiting.

She hugged and kissed me without me doing a thing but just standing there. I didn't even put my arms around her. Kind of funny the way it was. That hugging and kissing wasn't like it used to be. The earth didn't shake. I didn't hear any bells ringing. I didn't even see any fireworks.

All I could think was that here was a woman smart as Barney Nolan, looking ahead, figuring everything out. Smart. Both of them. Well, I walked right past her and got on my horse and rode up the river. I aimed to spend the night on my new ranch. It was a rightdown good feeling to be a land owner—even if I wasn't smart.

Mean Men Are Big

My sister's name is First Merrybelle Dorcas. I'll bet you think that's the funniest name you ever heard. I think so, too. She wasn't really the first Merrybelle. Mamma was. Her name is Laura Merrybelle Dorcas, so my sister should be named Second, but she wasn't because we happened to move to Antioch just when we did.

Papa's name is James Finley Dorcas and he was a famous peace officer in a Kansas trail town. That was before I was born, but people have told me about it. I forgot to say I'm Tuck. That's a nickname. Mamma named me James Finley Dorcas, but I hate being called Junior.

I guess it all started in that Kansas town when Papa was standing on the street talking to a big cattle buyer. Mamma was riding along in her buggy when a cowboy let out a yell and fired a gun and Mamma's horse ran away. Papa jumped into the street and stopped the horse and that's how she turned out to be my mamma.

Papa had to put his guns away and give up his job before Mamma would marry him. She said he had to have a respectable business. That's why they moved to Denver, where Papa bought a hardware store. That satisfied Mamma, so I guess it was respectable.

I was born in Denver but I don't remember it. I don't remember anything about Denver except that Aunt Minnie came to keep house when Mamma got sick. Aunt Minnie is Grandpa's sister and keeps house for him in St. Louis, but she isn't like Grandpa. She has a mustache like he does but she doesn't have a beard.

Aunt Minnie has the biggest chest I ever saw. She wears a gold watch on one side. Her eyeglasses hang down on the other side. Papa

153

says she has a "sea chest." When I asked him why he called it that, he said, "Why, when you see Aunt Minnie, you can't help seeing her chest."

Mamma said, "Jim, you ought to be ashamed to talk that way."

Papa said, "Well, it's the truth."

What Papa said made sense all right. When you see Aunt Minnie, you sure can't help seeing her chest.

We moved to Pueblo, and Aunt Minnie went back to St. Louis. Papa bought another hardware store but he wasn't happy. He'd walk the floor and say, "A man can't get ahead in a town like this. The course of empire is westward."

He'd fling a hand out toward the mountains. "That's where fortunes are being made. Gold is being discovered. Railroads are being built. Towns are being born. Here I am, missing opportunities because we're held down by a hostage to fortune."

"I won't go where there aren't any schools or doctors," Mamma said. "Aunt Minnie says we should have stayed in Denver."

"Hang Aunt Minnie," Papa said, sounding pretty mad. "I wish I could. We had to leave Denver to get rid of her."

"I'm still not going to some terrible old mining camp where there aren't any schools or doctors," Mamma said.

"Our little hostage looks mighty healthy to me," Papa said, "and you were a schoolteacher before I saved you from being an old maid."

"Being healthy won't keep him from taking smallpox or scarlet fever," Mamma said, "and just teaching doesn't take the place of a school." Her mouth was a long white line. "I won't go."

Her mouth didn't get that way very often but when it did, Mamma looked a lot like Aunt Minnie. In the face, I mean. She didn't really look like Aunt Minnie because she didn't have Aunt Minnie's sea chest. Anyhow, Papa always quit talking when she got that Aunt Minnie look on her mouth. He'd just walk out of the house.

After we lived in Pueblo for quite a while, Papa left on the train and was gone for a long time. I asked Mamma where he'd gone, and she said, "He took a lot of mining machinery over the mountains." Then she hugged me. "We miss him when he's gone, don't we, darling?"

I said, "He'll be back pretty soon, won't he?"

Mamma cried a little then and said, "Yes, I think so."

When Papa got back, his mustache just kind of bristled. He

laughed and hugged Mamma and joked a lot. Then he said, "I found the right place, honey. There's a school and a doctor and fortunes are being made overnight. It's the opportunity of a lifetime, and you know what they say. Opportunity only knocks once on a man's door."

Mamma asked, "What's the name of this great town?"

"Antioch," Papa said.

"Never heard of it," Mamma said.

"You will, honey. You will. It's going to be a big place."

Mamma folded her hands and put them on her lap. She stared down at them as she said, "Jim, we're going to have another hostage to fortune."

Papa just stood there looking at her and the funniest thing happened. His mustache didn't bristle any more. It kind of wilted. He said, in a low voice, "Not . . . another one?"

"Yes," Mamma said. "Another one," and she began to cry.

Papa got down on his knees and kissed her. "That's wonderful, honey."

Mamma kept on crying. "All right, Jim," she said. "I'll go. Living with you like this is like living with a hungry lion in a cage. You've just got to go and try it."

Papa's mustache got bristly again right away. He said, "That's my girl, Laura. That's my girl."

After that there was a lot of bustling around. Mamma felt puny but she got things packed up. Papa sold his store and the house and we took the longest train ride. It was a little train. Papa said it was a narrow gauge. It wound around through the mountains and it tooted its whistle. We traveled awfully fast. I guess we were going twenty miles an hour.

We slept on the train and it was about noon the next day when we got to Antioch. It was the funniest-looking town I ever saw. Not like Pueblo at all. It was down in the bottom of a canyon with a creek running along one side. All the buildings were kind of brown like an old leaf. But the funniest part of it was that right in the middle of Main Street there was an open spot.

"Two vacant lots," Papa said. "They haven't found out who to give them to yet."

Maybe they were vacant lots. Papa ought to know, but it looked to me like my upper teeth where the two front ones were gone.

We went to the hotel and had dinner. Mamma got mad at me because I dumped all the little crackers into my soup. She made me eat every bite, and then I was so full I couldn't eat anything else.

Just about the time Papa finished his pie, a man with a long white beard came to our table. Papa introduced us. He said his name was Uncle Luke Mattingly. I thought that if he was my uncle, he must be married to Aunt Minnie, so I asked him if he was.

He laughed and slapped his leg. "No, son, I ain't."

Papa said, "That's the luckiest thing that ever happened to you. Since you discovered the Yankee Doodle, that is."

Mamma said, "James!"

"It's the truth," Papa said. "There's just two ways of looking at Aunt Minnie. Front or back, and sideways. You can't miss her either way, but I'd like to."

"What do you think of our town?" Uncle Luke asked Mamma. "I'm the town daddy, you know. Started it twenty years ago when I discovered the Sweetheart Mine, then we lost the vein and the town died. I stayed right here and kept looking. Folks said I was crazy but they changed their tune when I struck the vein again." He pointed at the hill across the creek. "Up yonder on that there ridge. This time I called it the Yankee Doodle."

"I never saw a town like it, " Mamma said. "Do you have a doctor in town?"

"You bet we do," Uncle Luke said. "Doc Pettybone. He's the best doggone pill roller in all the San Juan. Just one thing wrong. He's treated broken bones and taken out more bullets than you can shake a stick at, but he ain't brought a baby into the world since he came to this camp. It sure grieves all of us. I figured I'd take care of it when I reserved them two lots for the first baby born in Antioch, but it's been twenty year and it ain't worked yet."

"Give us time, Luke," Papa said. "Just give us time."

When we got upstairs to our room, Mamma began to cry. She said, "Jim, I've got to have a doctor, and all there is in this awful wilderness is a pill roller."

"He's a doctor," Papa said.

But Mamma kept on crying. "Pills won't do me any good when my time comes, and I don't care how he rolls them."

Papa got up and went out. Pretty soon he came back with a tall man who had a little mustache and a goatee and carried a black bag. He was wearing a boiled shirt and a string tie and a long-tailed coat. I guess he was just about the most handsome man I ever saw, and Mamma quit crying the minute she saw him.

Papa said he was Doc Pettybone. Mamma said, "I'm happy to know you."

"And I'm happy to know you, Mrs. Dorcas," he said. "You're going to have the best of care it's possible for me to give you. I practiced in Durango before I came to Antioch and I delivered lots of babies."

For some reason that made Mamma happy. Doc Pettybone sat down and held her hand for a while, then he opened his bag and took out a little silvery-looking thing and put it into her mouth. He pulled it out after about a minute and looked at it and nodded.

"You're strong and healthy, Mrs. Dorcas," he said. "I'm sure you won't have a bit of trouble."

"Unless you're taking a bullet out of some man or putting broken bones together," Mamma said.

"The biggest thing that ever happened in this camp will be the birth of the first baby," Doc Pettybone said. "You'll come ahead of everything else. Believe me." He put the little silver thing into the black bag and closed it. "How long will it be, Mrs. Dorcas?"

"Six months," Mamma said.

He nodded. "That's going to be real fine. It will all be over with before cold weather starts. Now any time you don't feel good, you come and see me. Or send for me."

After Doc Pettybone left, Papa said, "He's a good doctor, Laura. Everything's going to be all right just like I told you."

Mamma looked happier than I'd seen her since we'd left Pueblo. She said, "Yes, I think it will. As soon as we get settled, I'll send for Aunt Minnie and she can take care of you and Tuck."

Papa threw up his hands and started to say a bad word. The he choked and coughed and said, "By the great horned toad, you won't do any such thing. We'll find somebody right here in Antioch."

Mamma's mouth turned into a long white line again. She said, "I'll feel better with Aunt Minnie here."

Papa walked out. I don't know when he got back. I was asleep.

The next day Papa bought a house and we moved into it that

afternoon. It was on the creek clear up above town and you could see a long ways down the canyon. It was two stories and had a long bannister beside the stairs. I slid down it until Mamma made me stop. Then I went outside and turned the doorbell until Mamma told me to stop doing that, too. She said it made her nervous.

After that I went inside and shut the front door. It had one big glass pane and a bunch of little colored panes all around it, blue and red and yellow. I'd shut one eye and put the other one up close to a colored pane and look through it. Then the funniest thing happened. The whole world turned blue or red or yellow, depending on which pane I looked through.

Mamma and Papa got along pretty well after that. He went to work for Uncle Luke Mattingly, and Mamma got bigger and bigger. She said that was what always happened when a woman had a baby. That's all she'd tell me, but I asked Uncle Luke about it one day and he said he didn't know why that was, either. He said babies came out of a cabbage patch.

I hunted all over town for a cabbage patch but I couldn't find one. Uncle Luke took me fishing the next day and I told him I didn't think there was a cabbage patch anywhere in Antioch. He got red in the face and his mustache and beard kind of quivered. Then he said, "I didn't tell you all of it, Tuck. You see, it don't make much difference where the cabbage patch is. I seen some real nice ones the last time I was in Durango." He choked up and wiped his eyes. Then he said, "Tuck, you ain't getting no bites today. Let's go to the store and see if they've got any licorice."

That was what we did, but I kind of hated to get licorice. It made my face dirty and Mamma always scolded me. I decided I could wash my face in the creek, so I walked along with Uncle Luke. The more I thought about the cabbage business, the more I wondered about it. It seemed to me there had to be some way to get the baby from the cabbage patch in Durango to Antioch.

When we left the store, I had a stick of licorice in my mouth. I was going to ask Uncle Luke about the baby business when a man called, "Mattingly."

He turned around, and there was the biggest man I ever saw. He had the biggest mustache I ever saw, too. It was red and went way out on the sides of his face and hung down on both ends. He had a beard, too. It was short and seemed to stick out and point right at Uncle Luke.

"What do you want, Dunbar?" Uncle Luke asked.

"You know what I want," the man said. "You've pussyfooted around long enough."

Uncle Luke looked like he wished he was somewhere else. He sucked in a long breath and stood on one foot and then the other one. Finally, he said, "Doak, this here boy is Jim Dorcas's son. Tuck, I want you to meet Doak Dunbar."

I guess the big man hadn't even seen me until then. He stared at me when I said, "How do you do, Mr. Dunbar." He growled kind of like the dog I used to have in Pueblo did when he had a bone and I tried to take it away from him.

I didn't know Dunbar was a mean man until he turned his head and looked at Uncle Luke. He said, "So this is the Dorcas brat. Now you're figuring on another one, ain't you? You're cute, Mattingly. Mighty cute."

Nobody had ever called me a brat before. I hadn't done anything to him. I'd been just as polite as I could. I said, "I'm not a brat and you don't have any reason to call me one."

"He's right," Uncle Luke said. "Just as right as rain. When I tell Jim about it, you'd better hunt for cover."

Dunbar laughed and said a bad word. He pulled his coat to one side and I saw he had a gun in a leather holster. Nobody in Antioch carried a gun except Pete Jones, the marshal, and he didn't carry his except on Saturday night.

"There was a time when I'd have believed that," Dunbar said. "They say when he was in Kansas he was a tough hand, but he ain't no more. Don't even pack his iron, and I've given him plenty of excuses."

Uncle Luke didn't say anything to that. He turned around, and we started off down the street. Dunbar said another bad word and grabbed Uncle Luke by the arm and whirled him around.

"I'm giving you till tomorrow night, Mattingly," Dunbar said. "Then I'm going to run you and Dorcas out of town if you don't sell me them lots."

He raised a thumb to his hat and shoved it back on his head, and I saw that his hair was just as red as his beard and mustache. "Use your noggin, man. I'm offering you five thousand dollars for them lots and

I'm promising I'll build the best saloon and gambling place on the western slope. You owe that much to the men in this camp and they know it."

He let Uncle Luke's arm go and turned around and walked off. Uncle Luke said, "You run home, Tuck."

So I didn't get to ask him any more about the cabbage patch being in Durango. When I got home, Mamma said he was coming for supper, so I thought I'd get another chance, but I didn't because as soon as we started eating, Mamma said, "Jim, Aunt Minnie will be here tomorrow on the train. You be sure to meet her."

Papa didn't say a word but he looked just like he did the time he hit his thumb a hard whack with the hammer and started to say some bad words and Mamma yelled, "Stop that. Little pitchers have big ears." After that he just swelled up and got purple in the face and I thought he'd bust.

When Mamma went into the kitchen to do the dishes, Uncle Luke said, "I want to talk to you."

Papa said, "I know what about, too. The Lord doesn't do it halfway when He sets out to punish a man. It ought to be enough for Him to send Aunt Minnie."

"I should think you'd be thankful to have her here to take care of Laura," Uncle Luke said.

"Thankful?" Papa looked surprised. "Do you thank the Lord when he sends a blizzard? Or a snow slide? Or an earthquake?"

They got up and went into the parlor. I crawled behind a big chair to play with my blocks. I thought they'd talk about the cabbage patch, but instead they talked about that Doak Dunbar.

"He's been after me for weeks to sell him those lots," Uncle Luke said. "Now he's telling everybody it's a put-up job. You're working for me and your wife's about to have a baby and that's why you came to Antioch."

"That's true as far as it goes," Papa said. "I expect to build a hardware store as soon as the baby comes and I get a deed to those lots. You knew that all the time. If you sell them to Doak Dunbar. . . ."

"I know how you feel," Uncle Luke said, "but we've got to be practical. Dunbar's got the reputation of being a killer. He says he'll run both of us out of town if I don't sell to him. Of course if you'd take your guns and. . . ."

"I've told you before how it is," Papa said. "I promised Laura."

"Then I'll have to do it," Uncle Luke said.

Mamma called me to bed, so I didn't get to hear any more. I thought about it before I went to sleep. I wondered who Papa thought was worse, Doak Dunbar or Aunt Minnie. I decided he was scared of Aunt Minnie but I know he wasn't scared of Dunbar.

I'd seen Papa's guns lots of times when I got into the trunk in the attic. In the morning soon as I finished breakfast I went upstairs and looked in the trunk. The guns were gone, but I didn't tell Mamma.

I went with Papa to meet the train. Aunt Minnie was on it, all right, with her sea chest and everything. She kissed me and hugged me till I couldn't get my breath. She said, "Sakes alive, Tuck, how are you going to eat an apple with those front teeth gone?" Then she looked at Papa and kind of grunted. "Well, James, you haven't changed any."

"Neither have you," Papa said.

He put her valises in the bed of the buckboard, and I heard him say under his breath, "Looks like it's going to be a long hard winter."

Aunt Minnie hugged and kissed Mamma when we got home, then she said, "Laura, you wrote me you were eight months along."

"I am," Mamma said.

"Then I guess you can't count," Aunt Minnie said. "You're nine months. I can tell just by looking at you. You're not well, either. I can tell that, too. James, you stay home. You hear me?"

"I'll stay home when I'm needed," Papa said.

He walked out. Aunt Minnie said, "Laura, I told you that you were making a horrible mistake when you married that man. When are you going to get enough sense to leave him and come home to me and your father?"

"I'll never get that kind of sense," Mamma said. "Jim's my husband, and I love him."

Then Aunt Minnie saw me and made me go outside. I got a stick of wood and whittled with the new knife Uncle Luke had bought me. I cut my hand and it bled like everything, but I didn't go in and tell Mamma. I guess I was like Papa. I was afraid of Aunt Minnie.

That afternoon Mamma went to bed. She said she didn't feel good. When Papa got home for supper, Aunt Minnie said, "Laura's going to have your baby tonight. You stay here and you'd better get the doctor."

Papa didn't say anything. He didn't say anything when Aunt Minnie brought the big dish of dumplings to the table, either. If there was anything he hated, it was dumplings. I tried to eat one, but it was big and doughy and tasted awful. Papa excused himself and went into Mamma's bedroom. He stayed until it was dark and then he left without saying a word to Aunt Minnie.

I had to sit there until I finished my dumpling. Then Aunt Minnie said I looked bilious, and I went out on the front porch and sat down. I stayed there quite a while, getting sicker all the time until I heard some shooting down town. I forgot about being sick when I remembered that Papa's guns were gone from the trunk. I got up to go find out about the shooting when Aunt Minnie ran out of the house.

"Your mamma's got to have the doctor right away," she said. "You go get him. Fetch your papa, too. Just wait till I get my hands on that man."

Something in her voice scared me, and I ran. Doc Pettybone wasn't in his office, and there wasn't anybody on the street. Then when I got to the Antioch Bar I looked in and saw a crowd of men. Doc was in the middle of the room bending over someone laid out on a billiard table.

I squirmed between men's legs until I got to the table. Doc was leaning over Uncle Luke. He had his sleeves rolled up, and Uncle Luke had his shirt and undershirt off and he was lying awful still. There was a little round hole in his chest.

I grabbed at Doc's pants legs and started to yank on it and tell him Mamma needed him when somebody grabbed me and put a hand over my mouth. I kicked and tried to get free, then I saw it was Papa who was holding me.

Just then Doc straightened up and held something between his fingers. "There's the bullet," he said. "Didn't hit anything vital. I think he's going to be all right."

Papa took his hand off my mouth and I yelled, "Mamma's sick. She needs you right away."

Doc looked at Papa. "I can't go now."

"You promised," I said. "The first night we were in Antioch. You said Mamma came first. You said broken bones and bullets could wait."

"The boy's right," Uncle Luke said. His face was white as anything, just as white as his beard. "You take care of her first."

Doc grabbed his black bag and went out of there on the run, Papa a jump or two behind him. I tried to keep up but I couldn't. When I got home, Doc came tearing out of the house, still holding his black bag and headed back down town.

I went inside but I didn't go into the bedroom. The door was open and I heard Papa say, "I'm sorry I had to break my promise to you but I never should have made it. You wouldn't have asked me to if it hadn't been for Aunt Minnie. She tried to bust us up in Denver and she's trying it again, scaring you into going to bed and sending for the doc and maybe causing Luke to die because Doc had to leave him."

I peeked through the door. Mamma was in bed and she was crying. I jerked back real quick because Papa had hold of Aunt Minnie's shoulders and was pushing her toward the door. They didn't see me. Aunt Minnie was too scared and Papa was too mad.

When they got out into the parlor, Papa said, "I've put up with your cussedness because of Laura but I'm done. You're leaving on the midnight train. You're a mean old woman who never had a man and so you think there's something wrong with Laura loving me and me loving her. The only thing wrong is you. Now you pack up and get out of here."

Aunt Minnie climbed the stairs to her room real fast. Papa went back into the bedroom and got down on his knees beside the bed. I peeked through the door again and heard him say, "I love you, Laura. All I want is to have our home away from your father and Aunt Minnie. I'm not the only one that loves you here in Antioch. Luke told Doc to come to you. Maybe he's bled to death by now but he wouldn't have cared. You came first to him just like you did to me and Doc. To everybody, I guess." He kind of choked up, then he said, "You wouldn't have been scared of having babies if it wasn't for your Aunt Minnie. You've got to stop it. Lots of women have babies."

Papa leaned over and kissed her. "You don't really care about me? I mean, you aren't mad because I had to kill a man?"

"No, Jim," Mamma said. "You go find out how Luke is. I guess I can be as brave as he was tonight."

Well, Aunt Minnie left and Uncle Luke got well and Mamma had the baby a month later. That's how my sister happened to be named First Merrybelle Dorcas. She was the first baby born in Antioch, you see, so Papa got those lots and he built a big, fine hardware store on them.

It was a whole year before I found out there wasn't anything to that cabbage-patch business. That was when Mamma had another baby. She named him Luke Mattingly Dorcas and Mamma wasn't scared any more. She didn't even worry, Papa said, and I guess he was just about the happiest man in the whole camp. He's going to build another room on the back of the house. This one's going to be a girl, he says, to keep First Merrybelle company.

The O'Keefe Luck

The night was a dark one, with a heavy overcast covering the stars, so John O'Keefe heard Dave coming long before he saw him. He called to Mrs. Hascall, his housekeeper. "Get Dave's supper ready. He's riding in." He stepped off the porch and crossed the yard to the corral, the uneasiness that had been steadily growing in him becoming intolerable.

O'Keefe waited by the corral gate; he heard the incoming beat of Dave's horse's hoofs on the county road, the call of some night bird over the river to the west, the bursts of laughter and loud talk from the bunkhouse where a poker game was in progress. The sounds were familiar ones, but he was hardly conscious of them.

A question that had been nagging him for hours left no room in his mind for anything else. Had he sent his boy to do a man's job? Or would the boy become a man when the chips were down? Would the O'Keefe luck hold for Dave, too? He didn't know.

John O'Keefe was sixty-two. The good, green years were behind him. He could not recall them. Actually he had no desire to do so. He had lived the kind of life he wanted. If he had the years to live over, he would have made few if any changes. His decisions, the major ones at least, had been right. He didn't believe in luck as such, although it was a word he liked to use. He did believe a man made his own luck, and that was exactly what he had done.

The future was something else. O'Keefe knew what he was, a relic from an era that was nearly gone. The future belonged to Dave. He did not see things the way his father did and that was good. Growing up in an age of barbed wire, railroads, and homesteads, Dave did not approve of the direct and violent ways which had made the O'Keefe luck what it was.

Probably Dave would survive in these days when individualism was a thing of the past, when compromise was the rule and half a loaf was better than no bread at all. John O'Keefe had never been one to compromise. He never had and he never would. Maybe it was time he turned the outfit over to Dave, but his doubts lingered. Was Dave man enough to run the OK? Well, he would soon know, O'Keefe thought.

Dave swung off the county road and reined up at the corral gate. As he dismounted, O'Keefe asked, "You all right, son?"

"Sure," Dave said, surprised. "Why wouldn't I be?"

"No reason, I guess," O'Keefe said, and let it go at that. He would not ask how it had gone. Dave would tell him in his own good time.

Dave stripped gear from his horse and turned him into the corral. They walked to the house together, O'Keefe saying, "Mrs. Hascall kept your supper warm. I told her you were coming when I heard your horse, so I reckon she'll have it ready."

"Good," Dave said, and went into the house and on back to the kitchen where he washed at the sink, then sat down at the table.

Mrs. Hascall brought his supper from the warming oven and he began to eat with the ravenous appetite of the young and hungry. O'Keefe sat down across from Dave and rolled and lighted a cigarette.

"You want a cup of coffee, Mr. O'Keefe?" Mrs. Hascall asked.

"No," he said.

It irritated him that coffee kept him awake if he drank it this late in the evening. He was more than irritated when he remembered the gallons of strong, black coffee he had drunk at all times of the night beside a roundup campfire when he was Dave's age. It had never kept him awake then. The fact that it did now was another proof that the good years were gone.

Not that he needed additional proof. The rheumatism that gripped him during rainy spells and made it misery to even step into the saddle was all the proof a man needed. He was like an old horse that should be shot or put out to pasture, but he wasn't ready for either.

"If there's nothing else you need, I'll go to bed," Mrs. Hascall said.

"Sure, go ahead," Dave said. "Thanks for keeping my supper warm."

"Glad to," Mrs. Hascall said, and left the kitchen.

O'Keefe finished his cigarette and rose, and going to the stove, lifted a lid and tossed his stub into the flames. He turned and stood waiting until Dave finished eating. He was a big man, but Dave would be even bigger in another year or so when he filled out. O'Keefe had a rough-featured, craggy face; Dave resembled him except that his chin wasn't quite as strong, his nose not quite as sharp.

O'Keefe had learned long ago that it was important to look the part of a ruthless cattle baron if that was what you aimed to be, and O'Keefe had aimed to be exactly that from the time he had been Dave's age and had brought a herd of cattle from California to this lush Oregon valley.

But you had to do more than look the part. O'Keefe had done that, too. He had killed five men in the forty-one years since he had started the OK here on Buckshot River. Besides the five, he and his men had hunted down and hanged three horse thieves and seven cattle rustlers. These, of course, were in addition to the Indians he had shot during the Piute-Bannock War over thirty years ago. That had been his way of meeting opposition; it was what had made the O'Keefe luck.

None of these killings had caused him to lose a moment's sleep. They had all been justified in his eyes. Killing had been the natural way of the times. A man did not survive without killing. Now, according to Dave, a man didn't survive if he killed.

The boy might be right, O'Keefe thought, for law had come to the Buckshot along with homesteads and the railroad, law that was not O'Keefe law. Sheriff Ira Tate was a homesteader man who would like nothing better than to drop a noose around O'Keefe's neck.

Still, O'Keefe wasn't sure Dave was right. You couldn't lie down and play dead when the wolves were yapping at your heels. It wouldn't do any good to make a complaint to Tate. There had been a day when the sheriff's office and the courts were tucked into John O'Keefe's pocket, but that day was gone.

So what was there to do? Dave had no answer. That was the reason O'Keefe had sent him out this afternoon. You had to do more than look tough; you had to be tough, and O'Keefe had never been sure that Dave had the substance as well as the appearance. You controlled luck or luck controlled you. It was that simple.

Dave yawned. He rolled and lighted a cigarette, then he said, "This

Sam Runyan is a tough bird. Your bluff didn't work. I didn't think it would."

O'Keefe had ordered Runyan to get off OK range by sundown, July 31st. Today was the 31st. O'Keefe knew Runyan was a tough bird the first time he had seen the man. He couldn't prove it, but he'd been convinced right along that the homesteaders couldn't let well enough alone. They were afraid of John O'Keefe and the OK, so the way he figured, they'd sent for a hardcase to come to the valley with a covered wagon and a woman who posed as his wife and pretended to be just another family of homesteaders.

In reality Runyan was making a test to see if the OK was as tough as it had been in the days before Ira Tate had started wearing the star. Right there was the pinch, but Dave didn't seem to realize it. Once the OK let a man settle on its range and he made it stick, more would come in a flood, and John O'Keefe's forty years of work would be gone. That first man was the important one, and right now he was Sam Runyan.

"So he's still there," O'Keefe said softly.

"He's there and aims to stay," Dave said. "He claims it's time we woke up and realized we can't go on blocking off 10,000 acres of public domain. He's right, Pa. In the long run, I mean."

"The hell he is. I suppose you want to tear our fences down and invite the buzzards in?"

Dave laughed. "No, I didn't figure on inviting them. I'm going to town in the morning and see Tate. We can get Runyan for trespassing. He cut our fence and crossed a mile of our land. He can't deny it, so Tate will have to move him."

"Tate won't do it," O'Keefe said. "He knows who voted him into office."

Dave rose. "Sure he knows, but he likewise knows his job and he knows the law. Sooner or later the grangers will get a government man in here and we'll be ordered to give access to the land we don't own, but they can't get the job done by cutting our fences and crossing our land anywhere they take a notion. You'll see." He yawned again. "Well, I'm going to hit the hay. Good night, Pa."

"Good night, Dave."

O'Keefe waited until he heard Dave's steps on the stairs and his bedroom door close, then he picked up the lamp and, leaving the kitchen, crossed the living room to his office. He set the lamp on the desk and looked around the cluttered room. Here were forty years' gatherings: bits of leather, old ledgers and tally books, legal documents, boxes of cartridges, and an assortment of guns. When Dave took over, the first thing he'd do would be to clean the room up and throw half of this stuff away.

O'Keefe picked up the picture of his dead wife. He shook his head and put it down again. Funny how his life had fallen into three periods of approximately twenty years each: twenty years of growing up in California, twenty years of working and shoving and fighting to make the OK what it was today and being too busy to get married, and the last twenty years of marriage and raising Dave and hoping like hell that the boy was tough enough to hold the OK together. The middle twenty was the period that had established the O'Keefe luck, the years that had made folks afraid to buck the OK and afraid to cross John O'Keefe.

His wife had died last year. He had never fully understood her and her soft ways any more than she had understood him and his hard ways, but they had loved each other and they had been reasonably happy. Folks had always treated her with respect. He had seen to that.

O'Keefe found it hard to even think about love. Hating had always been easier for him than loving. When it got down to cases, he guessed he had never loved anyone in his life except his wife and Dave. He couldn't do anything more for her, but he could do something for Dave; he could leave him the OK just as it was, a big, sprawling ranch with 10,000 head of cattle, the biggest spread in this corner of Oregon. More than that, he could give Dave an illustration of what he had to do to hold the ranch together.

He turned to the map on the wall. He knew it by heart; he could draw it on another piece of paper with his back to the wall map. The county road that followed the river for miles, the double line of quarter sections belonging to him that lined both sides of the road running north and south, and the second line that formed the top of the T and ran east and west from the high shoulder of Horn Mountain clean across the valley to the rimrock on the other side.

Years ago O'Keefe had had his buckaroos file on these claims and prove up on them, then he had bought the land from them. It had been legal enough, and he was within his rights when he had fenced both sides of the road and the north edge of the OK range.

O'Keefe had been all right as long as he had been able to keep his man in the sheriff's office. But now . . . ! He turned his back to the map. The fact that Dave was foolish enough to think he could get anything out of Ira Tate was what bothered him.

O'Keefe had killed men before there was a county and a sheriff to call on. After that he had used the law to do what he had been forced to do himself. Now that he could not longer use the law, he had to go back to the old ways. He had no choice.

Maybe Dave could hold the OK together, maybe not, but one thing was sure. A dead man was the kind of grim warning that would keep the live ones in line for a long time. It had always worked; it still would. Human nature hadn't changed, even with barbed wire, railroads, and a crowd of homesteaders. He had no cause to worry about being convicted of murder. There was always the O'Keefe luck.

He picked up his Winchester, filled the magazine, then dropped a box of ammunition into his pocket. He was surprised at the way the talk had gone in the kitchen. Dave seemed to think it was his place to do something about Runyan.

In one way that was good. He was assuming his responsibility, he was no longer a boy. But he hadn't been man enough to put a bullet into Runyan. That was what disappointed O'Keefe and showed him that Dave wasn't ready to take the OK over. Maybe he never would be.

O'Keefe left the house, saddled his horse and, mounting, took the county road, riding north. He would reach Runyan's camp just about dawn. Two hours later he opened a gate, rode through it, and closed it, then struck off across the grass.

An hour later with the gray of first dawn lifting the night from the valley, he made out Runyan's covered wagon ahead of him. Beside it Runyan squatted over a small fire. The man didn't turn as O'Keefe rode up, although he must have heard him.

This struck O'Keefe as strange, so strange that he levered a shell into the chamber and eased back the hammer.

He said, "You were told to be off OK range by sundown of last night, Runyan. Turn around. I don't like to shoot a man in the back."

Runyan turned, moving very fast, his revolver in his right hand. He fired, the bullet passing close to the side of O'Keefe's face. He let go with his Winchester, as much by instinct as intent, for he had not expected this. In that one brittle instant he had been a fool for not expecting it. Dave had said Runyan was a tough bird and O'Keefe had known it all the time.

Fool or not, the O'Keefe luck held. His bullet smashed into Runyan's chest and knocked him flat. His right hand went slack and he dropped his revolver. O'Keefe rode toward him, keeping him covered. The job was finished. He turned his horse and rode away. His bullet had caught Runyan squarely in the chest and must have killed him instantly.

Now O'Keefe was weak with a strange and disturbing sense of relief. He realized how far he had gone back in the years since he had lived by the gun, protecting the OK in his own hard and ruthless way, making the O'Keefe luck what it had been through the years.

The sun was up when he met Dave who was riding north on the county road. O'Keefe said, "Runyan's gone." Dave gave him a long, searching look. O'Keefe added sharply, "Come on back with me. You've got to get those heifers moved off the lower field today. You should have done it last week."

Dave nodded and swung his horse around. "I know," he said.

O'Keefe spent the day on the front porch waiting for Tate. The homesteaders knew that yesterday had been the deadline for Runyan to get off OK range, so somebody would trespass today to see if he was still there, probably the sheriff himself.

O'Keefe didn't have anything to worry about. There had been killings for which he might legally have been hanged, but they had been a long time ago. This was a strange twist, he thought. He'd had every intention of shooting Runyan down in cold blood, but the homesteader had tried to shoot him first. Any way you looked at it, O'Keefe had killed in self-defense.

At four o'clock Tate rode into the yard. He was a big man, as big as O'Keefe, and he had hated O'Keefe as long as he had been in the county just as O'Keefe hated him for winning the last election. Now Tate said, "You're under arrest for the murder of Sam Runyan. Saddle up. I'm taking you to town. You'll hang for this one certain."

O'Keefe's lips made a tight grin. "You're wrong, Tate. I rode out there to kick him off OK range. His deadline was last night, but he hadn't gone. When I rode up, he had his back to me. He whirled and took a shot at me. I guess he'd have got me if he hadn't been moving so fast, but it turned out I got him."

Tate shook his head. "That's a hell of a poor story for you to tell and I'm surprised you even tried it. You've run roughshod over people in this valley for years. Nobody but you know how many men you've killed. Some say as high as ten. You was born to hang, O'Keefe, and the sorry part of this mess is that you didn't hang for the first one you smoked down."

Angry, O'Keefe said, "Tate, even if you are a homesteader sheriff, you can't just come in here and arrest me because you like the idea. I admit I shot Runyan, but it was in self-defense, I told you."

"You're a liar, O'Keefe, and the jury will call you a liar. All you had to do was to come to me and charge Runyan with trespassing which he done and for cutting fence which he done, and I'd have moved him off your range. I wouldn't have liked it, but I'd have done it because he was guilty on both counts. That's what Dave would have done because he's got some brains in his head, but not you. You had to take care of it yourself and to hell with the law. This is the last time you'll try it because I promise you that you'll hang."

Staring at the lawman's dark face, his narrowed eyes, the thin-lipped expression of implacable hatred, John O'Keefe was suddenly afraid. It was the first time in his life he could remember being afraid, like this, anyway. He realized again he had gone back a long ways these last years, or he'd have had his Winchester in his hands and he'd have kept Tate covered from the time he turned off the road.

"I told you it was self-defense. You can't prove. . . ."

"You bet we can. Runyan's wife was in the wagon and she saw the whole thing. You should have killed her, too, O'Keefe. I never heard you were a woman killer, but I wouldn't put it past you. She says you rode up, shot Runyan, and rode off. She says you didn't say a word and Runyan didn't have a gun."

O'Keefe stared at Tate, his head tipped back, sweat running down his face. Sure, he had known the good, green years were behind him, but he wanted to live out the ones that were left; he didn't want to die. For John O'Keefe to hang . . . ! He had known Runyan had a wife, but he had completely forgotten about her. He had never thought of looking in the wagon. He should have killed her. It would have been the only sure way of being safe. Now she could go to court and lie him right into the gallows.

They'd never hang O'Keefe. Not all the homesteaders in the world could do that. Or the barbed wire or the railroad. He wheeled and ran headlong toward the house. His Winchester leaned against the wall. If the O'Keefe luck held long enough for him to get his hands on it, Ira Tate wouldn't be riding back to the county seat.

Tate's bullet caught him between the shoulder blades before he had covered half the distance. He stumbled and fell forward into a long spiraling tunnel that was without bottom. Before he reached complete blackness, the thought came to him that Dave would succeed in holding the OK together because he didn't believe in the O'Keefe luck. Then the blackness was all around John O'Keefe.

Beecher Island

Sam Burdick had no notion of passing time. All he knew was that the sun was well above the eastern rim of the prairie and the morning was beginning to lose its chill. Only an hour ago, or maybe it had been two, he was camped with the rest of Forsyth's civilian scouts on the bank of the Dry Fork of the Republican when the Indians had tried to stampede the horses and failed. Minutes later the Indians had appeared by the hundreds as suddenly as if they had sprouted out of the ground.

Someone had yelled, "Get to the island," and the scouts had plunged pell-mell across the sandy, nearly dry bed of the stream to an island that was covered by brush and weeds. Sam had heard the command above the frantic commotion, "Dig in! Dig in!" That was exactly what they had done, dug in with butcher knives and tin plates and anything they could use while Indian bullets and arrows swept over their heads.

The scouts' horses were shot down; now and then a man was hit. The Indians had attacked and had been beaten off, but they would come again. No one had told Sam that they would, but he was as sure of it as he was sure of death and taxes.

The old mountain man, Bill Smith, lay behind his dead horse in the pit next to Sam. A bullet had slashed a bloody furrow across Smith's skull, but he had wrapped a bandanna around his head and kept on fighting.

The only firing now was from the Indian sharpshooters who were hiding in the tall grass along the banks, and the answering shots from a few scouts who were equally well hidden in the brush on the low end of the island.

Now that there was this lull in the fighting, Sam had time to draw a deep breath and look at the sky and wonder why he was here. Sure, he was like the others in one way. He felt he was doing something that had to be done.

The Cheyennes had swept across the western end of Kansas, burning and torturing and killing, and they had to be punished. There weren't enough soldiers to do the job in the skeleton army that survived the Civil War, so General Sheridan had told Colonel Forsyth to enlist fifty civilian scouts and see what he could do with the Cheyennes.

They had set out to find Indians and punish them. Well, they had succeeded in finding them, succeeded too well. They'd found hundreds, maybe a thousand, so now it was a question of who was going to punish whom. It was even a question of whether any of the scouts would live to leave the island with odds like this.

"They ain't pushing us right now," Sam said, and then, although he knew better, he asked, "Figure we whipped 'em?"

"Hell, no," the mountain man answered. "They'll hit us again purty soon. We ain't seen hide nor hair o' Roman Nose, and when we do, we'll know it."

Sam closed his eyes, his pulse pounding in his temples. He pressed hard against the body of Sam's dead horse, which lay between him and the edge of the island. You do something like joining the scouts because it's your duty, but there were other reasons, too.

Maybe you're bored by the monotony of farm life or you want to be a hero, or maybe you're in trouble with the law and this is one way you can keep ahead of the sheriff. Or maybe, and Sam guessed this was the most important reason, you see a chance to pick up a few dollars at a time when dollars in central Kansas were about as hard to find as feathers on a fish.

With Sam it had been a proposition of needing the dollars. At the time the farm work wasn't pressing. Still, he hadn't figured on this kind of fight. One scout, William Wilson, had been killed, and several others including Colonel Forsyth were wounded.

Someone holed up in the middle of the island called, "If you men on the outside don't do a little shooting, them red devils will be on top of us again."

"That feller's a fool," Smith said in disgust. "He better git over here and do some o' the shooting he's talkin' about."

Two of the scouts, McCall and Culver, were needled into action by the man who had yelled. They raised up to locate an Indian to shoot at. Smith bellowed, "Git down," but he was too late. One of the sharpshooters shot Culver through the head and caught McCall in the shoulder.

Smith swore bitterly. "Every time we lose a man, we cut down our chances of knocking 'em back on their heels the next time they charge us." He motioned toward the bluffs. "There's the old boy hisself. I knowed Roman Nose would be in it sooner or later. He's got more fight savvy than any other Injun I know."

Quickly Sam rose up to see what was happening and dropped flat again. He'd had time to see hundreds of mounted braves gathered at the foot of the bluffs out of rifle range. One big brave who was wearing a red sash around his waist was haranguing them and making wild gestures as if he was furious over something.

"It was a good thing for us Roman Nose wasn't in on the start of this ruckus," Smith said, "or they'd have grabbed the island afore we got it. The trouble with Injuns is that they want to count coup so bad that even a good fightin' man like Roman Nose don't have no luck gettin' 'em to foller orders."

"How many do you figure are out there?" Sam asked.

"Maybe a thousand," Smith answered, "though it's hard to say for sure, with some of 'em hidin' in the grass and sharpshootin' the way they are. Damn that Forsyth! I tried to tell him yesterday we was follerin' a big party, but you can't never tell an Army man nuthin'."

"Are they all Cheyennes?"

"Mostly, but there's some Oglalas with 'em. Arapahoes, too, chances are, though I ain't spotted any yet."

An arrow flashed over Sam's head, and a moment later a bullet hit the body of his horse with a sodden *thwack*. He dug his nose into the sand, then realized he'd be no good to anyone if he remained in this position.

He raised his head to look and dropped back quickly, puzzled by what he saw. The mounted braves were riding downstream toward a bend in the creek below the island. There didn't seem to be any sense in this maneuver, but the warriors were undoubtedly following Roman Nose's orders. If Smith was right about the great Cheyenne's fighting savvy, there must be very good logic back of what the Indians were doing.

Again there was a momentary lull in the firing. A bugle sounded from somewhere among the Indians, surprising and shocking Sam. He asked, "Where in tunket would a Cheyenne learn to toot a bugle? And where would they find one?"

"They'd find one easy enough," Smith said. "Kill a bunch of soldiers and you get yourself a bugle. Tootin' one's something else. But I don't figger it was an Injun. Chances are one o' William Bent's sons is out yonder with 'em. Some of 'em have turned renegade, and it wouldn't be so hard for one of 'em to have learned a bugle afore he left Fort Bent."

"Looks to me like they're riding downstream," Sam said. "I don't see any reason for that."

"Kind o' funny about Injuns," Smith continued, apparently not hearing what Sam had said. "Now there was Fetterman, who got massacreed by Red Cloud. I'll bet you that right now Roman Nose is thinkin' about what happened to Fetterman and he's tellin' hisself that if he can give us the same treatment, he'll be great like Red Cloud."

Sam had been paying little attention to Smith. He was still puzzling over the reason for the movement downstream, and now a possible explanation came to him. He asked, "You think Roman Nose is taking them downstream to get them lined up for a charge?"

"Downstream?" Smith bellowed, and sat up to get a quick look. He got his head back a second before a bullet whizzed above him. "That'n was a mite close," he said as if he had been annoyed by a passing mosquito.

Sam grinned, thinking he couldn't have been that calm about it. But then the mountain man had been ducking bullets longer than Sam Burdick had been alive.

"Well sir, I'll tell you what you'd better do," Smith said thoughtfully. "The colonel ain't one to listen to me. I ain't his official scout, and Sharp Grover is. One thing's sure. Grover ain't gonna listen to anything I say neither. But Forsyth oughtta be told what them damn brownskins are doin'.''

"Grover's probably told him," Sam said.

"Mebbe so, mebbe not," Smith said. "Just the same, you'd better make a worm out o' yourself and git over there to the colonel and tell him. If we ain't fixed to roll 'em back, they'll roll over us. That's as sartin as there's sin in hell."

"I'll try to get to him," Sam said, and slid out of the shallow trench he had dug behind the body of his horse.

He snaked through the grass, hoping he had time to reach Forsyth. He moved slowly, his body flat against the ground, pushing himself forward with his hands and feet. Once a burst of firing lashed out from the low end of the island. Sam stopped until it was over. Jack Stillwell was hiding there in the tall grass with two older scouts. The three were the best shots in the command.

Sam felt good just remembering they were there. Stillwell was very young, younger even than Sam, but he was not a farm boy. Even though he was still in his teens, he had the reputation of being one of the best scouts on the frontier. Although it had seemed incredible, Sam had heard that Stillwell had once guided a wagon train when he was only twelve. Now that he knew Stillwell, he could believe it.

He went on, still keeping low. He felt as if he were moving at a snail's pace, but he had not been far from Forsyth's trench when he started. Now, not certain where he was, he called, "Colonel."

"Here," Forsyth answered.

Another minute was all it took Sam to reach Forsyth. He saw that the man was suffering. He kept biting his lower lip against the pain that racked his body; sweat made a shiny film across his forehead. Suddenly it occurred to Sam that the colonel was a soldier all the way down to his boot heels, and if they lived through this fight, it would be Forsyth who brought them through.

"Can't the doctor do anything for you?" Sam asked.

"Dr. Mooers has suffered a head wound and will not live through the day," Forsyth said. "To make our situation worse, we lost all our medical supplies. We left them in camp when we headed for the island. Of course it's impossible for us to get them now. By the time we have a chance to go after them, the Indians will have carried them off."

Sam considered this, wondering how anyone could have been careless enough to go off and leave the medical supplies. This, plus the loss of the doctor, could be a fatal blow if the battle lasted any length of time. With the possible exception of the officers, Forsyth and Beecher, the scouts could not have lost a man who would be missed as much as Dr. Mooers.

"Was there something you wanted to say?" Forsyth asked.

"Yes," Sam said. "I wasn't sure whether you knew or not, but the Indians are drifting downstream toward the bend. Bill Smith and me figure Roman Nose will lead a charge against us as soon as he gets them lined out."

"We're whipped if they run over us," Forsyth said. "They'll trample us to death or shoot us." He hesitated a moment, then called, "Beecher, get ready to repel an attack. It's up to you to see that all the men have their rifles and revolvers loaded. Take the guns of the dead men and the badly wounded and see that the scouts on the low end of the island have them."

Sam crawled back toward his trench, momentarily exposing himself as he left Forsyth's pit. He lay motionless for a few seconds in the tall weeds, thankful he had not been hit, then went on. A minute or so later he was back in his own trench.

"The doc's hard hit and expected to die before night," Sam said. "What's almost as bad is the loss of our medical supplies. They were left in camp this morning."

Smith shrugged at the news. He said, "Well, that whittles down our chances a little more. All we need now is to run out of ammunition, and Roman Nose has got us."

A moment later Sam heard the command, "Load up. Hold your fire till you're given the order."

"Look at 'em come," Smith said, his voice holding a note of admiration. "If I was where I could see this but knowed my hair was gonna stay on my head, I'd say it was a real purty sight."

Sam nodded agreement. In an oblique sort of way he admired the Indians. They were a people fighting for their homes against impossible odds. Now, easing up so he could look over the top of his dead horse, he saw the Indians sweep up the creek. For the time being the sharpshooters' fire had died, so it seemed safe to keep his head up.

Sam's heart began to pound as he watched the great mass of riders gallop up the stream toward the island, sixty wide and eight deep, Roman Nose in the front rank. Then Sam reminded himself it was no time to feel compassion for the Indians. They would kill him as readily as they had killed his saddle horse if they could.

The deadly cold that had nested in the pit of his stomach spread through his belly as his sweaty hands tightened on the Spencer. The Indians were fighting for their homes, but he, Sam Burdick, and his friends Bill Smith and the rest of the scouts, were fighting for their lives.

The Indians swept on up the creek, the painted braves naked except for their moccasins and breechclouts and cartridge belts. They rode bareback, their horse-hair ropes knotted around the middle of their ponies so that it went over their knees. They gripped their horses' manes with their left hand, their rifles held above their heads in their right hands.

Unexpectedly the Indians pulled up just out of rifle range, the sudden silence bringing a tension to Sam's taut nerves that seemed more than he could bear. Again Forsyth shouted, "Hold your fire until I give the order."

Roman Nose had swung out of line to face his men. He talked to them briefly; then he turned back to the scouts and shook his fist at them. He tipped his head and let out a great war cry, hitting his mouth with his hand. Sam, crouched there in his pit, felt a chill travel down his spine. He had never heard such a sound in all his life, a sound he would not forget as long as he lived.

They came on again at a gallop, the long lines as perfect as those of a well-trained drill team. Sam kept his gaze on Roman Nose. *Cruel and brutal*, Sam thought, *but certainly a magnificent physical specimen.* He was big, six feet three or more, and unusually muscular for an Indian. He sat astride his great chestnut horse with perfect balance; his war bonnet was beautiful, the curved buffalo horns just above his forehead, the eagle and heron feathers floating behind him.

Now the sharpshooters opened up from the grass, bullets whistling past Sam's head. Smith said, "They're just figgerin' on keepin' us down, but it won't last long. They'll have to stop shootin' in a minute, or they'll plug their own men."

Smith was right. The firing stopped; the bugle sounded its clear, sharp call as it rang out into the war cries of the charging avalanche of painted warriors.

"Now," Forsyth called.

An instant later Beecher picked up the order, "Now."

The volley made an ear-hammering roar as powder flame lashed out from the Spencers, the bullets tearing great holes in the front rank of the Indians as men and horses fell. They closed ranks and came on . Roman Nose was still in the front, yelling his frightening war cry and holding his rifle above his head.

Another volley and a third and a fourth. Far out on the left flank a medicine man was knocked off his horse. Sam, squeezing off another shot, thought for an instant the charge was broken, but once more they closed ranks and swept on, the prarie grass behind them littered with dead and wounded men and horses.

They were almost to the island now, charging straight into the death-dealing fury of the Spencers. A fifth volley and a sixth, and then Roman Nose was knocked off his horse, the medicine that had brought him through so may savage fights failing him at last.

The big warrior was the key to the charge, the very heart of the attack. When he fell, the charge stopped as if it had rolled up against an impenetrable wall. One more volley, and even in the face of this leaden death the Indians picked Roman Nose up and carried him off the battlefield.

Sam jumped to his feet with the rest of the scouts who could stand, all yelling and emptying their revolvers at the Indians, who were racing away across the prairie. A handful of braves had reached the lower end of the island. If they had come on . . . if Roman Nose had not fallen, they would have overrun the island, and the scouts would have been trampled to death just as Roman Nose had planned.

Sam had been surprised to find himself on his feet, his empty revolver in his hand as he cheered with the rest. This was not like him, but now he felt a great wave of pride engulf him, pride because he was a member of this body of scouts, pride because they had fought hard enough to stay alive, pride in having the courage it took to stay and keep firing in the face of five hundred horsemen who wanted only to kill him and his fellow scouts.

"Get down," Forsyth yelled. "Lie down."

And Beecher, "Get down or you'll have your heads blown off."

Smith reached over and yanked Sam back into his pit just as the sharpshooters opened up once more from the grass, raking the entire island with a vicious, deadly fire. Sam lay in his trench and reloaded his Spencer and revolver, thinking briefly of the insanity of war, of the squaws who loved the Indians who had fallen just as much as some white women loved the scouts who had died since the first dawn attack, just as his own mother loved him.

He lay on his back, the hot morning sun hammering down on him. The powder smoke that had been a drifting cloud above the island was gone now, its acrid smell still lingering in Sam's nostrils. Then it came to him. This was the best the Indians could do. They would never do any better.

He would walk away from this island, he told himself; he would be back on the farm in time to help his father harvest his corn.

Steel To The West

My name is Jim Glenn. I had come to Cheyenne months ago—when it was no more than a collection of tents and shacks—knowing the Union Pacific would soon reach it. I believed in the future of Cheyenne, so I invested everything I had in town lots and was building on one of them.

I had heard that steel would reach Cheyenne on November 13, 1867. After breakfast that morning I told my girl Cherry Owens and my preacher friend Frank Rush that it was a historic occasion and we'd better be down there somewhere along the grade and watch the spectacle. That was exactly what we did. Frank's wife Nancy came along.

Cherry was running a restaurant at the time and had all the business she could handle, so she was reluctant to leave, but I told her every man and his dog would be standing somewhere beside the grade watching the rails being laid and she might just as well enjoy the show. Besides, she wouldn't have any business if she stayed in her restaurant all day. When we arrived, we found that I was right. Every man and his dog was there, particularly the dogs.

We weren't disappointed. Laying the rails was the most interesting show I had ever seen, and the others agreed. The surveyors, bridge builders, and graders were all working miles west of Cheyenne. There had been some Indian trouble, even though soldiers out of Fort D. A. Russell near Cheyenne were constantly patrolling the route the railroad would take.

Most of the men employed by the Union Pacific were Civil War veterans who worked with their guns close at hand, but still we were constantly hearing of Indian trouble—particularly with the surveyors who had to work far out ahead of everyone else. They were the most likely to get killed, and many of them were.

The Casement brothers, General Jack and Dan, were responsible for laying the track, and much of the grading, too. Jack Casement had been a general during the War and had put together a well-organized, disciplined group of men. Most of them were Irish, a tough, brawling, hard-working bunch who would have been hard for anyone else to manage, but the Casements handled them well.

As we stood in the crowd and watched the rails being laid, I was amazed at the proficiency and speed with which the job was done. A light car pulled by one horse came up to the end of steel, the car loaded with rails. Two men grabbed the end of a rail. Other men took hold of the rail by twos, and when it was clear of the car, all of them went forward on the run.

At exactly the right second someone yelled a command to drop the rail. They did, being careful to put it into place right side up. Another gang of men was doing exactly the same thing on the other side of the track. I held my watch on them several times and noted that it took about thirty seconds per rail.

The instant the car was empty it was tipped to one side while the next loaded one moved up, then the empty car was driven back for another load, the horse galloping as if the devil was right on his tail. The gougers, spikers, and bolters kept close on the heels of the men dropping the rails.

Just a few minutes watching these men gave me an admiration for them I had never felt for a group of laborers before. I had not seen anything like it, and I never saw anything like it afterwards. It was cooperation to a T.

Then the thought came to me that I would make a fortune out of the lots I'd bought and the buildings I was putting up, and I owed it all to these men who were laying the rails and spiking them into place along with the graders and bridge builders and surveyors.

Of course, I really owed something to the Union Pacific company and General Dodge who headed the operation and the Casement brothers, but the men on top were making good money whereas the Irishmen who did the sweating and ran the danger of getting an Indian bullet in their briskets weren't getting rich.

There was a hell of a lot of banging as the end of the steel moved past us. I did some quick calculating as I watched: Three strokes to the spike. I counted ten spikes to the rail. Somewhere I had heard it took four hundred rails for a mile of track. About that time I quit calculating, but one thing was sure. Those sledges were going to swing a lot of times before the line was finished between Omaha and Sacramento.

We walked back to Cherry's restaurant in a kind of daze. The whole operation was incredible. Sherman Hill lay west of Cheyenne, then the desert that offered a different kind of resistance, with the Wasatch mountains on beyond the desert. Of course the Central Pacific with its Chinese labor had a worse kind of terrain to cover, with the Sierra an almost impenetrable wall.

Cherry invited us to dinner. Her hired woman, who had stayed behind, had the meal almost ready by the time we got there. We ate hurriedly, having heard the first train to Cheyenne would arrive that afternoon. The whole town would be down there beside the tracks to welcome it.

It was the day we had been waiting for, but still I had an uneasy feeling in the pit of my stomach every time I thought about an offer I'd turned down recently for my property. A thousand dollars was a lot! I'd paid a fraction of that, so it would have meant one hell of a big profit. I thought we hadn't reached the peak yet, so I'd said no, but I wasn't much of a gambler, and now I wasn't sure whether I'd made a mistake or not.

I'd heard plenty about Julesburg, the end-of-track town to the east of us. It had been on the boom for months. Early in the summer—or maybe it had been late in the spring—there had been only about fifty people in Julesburg. By the end of July it had exploded to about four thousand, with streets of mud or dust—depending on when it had rained last.

The prices the merchants had charged for their goods were outrageous. Apparently it was the grab for money that had made Julesburg the hell hole it had been, but it was the absence of law and order that worried me. I think all the businessmen of Cheyenne felt the way I did and had no intentions of letting the same thing happen here. Still there was the question of what we could do about it.

Julesburg had had more than its share of whore houses, dance halls, gambling places and saloons. The women, it was said, walked around town with derringers carried on their hips. They would rob a man by putting something in his drink, but he would not be allowed to take proper measures against them after he came to.

One reporter wrote that Julesburg had people who would kill a man for five dollars. I believed it. Dead men had been found in the alley every day, their pockets emptied of whatever they had been carrying. The part I could not understand was the obvious fact that the people living in Julesburg were indifferent to what was going on.

All of this ran through my mind as I ate. I didn't say much to Cherry, sitting beside me at the counter, but the thought began nagging me that neither Cherry nor Nancy Rush would be safe if we allowed Cheyenne to go the way Julesburg had.

In the long run it was the good women like Nancy and Cherry who built the towns and brought civilization to the frontier, not the whores who too often worked hand in glove with the sneak thieves and murderers who had made Julesburg a literal hell. Now that Cheyenne was the end of track, Julesburg would cease to exist as a town. I knew exactly what would happen. The riffraff from Julesburg would move to Cheyenne.

I knew what most of my friends thought: A vigilance committee was the only answer. As we hurried back to the track, I wondered if they were right. A few minutes later when the train pulled in with the cars banging and the bell ringing and the whistle shrieking, I decided I'd better think about it some more. Maybe they were.

A man on the train yelled, "Gentlemen, I give you Julesburg." That wasn't any news to me. While everyone else was whooping and hollering as the passengers left the train, I stood there as if paralyzed.

Frank nudged me in the ribs. "What's the matter with you, Jim?" he asked.

I shook my head and came out of it right away. I managed a weak holler, but my heart wasn't in it. I could see that the train was carrying the frame shacks and tents that had made up most of Julesburg, along with the barroom equipment and gambling devices that had given Julesburg the reputation of being the most notorious sin city in the West.

Along with the railroad men, mule skinners, and hunters who were on the train, there were the whores and the pimps and professional gamblers and con men. Within a matter of hours the Cheyenne of today would be a city of sin that would match the Julesburg of yesterday. It struck me that this historic occasion was not what I had expected it to be. Certainly I was having second thoughts about it.

Cheyenne had planned a big celebration, with a platform for speakers and big signs that read "The Magic City of the Plain greets the transcontinental rail way" and "Old Casement we welcome you" and "Honor to whom honor is due." I wanted no part of it, and I wondered if progress always meant that you had to swallow the bitter with the sweet.

I'd had more than enough. I said, "Cherry, let's get out of here."

She nodded. As we walked back along Ferguson Street, she glanced at me and asked, "What's the matter, Jim?"

"It's funny how it is when you actually see something that you knew was coming," I said. "Cheyenne will be the hell on wheels that Julesburg has been. It scares me. Have you got a gun?"

"Yes," she said. "I knew this was coming and it scares me, too. I bought a pistol just the other day. I'll use it if I have to."

"Good," I said. "If you need any help, get word to me as fast as you can."

She laid a hand on my arm and squeezed it. "Thank you, Jim," she said.

I left her at the restaurant and went on home, more worried and upset than I wanted to admit. We had policemen, and we had a civilian auxiliary police force in which I had very little confidence. I knew damned well that our official law enforcers simply could not handle the number of toughs who had come in on that train. To make it worse, more would come. I had no doubt of that.

Frank Rush stopped in later and said it had been a festive day and wanted to know why I was so glum. I told him, adding, "If you're the kind of preacher who is looking for souls to save, a lot of them came in on the train today. I guess the people who have been in Cheyenne from the day the first settlers arrived aren't angels, but we've been pretty close compared to the riffraff that was on the train."

He frowned and scratched his chin thoughtfully, then he asked, "How do you know the train was carrying that kind?"

"I saw enough of them to know," I said. "All you had to do was to look at them to know what they were. Besides, we saw the stuff they were bringing in from Julesburg. I guess there isn't any way to keep the undesirables out, but we've got to control them once they get here."

He hadn't even thought of it, I guess. He was about like most of the Cheyenne people. He finally nodded and said as if only half convinced, "I guess you're right?"

"Has Nancy got a gun?" I asked. When he shook his head, I said sharply, "Damn it, Frank, get her one."

He nodded again and said, "I guess I will."

I didn't think he would. If one of those hardcases ever so much as touched his wife, I'd kill him if Frank didn't, but killing a man after it was too late wouldn't help Nancy.

I had another visitor that day after Frank left, a man who introduced himself as Jess Munro. He came after it was dark and for a moment I didn't know who he was. After he came inside and I saw him in the lamplight, I knew I had seen him around town, but I had never actually met him or talked with him.

He was about thirty, I judged, a dark-faced man with a black mustache and beard and black hair. His eyes were dark brown, his jaw square, the kind of jaw you'd expect to see on a forceful man. He was stocky in build with large hands and muscular shoulders. He'd be a hard man to whip, I told myself.

Munro carried himself with a straight-backed military stiffness that I associated with army men. I suspected he had been an officer during the war, probably on the Union side because his speech gave no hint that he was a Southerner. I had never seen him without a gun on his hip. He had one now, and I wondered about it because he claimed to be a real estate dealer and had an office on Ferguson Street.

He shook hands with me, his grip very strong. He pinned his gaze on my face as if making a judgment about me, then he said, "Some of your friends have told me you're a tough hand. I can believe it because I've seen how you handle yourself in fights. I think you'll do."

"Do for what?"

"You saw what the train brought in this afternoon," he said, ignoring my question. "Not that it had any surprises. The police can't do the job, even with the help of some of us who have been appointed law officers on a standby basis." Then he shrugged, and added, "I guess we would be of help in case of a riot, but that's about all."

I nodded as if I agreed, but I wasn't convinced the standby police would be of any help if the chips were down. Still, I had considered volunteering for police duty, in the hopes that something might be better than nothing.

When I told him I'd been thinking about volunteering, he said, "Good. Then you'll be willing to serve on the vigilance committee we're organizing. Several men, just four as a matter of fact, will serve as chiefs. That's why we want you. You'll have fifteen men under you to carry out any job that the central committee decides on. Will you do it?"

Here it was at last, laid out in the open. I had to make a decision now, one way or the other. I hesitated, looking straight at Jess Munro. I'd had doubts of the vigilantes for years, but I'd been worrying about the situation here for a long time, too. Something had to be done if Cheyenne was to be saved.

Still I hesitated, saying, "I've always been leery of vigilante rule. They operate outside the law. It can become mob law very easily."

"That's right," he said grimly. "That's why we're seeking men like you to be leaders. We intend to take steps to safeguard against that very thing. I have appointed myself chairman of the committee for the simple reason that I've had some experience with vigilance committees and I know the dangers. Of course I will be subject to removal by a majority of the committee."

He paused, scratching his chin, then added, "Glenn, damn it, we just don't have much time. The toughs will be in control of the town before we know it if we don't do something. We've got to get on the job and do it quick. I'll be surprised if we don't have two or three murders before morning. We've got to organize and stay organized as long as Cheyenne is an end-of-track town."

I realized then I had no choice, doubts or not. I had as much responsibility as any man, maybe more than some because I was aware of what would happen if we let things go. I had to become involved because I knew damned well that the average Cheyenne resident wouldn't, any more than the good men in Julesburg had.

"Fine," he said. "We're meeting in the hall over Miller's store tomorrow night at eight o'clock. Don't mention this to anyone. Just be there."

We shook hands again and he left. I still wasn't sure I had done right, mostly because there was no certainty that Jess Munro wouldn't

use the vigilance committee for his own purposes. But it was a chance
I had to take. Maybe it would be wrong to particpate in the vigilante
movement, but it would be more wrong to sit on my hind end and let
Cheyenne go to hell.

   We saved Cheyenne so that in time it really did become the Magic
City of the Plains. You know, during all the years that followed, as I
watched Cheyenne settle down from an end-of-track town to a solid
city with schools and churches and women and children, I was never
sorry about the decision I made that day when steel came to us from
the East.

The Wooing of Rosy Malone

I am not by nature a philosophical man, but I have often wondered about the part that fate plays in one's life. How much of our lives is determined by destiny, or how much depends on our decisions? Just being at a certain place at a certain time when a certain thing happens is the kind of thing I mean. My presence in Garnet when the Rawlins gang rode into town is a case in point.

My name is Jim Dance and I have a little spread a couple of miles south of Garnet. I own about fifty head of cattle, enough to scratch out a living along with the work I do for one of my neighbors. I've also planted an apple orchard and in another five years I should turn a profit. Of course I aim to build up my herd, too. I figure I'm about as well fixed as any young cowboy in the county.

I'm also in love with Rosy Malone, the Garnet schoolteacher, and I want to give her a comfortable life. The problem is she won't marry me. I thought she loved me and liked my place. She came out every week or so to clean it up and she always cooked a big meal for me when she was there, so I had trouble figuring out why she wouldn't marry me.

Rosy had other men chasing her, so she had plenty of choice, but I always thought I had the inside track. She'd give me phony excuses for saying no, like, "I'm not ready to give up my independence." Or, "The children need me." Or, "I just can't face the responsibilities of marriage."

That's the way it stood that October afternoon when I rode into Garnet to pick up my Winchester. I'd gone hunting the day before and had had two good chances to bring in some camp meat, but I missed both shots. I'm a good shot with a rifle and there was no excuse for missing either one, so I told myself my sights were off and I wanted the gunsmith in Garnet to check them.

I hated to admit it, but the truth was I'd got worked up over Rosy's last turndown. We'd been to a dance on Saturday night and I'd had a hell of a good time and I thought Rosy had, too.

The schoolhouse is on the edge of a thick growth of lodgepole pines north of town, and the teacherage, a one-room log cabin, sits behind the schoolhouse and is hidden from the road. I didn't like her living there by herself and had told her so more than once, but she said she wasn't afraid, the cabin was comfortable and free, and she had a gun and was a good shot. That ended the discussion.

When we got to her place after the dance, she made a pot of coffee and served me a slice of chocolate cake. Then I hugged and kissed her before I left, and she responded more than she usually did, so I thought that was a good time to ask her for the umpteenth time to marry me.

She pulled away from me and walked across the room and stood by the stove. She said, "Jim, I like you better than any other man I know, and I want to marry you, but I'm afraid to. You've got a violent streak in you that comes out once in a while and it scares me. Some day you're going to kill a man or be killed."

I stood there just kind of paralyzed and stared at her. I guess I stared about a minute, feeling as if she had taken a blacksnake to my back. She was a very pretty girl, with a figure that made men want to keep on staring at her. She had blue eyes and auburn hair that curled all over her head. I guess if I could have created a dream girl to marry, she would have looked just like Rosy Malone. Standing there just looking at her, I knew that for the first time she was giving me the real reason she didn't want to marry me.

I turned around and walked out. I mounted and rode home. The next day I hurt all over. I couldn't forget what she'd said. I thought it was unfair, and I wondered what kind of man she wanted. I just had never thought of myself as a violent man.

Sure, I had been considered a little wild when I was younger. I'd had my share of barroom brawls and I had a reputation for not taking anything off anybody, but I also knew I was steadier and worked harder and would give Rosy a better life than the other men she went with.

I didn't sleep any Saturday night. I steamed about it all day Sunday and on Monday I went hunting instead of staying home and working. Blaming those missed shots on my sights was an excuse and I knew it in my guts, but I sure as hell couldn't bring myself to admit it. I took my rifle into Garnet to check the sights and told the gunsmith I'd be back on Tuesday to pick it up.

That's how I happened to be in Garnet when the Rawlins bunch rode into town. I wasn't surprised when I walked into the store and the gunsmith laid my Winchester on the counter, saying, "Jim, there's nothing wrong with your sights. I wish all the guns I had in here shot as true as this one does. I'd like to buy. . . . "

I was reaching down to pick up the Winchester when I heard two shots. It took a second or two for me to realize they came from the direction of the bank which was about half a block to the east. At least that was the way it sounded.

I grabbed the rifle up off the counter and ran out through the street door. Three horses were in front of the bank. One man was in the saddle, one was trying to mount, and a third one was coming out of the bank, a couple of bags of coins in one hand and a gun in the other that he was holstering as he ran.

Levering a shell into the chamber, I cut loose, taking the man who was leaving the bank. I knocked him flat, then fired at the man who had just stepped into the saddle and sent him sprawling as his boogered horse bucked once and took off down the street. By this time the third man was cracking steel to his horse and had reached the end of the business block when I got off my third shot. I should have saved my fourth bullet because the bank robber disappeared around the corner just as I was squeezing the trigger.

It was all over in about ten seconds. A dozen men boiled out of the doorways along Main Street and surrounded the two men lying in the dust, Doc Muller among them.

By the time I got there, Muller had examined both men and was standing up announcing that they were dead. Somebody demanded, "Who got 'em?"

The gunsmith who had run on ahead of me said, "Jim Dance done it. I seen it all. Best shooting I ever saw."

They shook my hand and told me I'd saved the bank and their money and that meant saving the town and the county. Then someone came out of the bank, white-faced and trembling, and announced that Vic Sorrel, the banker, had been killed.

"Trying to get his gun out of a drawer, looked like," the man said. "They just gunned him down."

By that time I'd had a good look at the men I'd killed. They were young and bearded, maybe twenty or twenty-one. One had a hole through his head, the other one in his chest. A lot of blood was on the ground.

I guess it was the blood that did it. I knew I was going to be sick, so I headed for my horse that was still hitched in front of the gun shop. I didn't quite make it to my horse, so I had no chance to get out of town. I stood there in the street beside the hitchrack throwing up everything I'd eaten for a week. At least it felt that way.

By the time I was over it, the preacher, Paul Adams, had reached me. He said, "Don't have any regrets, Jim. They were bad ones. They've killed a lot of men including Vic Sorrel who was a good friend to everybody in town."

I had a bitter taste in my mouth as I took my bandanna out of my pocket and wiped my lips. I wasn't thinking very straight, but I knew what the preacher said was true. Vic had loaned me the money to get started, saying it was good business to help young, hardworking men who dreamed about working for themselves.

"The community needs men like you, Jim," he said as he shook hands with me.

Rosy's words about me having a violent streak came roaring back into my mind as I stood looking at the preacher. I guess she was right because I hadn't thought about what I was doing. I'd just started shooting. But Vic Sorrel had had the same streak of violence, I thought. He'd tried to defend the bank and other people's money and he would have killed the outlaws if they'd given him a chance.

I stepped into the saddle and rode home, not even thanking the preacher for what he had said. I didn't work any that day, either, not anything important anyhow, just stood around repairing harness and cleaning out the corrals and doing any busywork I could find to keep my mind off those two young men I had seen lying in the street.

Just before dark the sheriff, Don Bailey, rode out from town. He said, "You done a good job, Jim. I was out at my ranch when I heard what had happened. By the time I got to town and rounded up a posse, old Bill Rawlins was long gone. We couldn't pick up his trail."

"Rawlins?" I asked.

I was a little shocked. The Rawlins gang was well known in Garnet because they holed up in the mountains to the west of town when they weren't out robbing banks. They never bothered anyone within fifty miles of town. I guess they figured that if they let us alone, we'd let them alone. Why they had changed their pattern was more than I could figure out, so I asked the sheriff.

"Hell, who knows how an outlaw's mind works," Bailey said. "Maybe they figured on leaving the country and this was their last big job before they headed for Mexico. Anyway, I'm glad you got the boys. Old Bill will probably leave the country, now that he's alone.

"Then again, maybe he won't. He's just naturally a mean son of a bitch. He's abused women until they've died. He's shot men in the back. He's tortured them until they've begged him to kill them."

He cleared his throat, then went on, "If he finds out who shot his boys, he'll be back to get you. I don't know what to tell you, I just don't have the deputies to keep one out here to protect you. I can send a man out for a couple of nights just to be sure Rawlins don't sneak up on you."

"No, I can look out for myself," I said.

"There's a reward out for the Rawlins boys," he said. "Five hundred dollars for each of 'em. I'll see you get it." He hesitated, then asked, "You sure you don't want any protection?"

"I'm sure," I said.

He rode off and I walked over to my front porch and sat down. While the sheriff was telling me about Bill Rawlins, a terrible thought had upset the hell out of me. Suppose Rawlins holed up somewhere around here or stopped at some ranch for supper and heard about me and Rosy being my girl. He might come after her, knowing that would be the way to hurt me.

I hated like hell to face Rosy. By now she'd probably heard what had happened and she'd remind me that she had told me what I was and now I'd proved it. I figured that saving the bank wouldn't cut any ice with her.

Still, if it did happen to Rosy, I'd never forgive myself, so I saddled up and rode to her place. When she opened the door to my knock and saw who it was, she backed up and an expression came over her face I had never seen before. I judged from the looks of her red eyes she had been crying.

"Go away, Jim," she said.

That wasn't what I expected her to say. I thought she'd tell me I had the mark of Cain on me, that I was born to hang, that she'd be afraid to ever be alone with me again. But she didn't say anything like that. I had a feeling she was grieving because her opinion of me was right and therefore she knew she could never marry me.

I wasn't going to be run off before I said what I had come to say, so I just stood there and said, "You're going to listen to me. Then I'll leave you alone. The men I shot were part of the Rawlins gang, the sons of old Bill Rawlins. He got away. The sheriff told me he was a bad one, the kind who would dry gulch me if he found out who shot his boys. We don't know where he is, but he may have circled back and stopped at some ranch for supper.

"This kind of news travels fast, so he may have heard who killed his sons. He may also have heard that you are my girl. If he did, I'd say the chances are he'll come after you. I want you to sleep in town for a few days until we know he's out of the country."

"I'm safe here," she said.

She stood her ground as if she were frozen, her face set and cold. I got sore then, thinking she didn't want to hear my side of it. I guess I yelled at her when I said, "Damn it, Rosy, I saved the bank and maybe saved a lot of people. Those men deserved to die. They murdered Vic Sorrel."

"A human life is worth more than a bank or the money people have put in it," she said. "I could never have done what you did. All I know is that you killed two men."

"Then you won't go?"

"No," she answered.

I turned and left the cabin, knowing she had a stubborn streak a yard wide and I could stand there all night and argue with her without changing her mind. I mounted and started home, then I began thinking that if Bill Rawlins did come back, I couldn't bear to think of what he'd do to Rosy. Her being stubborn wouldn't help her a damn bit. If she wouldn't save herself, then I'd have to do it.

The Wooing of Rosy Malone

I rode back and left my horse in the lodgepoles far enough from the teacherage so Rosy wouldn't know it was there. An almost full moon was coming up in the east, and if I'd left the horse close to the cabin, she might see it if she stepped outside before she went to bed.

I lifted my Winchester from the boot and eased back through the trees until I was close enough to see her door. She'd surely have sense to lock her door, and by the time Rawlins kicked it in, I'd be on top of him. I wasn't sure how I'd handle him. I couldn't shoot because I might hit Rosy. Her bed was opposite the door and she'd rear up when she heard the door getting kicked in, so she could very well stop the slug instead of Rawlins if I wasn't careful.

When I sat down with my back to a tree, my Winchester cradled across my lap, I thought I wouldn't have any trouble staying awake, but I hadn't slept much since Saturday night and all of a sudden it caught up with me. I found myself nodding and then jerking awake and wondering how long I had slept. I got up and walked around through the pines for a couple of minutes, then came back and sat down to do it all over again.

I don't know how many times that happened, but the moon was riding high above me when I heard Rosy's door being kicked open. I jumped up and headed for the cabin on the run, but I was groggy and bleary-eyed and still didn't know just what I was going to do.

It had to be Rawlins. I cursed myself for staying as far from Rosy's door as I had, but I was lucky in one regard. He took time to light a lamp, saying, "So you're Dance's girl. Well, I'm going to carve you up good and I want to see what I'm doing."

I had a crazy feeling I was running through molasses and I wouldn't get there in time to save Rosy. Rawlins pulled a knife and turned to Rosy who was sitting up in bed so terrified she couldn't even scream.

I plunged through the door before Rawlins reached Rosy's bed. I yelled "Rawlins" just to turn him away from Rosy. I aimed to shoot the instant I could get Rosy out of the line of fire, but I never did. There was a two-inch lift of the cabin floor above the ground, and as I charged through the door, my Winchester on the ready, I caught a boot toe and went sprawling. As I fell, I cracked my head on the side of the stove. Somehow that turned me half over so I lay on my side staring at Rawlins who had wheeled the instant I yelled at him.

He came at me with his knife in his hand. I saw an explosion of stars and although I wasn't knocked cold, I couldn't speak and I couldn't move. Rawlins was grinning when he came toward me, not hurrying because I guess he saw I was paralyzed.

I tried to lift a leg to kick him in the crotch, but I couldn't move a muscle. I cursed myself for my awkwardness; I expected to feel his blade in my belly the next second, but it didn't happen. A gun roared and Rawlins toppled forward on his face to lie beside me.

Then I saw that Rosy was holding a gun, smoke slowly twisting from the muzzle. She couldn't seem to move, either, or at least not for a few seconds, and then she slowly put her feet on the floor and walked toward me.

She got down on her knees and held my head in her lap, kind of crooning to me. She was pale, but she had control of herself then. I don't know how long it took me to get over that knockout fall, but the first thing I did when I could move was to reach up and pull her face down to mine and kiss her. When she lifted her head and I could move mine enough to look at Rawlins, I saw that he was dead. She was right about being able to use a gun.

After that things began to take their natural shape and size, and although my head hurt like hell and blood was dripping down the side of my face, I felt good just to be alive. I got to my feet with a little help from Rosy, swayed there for a moment as I clutched the end of the table, then I got a blanket off the bed and covered Rawlins' body.

"You can't sleep here the rest of the night," I said. "I'll take you to Paul Adams. He and Minerva will be glad to put you up. Then I'll get the sheriff out of bed and tell him what happened. He'll move the body."

She didn't argue. She didn't say anything, but she nodded as she took my hand. I blew the lamp out and we walked through the pines to town. When we reached Main Street, we turned toward the parsonage. Rosy still hadn't said a word.

I had to pound on the parsonage door three times before Paul padded across the front room and opened the door. He was wearing a robe over his nightgown and held a lamp in one hand as he peered at us.

"Rosy has had some trouble," I said. "She'll tell you about it. I've got to go fetch the sheriff. I thought you could give her a bed for the rest of the night."

He nodded and said, "Be glad to. I'll go get Minerva up."

I started to turn away, but Rosy caught my arm. "Paul," she said, her voice shaky, "I guess it's no secret that Jim has wanted me to marry him for a long time. I kept turning him down for what I thought was a good reason, but tonight I discovered it wasn't a reason at all. I want you to marry us in the morning." She turned to me and tried to smile and failed. "I discovered I'm no better than you are, Jim. Now I know how it was."

I held her in my arms and looked past her at Paul Adams who was staring at us goggle-eyed as if he thought we were both out of our minds. I said, "Early in the morning, Paul."